THE QUARRY

THE QUARRY

Charles W. Chesnutt

Edited with introduction
and notes by
Dean McWilliams

PRINCETON UNIVERSITY PRESS

Copyright © 1999 by Princeton University Press
Published by Princeton University Press, 41 William Street,
Princeton, New Jersey 08540
In the United Kingdom: Princeton University Press,
Chichester, West Sussex

Library of Congress Cataloging-in-Publication Data

Chesnutt, Charles Waddell, 1858–1932
The quarry / by Charles W. Chesnutt; edited with introduction and
notes by Dean McWilliams.
p.   cm.
Includes bibliographical references (p.   ).
ISBN 0-691-05995-0 (CL: alk. paper).
ISBN 0-691-05996-9 (PB: alk. paper)
1. Afro-American—Race identity—Fiction. 2 Interracial adoption—
United States—Fiction.
3. Group identity—United States—Fiction.
4 Adoptees—United States—Fiction.
5. Harlem Renaissance—Fiction.
I. McWilliams, Dean. II. Title.
PS1292.C6Q37 1999   98-26422
813'.4—dc21

This book has been composed in Berkeley Ten
Designed by Jan Lilly

The paper used in this publication
meets the minimum requirements of
ANSI / NISO Z39.48-1992 (R1997) (*Permanence of Paper*)

http://pup.princeton.edu

Printed in the United States of America

2 4 6 8 10 9 7 5 3 1

CONTENTS

INTRODUCTION TO
THE QUARRY

"Post-Bellum—Pre-Harlem" is the title that Charles
W. Chesnutt gave to an autobiographical sketch written late in his career. But in this title, as in much else,
Chesnutt was too modest. If we wish a phrase that de-
scribes the unique trajectory of Chesnutt's life—and
the special perspective it offers on black American history—we might better write "*Pre*-Bellum—*Post*-Har-
lem." Chesnutt's seven decades, which began in 1858
and ended in 1932, carried him from before the Civil
War through the rise and decline of the Harlem Renaissance. Paul Laurence Dunbar, Chesnutt's co-pioneer
in the creation of black literary art, had been dead for
a quarter of a century when Chesnutt passed on.
W.E.B. Du Bois, Alain Locke, and Charles S. Johnson,
the elders of the Harlem Renaissance, were, respectively, ten, twenty-seven, and thirty-five years Chesnutt's junior. And yet, Chesnutt remained active and
sharply alert until the last, seeking publication for a
new novel in his seventy-second year. He failed to secure publication for the manuscript, as he had failed to
place another novel seven years earlier. His failure to

find publication for these texts is unfortunate, for, as a consequence, African American literary history records an oddly truncated picture of his literary activity, telling us virtually nothing about Chesnutt's writings during the last third of his long career.

Chesnutt was born in 1858 in Cleveland, Ohio, where his parents, both free Negroes, had migrated from North Carolina in the late 1850s. Chesnutt's father and mother decided to return to their native state after the Civil War, and thus Chesnutt spent his late childhood, adolescence, and early adulthood in the area around Fayetteville, North Carolina. Chesnutt decided, while still in his teens, that he wanted to become a writer, and, with that end in mind, he trained himself in Latin, German, and French and read widely in the world's literature. He was able to support himself as a schoolteacher, but sensing that this profession might not provide an adequate livelihood, he also taught himself stenography. In 1883, after the failure of Reconstruction, Chesnutt found it increasingly difficult to live in the South, so with his wife and children, he moved back to Cleveland. There he read law and passed the state bar with the highest score in his group. However, he found his hope of practicing law blocked by prejudice, and so he started a profitable career as a legal stenographer.

Chesnutt had not, however, forgotten his literary aspirations, and in the mid 1880s his stories and sketches began to appear in print. In August 1887 *The*

Atlantic Monthly published his story "The Goophered Grapevine," and in 1899 Houghton Mifflin brought out his collection of stories *The Conjure Woman*. These two dates mark signal events in African American literary history. Novels and stories written by black Americans had been published as early as the mid-nineteenth century, but these narratives were primarily polemical in purpose, and they were read and discussed in the context of the national debates on Abolition and Reconstruction. Before Chesnutt's, no fiction written by a Negro had received serious attention from America's white literary establishment. "The Goophered Grapevine" and *The Conjure Woman* were hailed as fictions of a high order, and the praise was justified, for these stories combined sensitive portraiture of American blacks with considerable literary skill. Chesnutt's historic publications helped African American fiction develop beyond social polemics into a self-conscious literary art form.

Chesnutt followed these path-breaking publications quickly with four additional volumes: another story collection, *The Wife of His Youth and Other Stories of the Color Line* (1899), and three novels, *The House Behind the Cedars* (1900), *The Marrow of Tradition* (1901), and *The Colonel's Dream* (1905). And then silence—or so it seemed. Chesnutt published a few essays and several more stories, but there were no more book-length publications before his death in 1932.

It is frequently believed that Chesnutt abandoned

fiction after the commercial failure of his third novel in 1905. Chesnutt, it is true, was discouraged by his inability to support his family by his writing, and after the disappointing returns on *The Colonel's Dream*, he turned his energies to his practice as a legal stenographer. But he did not give up fiction entirely, and pursued a number of fictional projects; the most important of these were two novels, *Paul Marchand, F.M.C.* and *The Quarry*, which he submitted for publication in the 1920s. Unfortunately, both were turned down.

Chesnutt submitted *The Quarry* to Alfred Knopf, Inc., in 1928 and to Houghton Mifflin Company in 1930. We do not have the letter of rejection sent by Harry Bloch, an editor for Alfred Knopf, but Chesnutt's answering letter to Bloch recapitulates the reader's criticisms. "I note what you say," Chesnutt wrote, "about the central idea in the story, and my failure to carry it out, and the lifelessness of the characters and the 'priggishness' of the hero. I suspect you are right about all of this, and in the light of your criticism I shall before I submit the book elsewhere, see if I can put some flesh on and some red blood in the characters" (Helen Chesnutt 307). Ferris Greenslet, responding for Houghton Mifflin, remarked that the book had "rather the color of a thesis novel and does not, therefore, quite succeed in making the reader lose himself in a complete illusion."

Modern readers will probably agree with Bloch and Greenslet's criticisms of Chesnutt's last novel. Students of American literature will, however, find that the book has considerable biographical and historical interest. Chesnutt was entering his eighth decade when he finished this manuscript, and it is very much the product of a Negro writer and activist looking back over the past, surveying the present, and trying to help plan the future. *The Quarry* was completed in 1928, at the high-water mark of the Harlem Renaissance, and its characters dramatize some of the political and aesthetic controversies of this movement. Booker T. Washington, W.E.B. Du Bois, and Marcus Garvey are among the figures who appear, slightly fictionalized, in Chesnutt's last novel. The book's optimistic tone captures the spirit of a unique and very brief moment in the history of black America. *The Quarry* also gives us Chesnutt's last extended reflection on racial identity. Throughout his career, Chesnutt was associated with the "assimilationist" position. He argued that racism would not disappear until the distinctions between the races were blurred by increased marriage across racial lines. This is essentially the solution proposed by the anthropologist Franz Boas, who appears in the novel as Donald Glover's mentor. Boas argued that Negroes and Jews should join the American melting pot. But, as George Hutchinson has shown, Boas's position was complex. At the same time that Boas argued for Negro "assimilation," he also promoted pride in the African American cultural heritage. The same complexity can be seen in Chesnutt's position in *The Quarry*. Donald Glover takes pride in the achievements of Negro Americans. He and his Jewish friend Isidore Rovelsky move easily in New York's cosmopolitan, multiracial intellectual circles, but neither is willing to renounce his ethnic identity.

Donald is clear and emphatic in his racial loyalty. He is tempted five times to renounce his Negro identity— by Mr. Seaton, by Amelia Parker, by Moe Silberstein, by Mr. Bascomb, and again by Mr. Seaton—and five times he refuses. The strength of Chesnutt's stand against passing in this novel can be seen even more clearly when it is read against James Weldon Johnson's fictional *Autobiography of an Ex-Colored Man*, first published in 1912 but reissued to a wider audience in 1927, when Chesnutt was preparing *The Quarry*. Johnson's anonymous protagonist is a mulatto who despairs of his situation as a Negro and decides to live as a white man. Johnson, of course, did not write the novel to encourage mulattoes to quit the black race but rather to express his disappointment in a America where a talented young African American would feel driven to do so.

Chesnutt's story echoes Johnson's in several ways. Both protagonists are talented, light-skinned males. Both begin life in the north, go south to study at Atlanta University, come north to Harlem, and travel to Europe with wealthy white patrons, who encourage them to pass as white. Johnson's protagonist narrates his story retrospectively, and he tells us that he has successfully passed over the line. However, he offers this sad confession in the novel's last line: "I cannot repress the thought that, after all, I have chosen the lesser part, that I have sold my birthright for a mess of pottage." Chesnutt liked and admired Johnson, but he rejected the pessimism of Johnson's fictional *Autobiography* in his own narrative. The last line of Chesnutt's novel, in the Ohio University manuscript, is Mr. Seaton's concession to Donald: "I'm not at all sure that you haven't chosen the better part." Chesnutt changed this sentence in the Fisk manuscript to read "I'm not at all sure that you didn't make the wise choice," but the echo of Johnson's conclusion is still audible. Johnson's biblical metaphor occurs elsewhere in Chesnutt's novel in Isidore Rovelsky's refusal to abandon his Jewish heritage "for a mess of pottage." Rovelsky's decision, of course, anticipates Donald's own refusal to surrender his black identity.

The Quarry, which might well be subtitled "The Biography of an Ex-*White* Man," turns the novel of passing on its head by recounting the story of a white man who decides to be colored. Assimilation, in Chesnutt's last novel, does not mean blacks becoming white as much as it does whites becoming black. In this novel, Donald Glover, a genetic European American, renounces a white identity for a colored one. Indeed, the logic of Chesnutt's assimilationism requires that whites must first become blacks before blacks can become white. Whites must be persuaded to enter the black

world, morally and spiritually, to see the black condition from inside. This spiritual metamorphosis of
whites is essential. Until it happens, whites will never
understand blacks, and they will never allow blacks to
enter white-dominated society as equals.

Whites *can* become black: this is the drama enacted
in Chesnutt's last novel, and it is the paradoxical hope
that animated Chesnutt's literary career from its beginnings. Chesnutt decided very early that he wanted to
write about the black condition for a white audience. A
journal entry by the young Chesnutt records what was
to become a key strategy in that writing: "Nothing," he
wrote, "will sooner show us the folly and injustice of
prejudice than being ourselves subjected to it" (96). He
believed that if whites could truly understand the black
situation—could live it vicariously from within—they
could be moved to change it.

Heretofore, the body of Chesnutt's published fiction
has stood at six volumes: the five books Chesnutt saw
into print and the volume of his previously uncollected
stories, which Sylvia Lyons Render edited in 1974.
Charles Hackenberry's recent edition of *Mandy Oxendine* gives us what was probably Chesnutt's first
novel. The publication of Chesnutt's 1921 novel *Paul
Marchand, F.M.C*, by Princeton University Press and
the University Press of Mississippi, and this edition of
Chesnutt's last novel expand Chesnutt's published cor-
pus of fiction by nearly a third, extending it through

the final decades of his career. Publication of Charles Chesnutt's last novel helps us see the full achievement of an African American literary pioneer who remained engaged in the concerns of his community until the end of his life.

The Quarry exists in two manuscripts. The first is in Ohio University Library's Special Collections. It was given to the University by Carr Liggett, a friend of Chesnutt and an Ohio University alumnus. The second is in the collection of Chesnutt materials donated by Chesnutt's daughter Helen to Fisk University. The Ohio manuscript is 404 typed pages, triple-spaced, with hand-written corrections and changes. These hand-written changes are legible and fairly numerous, but, for the most part, of little consequence for the novel's meaning. The Fisk text, 276 typed pages, double-spaced, is the same as the Ohio manuscript, re-typed and incorporating the handwritten changes. It seems likely that the Ohio text was the penultimate draft, and that the Fisk version was the one submitted for publication.

Chesnutt submitted *The Quarry* to Alfred Knopf in late 1928 and to Houghton Mifflin December 29, 1930. There was time for Chesnutt to have significantly revised the manuscript between submissions, but he was in very poor health during this period, and he also completed a volume of children's stories, which he submitted to Houghton Mifflin in 1930. It is quite likely that the manuscript Chesnutt submitted to Houghton Mifflin was the one returned by Knopf.

I have taken the Fisk manuscript as the basis for my edition of the novel. In editing the manuscript I have treated it as a manuscript submitted for publication, and I have confined myself to correcting inaccuracies and inconsistencies in spelling, grammar, and punctuation. I have explained the most significant of my corrections in my notes at the back of this volume. I also note changes in the Ohio manuscript when these changes help to clarify Chesnutt's references.

I have many individuals and institutions to thank for help in bringing these manuscripts to print. First, I wish to thank John Chesnutt Slade, Chesnutt's grandson, for permission to publish the manuscripts and quote from other unpublished Chesnutt materials. I wish also to acknowledge the assistance of the following: Gary Hunt and George Bain of Ohio University's Alden Library; Beth Howse of Fisk University's Erastus Milo Cravath Memorial Library; Susan Crowl and Vattel Rose of Ohio University, and Michel Perdreau, formerly of Ohio University; Etienne De Planchard of the Université de Toulouse–Le Mirail; Roy Rosenstein of the American University in Paris; and George Hutchinson of the University of Tennessee, Knoxville. I would also like to express my gratitude to Ohio University for a Research Committee grant and for a faculty fellowship; this support provided some of the resources and the time from teaching which enabled me to do most of my research. Finally, and most important, I am once again in debt to my wife, Alvi, for her help, encouragement, and good humor.

I dedicate this edition to my niece and nephew, Holly and Luke Stowell.

THE QUARRY

CHAPTER I

ONE SPRING DAY early in the present century a small red two-cylinder automobile, one of the earliest models developed, turned into the yard of the Columbus City Hospital and drew up before the main entrance. The structure which faced the occupants of the car was built of dark red brick, pointed with black mortar. Along the cornice ran a terra cotta frieze set with metopes containing portraits in bas relief of Aesculapius, Hippocrates, Galen, Harvey, Jenner, Pasteur and others of the world's great healers. The city was very proud of its new hospital, which had recently been erected at large expense and furnished with the latest and most approved equipment.

Angus Seaton, who first descended from the car, was a tall, rather slender man with a kindly face, sharp features, grey eyes and sandy hair. The lady whom he helped out of the car was a handsome woman in the early thirties, of medium height, with well-rounded contours, dark hair and eyes, and quick movements which suggested a nervous or neurotic temperament.

Angus and Grace Seaton had been married nearly six years but were still childless. They had been fellow students at the State University. Theirs had been a love match, and they had lived together in the perfect intimacy of happy married life. They had very much desired children, had looked forward to them and had been greatly disappointed as the years rolled on and did not bring them. Experts whom they consulted declared them perfectly fit—there was no physical reason why they should not have children. But they did not, and the fact had begun to prey upon Mrs. Seaton's mind. She felt herself a born mother and her maternal instincts clamored for expression.

Mrs. Seaton had not given up the hope of offspring without a struggle. She had read all the books she saw advertised as "Advice to Young Married Women," "Hints to Expectant Mothers," and others of a similar nature, and found them either of no merit whatever, or mere appeals to a morbid curiosity, or applying to a condition which did not yet exist in her case, but which she never ceased to hope for, and for which she wished to be prepared when it arrived.

She had gone to Cincinnati and had herself psychoanalyzed by an eminent practitioner of that esoteric art, which was then in its infancy. She told him her dreams, which were largely of children, and he made a weird diagnosis which embraced suppressed sexual desires, and a lot of other things which certainly had never en-

tered her conscious mind. He advised a temporary separation from her husband and for a couple of months
they slept in different rooms, but all to no avail.

At the suggestion of a friend of the family, and without the knowledge of her husband, who was above all
things a practical man, and would not have approved
of it, she consulted a well-known psychic and seeress,
with a local vogue, who pumped her dry and then told
her that the thing she wanted most in the world was a
child, and that she would have one within a year. A
condition of success was that she should believe the
prediction. However, perhaps from lack of faith, the
year passed without any favorable auguries.

A well-educated and sophisticated woman friend to
whom she voiced her desire suggested that she read
Maupassant's *L'Héritage*, which she procured in a
translation, read through to the clever, cynical and im-
moral solution of the problem presented, which was
her own with a different motivation, then threw it into
the fire and struck her friend's name off her calling list
for a long time, indeed until she became a mother in
the conventional way.

Of course, the idea of adopting a baby had been discussed in the household, but only as a last resort. Marriages for a long time sterile had sometimes proved
fruitful later on. Mrs. Seaton's desire was a child of her
own on whom she could pour out the flood of starved
mother love which surged through her heart.

Seaton, on his part, knew from the memory of his own upbringing, in a household of narrow means, what it meant to rear a child, and he, too, much preferred that the longed-for baby should be their own. But finally, out of love for his wife and concern for her health and happiness, he agreed with her that since it seemed extremely unlikely that they would ever have a child of their own, they should accept the alternative and adopt a baby. And as they wanted a child with no strings on it, no parents or relations in the background who might claim it or grieve because they could not claim it, they picked out the Infants Ward of the City Hospital as the most likely place to find a suitable candidate.

The visitors mounted the stone steps to the door, which stood invitingly open, after the manner of hospital doors in good weather. Near the front of the long and wide hall which extended toward the rear, there was a desk, and behind the desk an attendant in nurse's uniform, of whom they asked if they might see the superintendent. The young woman ushered them into a waiting room to the right of the entrance.

"Pray be seated," she said, "and I'll call him."

After a lapse of about ten minutes, a very capable-looking man in the forties came in, of typically professional appearance. He had dark hair greying slightly on the edges, wore a pince-nez secured by a long cord, and his manner was at once suave and businesslike.

The attendant introduced him as Dr. Freeman, the superintendent in charge.

"And how can I serve you?" he demanded, after they had given their names and exchanged greetings.

"We wish," said Mr. Seaton, "to consult you about adopting a baby. Have you some very young children we could select from? My wife is childless, and would like to assume all the responsibilities of a mother. If the child is old enough to be taken away, the younger the better."

"You're the sort of visitors we welcome," Dr. Freeman replied. "It is easy enough to get the babies—there are so many of them that nobody wants! Our problem is to dispose of them. By the way, would you care to visit the nursery? We keep the babies for a short time, until they are either adopted or ready to be sent to the orphan asylum. It isn't the best practice to admit visitors to the nursery, but we have been putting in some new equipment which you might find interesting. We have the most up-to-date hospital in the Middle West.

They assented and the doctor led them back through the hall, past the open door of the lying-in department to the nursery beyond, which they entered by another door from the corridor. The tiled floors, the whitewashed walls, the furniture and fittings, of the latest sanitary type, were all immaculately clean. On one side, at the front end of the large room, stood half a dozen couveuses or incubators, where, in a scientifically regulated atmosphere, prematurely born babies were encouraged to live and breathe. Dr. Freeman explained the method, which was quite interesting, and gave some statistics to show to what extent the law of the survival of the fittest was defied and nature's efforts to keep down the population thwarted.

Another section of the room held a row of bassinets containing newborn babies and a little farther along a line of little cribs with infants of one to two months old. Most of these looked more or less alike, but now and then there was one of marked individuality. For instance, in one bed there was a solemn-looking Negro baby, the whites of its big eyes looking soberly out from its little black face.

"How's young Booker T. getting along today?" asked Dr. Freeman of the nurse in charge.

"Fine," was the reply. "He's very well behaved."

"Do you get many colored children?" asked Seaton.

"A few," answered the superintendent. "Many of the mothers come here for delivery, but most of them take the babies away, even under circumstances where white mothers would leave them. Negroes are very fond of their children, though they often neglect them because of wretched home surroundings. We don't really care to have them leave them, because the orphan asylums dislike to take them—they are harder to get rid of."

"Oh, what a beautiful baby!" exclaimed Mrs. Seaton, as they paused beside a certain bed. The infant thus characterized was a boy about two months old, a well-developed child for its age. There was a rather thick thatch of dark brown curly hair on its finely molded head. Its features were, for a baby of its age, clean-cut and well-defined. Its complexion was a clear olive, suggesting a possible Latin strain. Its mouth was a little Cupid's bow, and there was a dimple in its diminutive chin. Even at its early age there was a perceptible twinkle in its dark brown eyes.

"He's smiling at me," exclaimed Mrs. Seaton. "I think he likes my looks, the little darling."

"How could he help it?" said the doctor gallantly. "He's an intelligent baby, as well as strong, healthy and promising in every way."

"Is he open for adoption?" asked Seaton.

"Oh, please say yes," exclaimed Mrs. Seaton. "May I have him? Let me hold him a moment."

The attendant nurse lifted the baby from its crib and placed it in the visitor's arms. Mrs. Seaton rocked it to and fro and cooed over it. The child exhibited pronounced signs of pleasure, kicking its little feet and clinging tenaciously with one hand to the finger Mr. Seaton extended.

"I guess it'll be all right," said Dr. Freeman, "but we'll first have to look up his pedigree and see whether he's the kind of child you want. We have a perfect recording system and you can rely on it implicitly. Ours is a very mixed population and most of these children are of foreign extraction. We have Italians, Greeks, only

rarely a Jew, and all the Eastern European types, besides our own English, Scotch-Irish and German mixture. I don't think we have ever had a full-blooded Chinese or Japanese child left for adoption, although an
occasional Eurasian child is delivered here."

"Is it necessary to look any further, doctor?" asked
Mrs. Seaton. "I want a child that is all my own. I don't
attach a great deal of importance to heredity. This is a
good and beautiful baby and I'm willing to take him on
faith. I don't see how he could have anything but a
good heredity. We'll give him a happy home in a good
environment, and I'm sure the little angel will turn out
all we could desire."

"Very well," rejoined Dr. Freeman. "The risk is
yours, but I don't think there is any. I don't know his
history without looking it up, but there are no strings
to him. He'll be all yours. No one will ever claim him."

And so it was decided. They were to make the necessary arrangements to receive the child in their home,
and were to call for him in a day or two.

"You can take him on trial," said the superintendent,
"and if you decide that you don't want to keep him,
we'll take him back within a reasonable time, though I
hope we won't have to."

CHAPTER II

—————⟫●⟪—————

THE REARING OF a modern infant is a complicated, and, for those who can afford it, an expensive process. Little Donald—they named him after Seaton's grandfather—had all the attention any young child needed. The science of babiculture had not developed, at that time, to its present advanced stage. The specialist who comes to the house once a week with his little black bag, looks the baby over, makes suggestions as to diet and clothing and sanitation, vaccinates it for all imaginable diseases from infantile paralysis to senile dementia, and leaves each time with his minimum fee of five dollars, was as yet unknown in the city; but the family doctor, who knew little about serums or vitamins or calories, with fewer visits and for a smaller fee did all that was considered necessary. The modern prepared baby foods were not yet invented, but mothers learned how to sterilize and otherwise prepare the milk for the baby's bottle. Young Donald was fed on schedule, his B.M.'s and P.M.'s were watched and regulated, his hours of sleep fixed. He was a good baby and conformed to these rules quite as well as most infants. If he did not always eat or sleep at the proper time, he always got enough food and sleep. Whatever further care he needed was supplied in ample measure.

Mrs. Seaton could not have nursed him more devotedly or loved him more dearly had he been of her own flesh. In caring for him she found a healthy outlet for the hitherto repressed maternal instinct which was so strong an element of her character.

Some three months after little Donald was taken into the household, Seaton moved to Cleveland. He was the inventor, patentee and manufacturer of the Seaton carburetor, an automobile appliance which was destined, with the increasing development of the automobile industry, to make the inventor a wealthy man. He had decided that Cleveland offered a better market for his commodity, and he moved his family to that already large and rapidly growing city.

All the conditions of the time were favorable to rapid economic progress. McKinley had come and gone; Roosevelt was sitting in the saddle, riproaring and swinging the big stick. The high tariff and the steel trust had made the country safe for plutocracy and were filling it up with new types of immigrants who lowered our living standard while they increased our production and our markets. Mr. Bryan, a voice fated to futility, was still chasing rainbows. Locally, Tom L. Johnson, having cleaned out the Augean stables of the city council, was riding high on his hobby horse of three-cent railroad fare, with Newton D. Baker, pipe in hand, argent of tongue and ardent of spirit, holding on to his leader's stirrup straps until he could get into his own stride.

The Seatons took up their residence in a suburban neighborhood on the West Side, in an eight-room house on Ethel Avenue, a pleasant, shaded side street, off Lorain Avenue. They added a sleeping porch and a sun room, and were able to live comfortably, with a room for a servant and plenty of space for the baby to play in.

Young Donald grew like a weed, and proved a most precocious infant. At six months he could babble a simple musical phrase. At twelve months he could pronounce simple syllables. At fifteen months he could make his wants intelligibly known. At eighteen months he could form simple sentences. When he was a year old he could walk. He reacted instinctively to musical sounds and at fifteen months could stagger through what would be called in these degenerate days a Charleston—an epileptic terpsichorean orgy to the formlessness of which the tender limbs and soft muscles of a growing child easily lent themselves.

He developed a Gargantuan appetite—not sixty cows' milk but part of one's was his daily portion. It was the day of one cow's milk. Pasteurization was in its infancy, and the organization of great dairy companies which monopolize the milk products industry and exploit both producer and consumer impartially had not yet begun. It was not lawful to keep a cow in the city, but one could find perhaps a dairyman who would, or at least would promise, to supply the milk of one cow; when he did not, and the milk was properly sterilized, the difference, if any, was not perceptible to the tongue of faith. In due course Donald's milk diet was varied with mashed vegetables, and he became a large consumer of fried bacon, spinach and carrots at a very tender age.

He cut his first tooth when he was three months old, far in advance of the normal time for his milk dentition. He was a husky little devil, as restless as a maggot, as playful as a puppy.

"It's a good thing I'm a strong woman," his mother was wont to say, "or Donald would wear me out."

The Seatons told no one that Donald was an adopted child. Mrs. Seaton was sensitive on the subject of her childlessness and revelled, without any sense of guilt, in the compliments she received on her wonderful baby. Indeed, she and Seaton made the child as much their own as possible. He was formally adopted through appropriate legal proceedings in the probate court of the county, by which little Donald relinquished by proxy the name which he was born to but never knew and which the Seatons did not themselves know, and assumed, or rather had thrust upon him the first of the several names he was destined from time to time to bear. By virtue of this proceeding he became the lawful son of his adopted father, entitled to all a child's rights, including support and education during his nonage, and the right to inherit should his parents die intestate.

Thus a little waif, of unknown and at best obscure origin, picked up casually at a public hospital, became the pampered child of a man who was destined to become a captain of industry, with all the opportunities open to the offspring of the favorites of fortune. When Donald Seaton came out of the court house in his adopted mother's arms, and for several years thereafter, his future seemed as certain as that of the child of any respectable and rising American family well could be.

CHAPTER III

THE SEATONS, upon their removal to Cleveland, had promptly formed neighborhood acquaintanceships which supplied them with an active and healthy social life. Among other connections, they became members of the Entre Nous Bridge Club, which met from week to week at the members' houses.

One evening in spring, when Donald was about twenty-two months old, Mrs. Seaton, at a meeting of the bridge club in her own home, heard from another room some of the women guests discussing little Donald. She held the dummy hand and had seized the opportunity to step into the adjoining sun room and look at the baby, who was lying there asleep in his little cradle.

"He's a darling child," said the eldest hand, "as pretty as a picture, with such lovely curly hair, and as bright as he is beautiful."

"You mean intellectually, of course," said the cynic, who is always present, and on this occasion held the third hand. "I should prefer my children somewhat brighter physically. The child looks almost like a little coon," she ended, using the epithet most in vogue in polite society at the moment for designating colored people.

"Perhaps he is," rejoined the first speaker. "The darky blood is very persistent, and some of the best families of the South are likely to be embarrassed by an occasional throwback to some ancestor of whose very existence they were ignorant. I think her grandmother came from Virginia, or was it Louisiana?"

At this point the baby woke up and distracted Mrs. Seaton's attention from this somewhat disturbing conversation. She went to call the nurse, and a few minutes later returned to the card table and resumed her hand, but she made so many bad plays that her partner's look became one of pained reproach, and when her husband returned home from his office at the heel of the afternoon, she excused herself and asked him to take her hand.

CHAPTER IV

⟿⟾

No matter how liberal one might be in the matter of birth, however one might decry heredity and rely upon environment for the development of mind and character, it would be unreasonable to expect, in the United States, that the suggestion that the adopted son of white foster parents might have some Negro blood should prove anything but disquieting, so the pedigree of little Donald became, instead of a negligible thing, a matter of very great importance to the Seatons. Seaton still had retained business connections in the state capital which required him to go there at stated intervals. The date for his next visit fell within the week following the bridge party, and he seized the occasion to seek the information he had formerly refused. He called at the City Hospital and asked for the superintendent.

Dr. Freeman greeted him cordially.

"Well, Mr. Seaton," he asked, "how's the boy getting along? You didn't bring him back, so I suppose you have come to report you have found him satisfactory. We are always glad to learn when our wards turn out well. I hope no congenital weakness has developed nor any disagreeable trait of character? He is rather young for those things, but they crop out very early in life."

"No," replied Seaton, "his health is perfect, he has an ideal disposition, and we are very fond of him. But for certain reasons we have decided that we would like to learn all we can about his parents and their heredity."

"It's always interesting," said Dr. Freeman, "to know those things about children. They often account for talents or aptitudes which are independent of environment. A knowledge of them is of value in directing the child's education. For example, a child may seem to have a faculty for music or for drawing. Many children have such tendencies for a while, but in most instances, they soon disappear. Little Willie, who could hum a tune or play chopsticks on the piano before he could talk, proves later to have no musical sense whatever, and is satisfied with the Jew's harp or the banjo or the guitar"—it was before the advent of the ukelele, the last musical refuge of the musical moron—"when he might learn to play the piano or the violin. His vivid lifelike sketches of cowboys and Indians prove to be mere flashes in the pan. But if one knew that he had a musical or artistic heredity, that some ancestor was a competent singer, or painter, or performer on a musical instrument, a parent or guardian would be criminally negligent not to insist upon his having competent instruction until his aptitude is tested out—otherwise the world might have lost many of its greatest artists. I'll send for the record, and we shall see what we shall see about the lad's origin."

He rang a bell and asked the attendant to bring the file containing the record of the baby boy who had been adopted from the institution nearly two years before by Mr. Angus Seaton.

"We keep these records," he explained while they were awaiting the attendant's return, "on two cards. On one we note the date of birth, names and residences of the parents where the father is known—in some cases the mother doesn't know who the father was—their race, religion, profession or occupation, their economic status, and all the facts which classify them socially. Then on another card we note the disposition of the case, whether adopted or sent to the orphan asylum, and the date; if adopted, the names of the new parents, their ages and residence, and the same information with regards to their means and social standing. These two cards bear the same number, and both are placed in an envelope, properly marked and filed. Thus we preserve a full history of each case. The system, so you see, is absolutely perfect, there is no possibility of mistake. But here is the secretary with the record."

Dr. Freeman opened the envelope and took out the cards.

"This is card number one," he said. "Now let's see who our young friend is."

He ran his eye over the card, and as he read it his face registered astonishment and concern.

"Oh, Wilson," he called to the secretary, who was leaving the room but turned back when Dr. Freeman spoke, "are you sure these are the right cards?"

"Absolutely certain," returned the secretary, "I made them out and placed them in the file myself."

"I assure you, Mr. Seaton," said the superintendent, "on my solemn word of honor, that I hadn't the least inkling of the facts disclosed by this record when I permitted you to adopt the child, and you'll remember that your wife didn't wish us to look them up."

He then read the entries on the card, according to which the mother was Maggie O'Reilly of Irish birth, who came to America when a child. Her parents were peasants from County Killarney. She was twenty-five years old, of the Catholic faith, employed as a waitress in a cheap restaurant. The father was Willis Johnson, described as a "light mulatto," thirty-one years of age, put down as a Protestant, but not a member of any church. A barber by trade, though not regularly employed, he sometimes played the violin in a dance orchestra. The father and mother were living together unlawfully. Johnson had a wife somewhere, it seemed, but had not lived with her for several years.

"I'm awfully sorry," concluded the superintendent. "May I ask whether the black drop, which in our social register makes the whole man black, has manifested itself, and if so, how?"

Mr. Seaton explained. He had not noticed or suspected it until the neighbors began to talk. He was not certain then. The child was dark, but no darker than many a white child. He had supposed that his complexion might be due to Spanish or Italian or possibly American Indian strain, any one of which was an acceptable ingredient of the American melting pot. His hair was very curly, but not kinky, it had the texture of a white person's hair. None of the physical stigmata of the Negroid except color were present, and he would not have believed the boy was colored without further knowledge of his origin. But the doubt was only less poignant than the verified fact.

"It's a sad case," rejoined Dr. Freeman, "under the circumstances almost a tragedy, but it is better to discover it now rather than later. Of course you'll not want to keep him as your son. He might, if well reared, turn out to be quite a decent chap, but, if there's anything in heredity, it is very improbable. I don't attach much weight to the mixture of blood as a source of degeneracy—there have been great men of mixed blood—and a white child with similar heredity would have little better chance. And again, we know nothing about the history of the parents beyond one generation. Many people of mixed white and Negro origin derive their white blood from the best families of the South, and by the laws of heredity, the mental and physical qualities, good as well as bad, may skip one or more generations and reappear in another. As to the mother, the Irish are a fine type and extremely viable, despite their long years of political oppression, famine, and a potato diet, and have produced many great men. From a scientific standpoint, I should like to see the boy brought up as white. It would be a psychological experiment of rare interest, and, if he turned out well, might shake some prevalent theories and prejudices.

"But of course," he continued regretfully, "you can't keep him. Under our rules you have kept him too long to return him to us, so we shall have to leave his future in your hands. I'll have a copy of this record made for you, if you wish. It will only take a few minutes to type it."

Seaton thanked the superintendent and when the copy was finished put it in his wallet and took his departure, and when he had gone, Dr. Freeman picked up the file cards again, scrutinized them closely, and as he laid them down shook his head as though puzzled, and muttered to himself: "Well, I wonder!"

Since Seaton's business would keep him in the city for several days, he set out at the first unoccupied moment to learn by himself anything further that he could about the child's parents.

He sent for the head waiter of his hotel and inquired of him if he knew one Will Johnson.

"Is he a white man or a cullud man?" asked the waiter.

"He's a light-colored man," replied Seaton, "a barber by trade."

"What you want 'im for?" demanded the head waiter, suspiciously.

"I don't want him at all," returned Seaton. "I've never seen him and never want to see him, but I'd like to find out what kind of fellow he is."

"You're not a detective or a fed'ral agent?"

"No. My interest in him is a purely private and personal one."

"Yas, suh," said the waiter, obviously relieved but not entirely convinced, "I knows 'im."

This particular waiter had been "raised" as a farm hand in the South, where any sudden or unusual interest by a white man in a Negro was viewed with alarm. He had left his more or less happy home in Georgia between two suns, after an altercation over wages which he claimed and which his white owner denied owing. The quarrel had resulted in an exchange of blows, by one of which the white man was knocked unconscious, and, before he came to, the Negro, having a wholesome regard for his skin, got started ahead of the "posse," and made his way to Cincinnati, from which he had drifted to Columbus. He had secured employment as a porter in a restaurant, had learned to wait on table, and in the course of time had mastered his trade and become head waiter at the Neal House, at that time the leading hotel of the city. But the memory of his own experience was still green, and he would not willingly have turned his hand over to put one of his people in the clutches of the law. The white people made the laws and administered them, and if the law had been violated, it was up to the white people to catch and punish the offender.

"He's all right, suh," continued the waiter. "He ain't much good, but he ain't nevah done nothin' s'ious. He's been in the wu'khouse fuh vag'ancy once or twice, and he lives with a white woman dat he ain't married to, but dat's 'bout all that can be said ag'inst him."

"Do you know where he came from?" asked Seaton.

"No, suh, I doan know fuh sho'. I've only been 'round hyuh 'bout five years mahse'f, an he wuz hyuh when I come."

"Do you know of anyone else who might know more about him?"

"You might ask the barber, suh. He's a' ole residenter and knows ev'ybody in town, white an' cullud. He c'n prob'ly tell you somethin' mo' 'bout him."

CHAPTER V

———❖———

SEATON THANKED the waiter, tipped him, and sent him away. He had shaved that morning, but he glanced in the mirror and decided that his hair would stand a trim. This would give him a better opportunity to talk to the barber than would a shave.

He descended to the barber shop, which was on the basement floor. An obsequious brush boy took his hat and asked him if he wished to be served by any particular barber. He mentioned the proprietor, and was told that he was engaged, but would be at liberty in about five minutes, and in the meantime, wouldn't the gentleman like to have a shine? He did not need a shine, but since he had come to the shop to ask a favor, he permitted himself to be relieved of a dime, to which he added another for the bootblack personally, in order to still further win the good will of the establishment. The barbers, including the proprietor, were all colored, and on account of little Donald, he felt nearer to them than, as a white man, he had ever felt before to their people.

When his shoes had been polished, the head barber was at liberty.

"Mistuh Davis kin take keer uh you now, Judge," said the bootblack, applying to his customer a title adequate to the size of the tip.

When he had removed his collar and necktie and the barber had adjusted the sleeved apron over his patron's chest and shoulders and taken up his shears, Seaton approached his subject.

"The head waiter tells me that you know everybody in town."

The barber smiled in appreciation of the implied compliment.

"That's quite a large order, sir," he replied, "but I've been 'round here a long time and I don't guess there's anybody in Columbus worth knowin' that I don't know, and some that ain't worth knowin'. Did you have anybody in particular in mind?"

"The man I am inquiring about is probably in the second class that you mention, but you may know something about him. His name is Will or Willis Johnson."

"I know Mr. Will Johnson, claim agent of the Big Four Railroad," returned the barber. "He's one of my patrons, and a mighty fine gentleman."

"No," said Seaton, "the Johnson I'm inquiring about is a colored man, a light mulatto. The head waiter says you probably know him or know of him."

"Yes," said the barber, "I know all about him. He come of a good family and had a good education. When he grew up he went in the best colored society— his sister is a hairdresser and manicure right around the corner, in the Blaine Block, a very nice woman. What's Will been doing now? What do you want him for?"

"What might he be wanted for?" asked Seaton.

"Well, he might be wanted for gambling or pandering, or using or peddling coke. He's a good lookin' fellow, and good-natured, and friendly, but as a man and a citizen, and a good Negro, he ain't worth a whoop in hell—I beg pardon, sir, I hope you're not a minister."

"No," replied Seaton, "I'm just an ordinary sinner, and from what I have already learned of Johnson, I guess you've sized him up about right."

"I had him in the shop a while," continued the barber. "His sister wanted him to enter the State University here and become a lawyer or a doctor, but he wouldn't study. He was a good barber, polite and affable, and got more and bigger tips than any man in the shop, but he was a born gambler, and was always borrowing from the other barbers and from the waiters upstairs. He generally owed the head waiter, Jones, at least a month's wages, which that bloodsucker discounted in advance at ten percent a month. I didn't mind that so much, but when he took up with a low-down white woman, and it was talked about in the hotel, and when he began to get drunk and to use cocaine, I couldn't stand for him any longer; for I cater to the best people, not only of the city but of the country.[1] The governor has his barbering done here. I shaved President McKinley when he was governor and since, and Senator Hanna is my very good friend and corresponds with me about colored men who are seeking office. Do you see that card on the wall? That was given to me by the famous Elbert Hubbard,[2] who always stops at this hotel and comes in here to be shaved."

"Does he ever get his hair cut?" asked Seaton.

"Not here," laughed the barber, in appreciation of the joke. "I suppose he gets it cut once or twice a year, but he's never had it done here."

Seaton glanced at the handsomely framed oblong of cardboard, painted in fancy letters in alternating red and black, and reading: "The best barbershop in the United States," followed by the well-known signature of the genial Fra Elbertus.

"I've got all his books," continued the barber. "He sent me an autographed copy of 'The Message to Garcia,' which is hanging in my library, along with signed photographs of President McKinley and Senator Hanna.

"You can see," he continued with pardonable vanity, as he shaved Seaton's neck, "that I keep a sanitary shop, with all the latest improvements. Next year I'm going to put in manicures and a chiropodist. So I couldn't put up with Johnson any longer and had to let him go."

"Do you know anything about Johnson's ancestry?" asked Seaton. "Do you know, for instance, the source of his white blood?"

"Not definitely," replied the barber. "I know where mine came from. My father was the son of a banker in Richmond. But we mulattoes don't talk much about our white blood. The white people resent our having it, at least they never talk about it, and call us all Negroes. As a rule we accept the designation. But Miss Johnson, Will's sister, is an exception. She is very nearly white, and is rather proud of her descent, which she will tell you about. Thank you very much, sir. Come in again, sir."

Seaton went around the corner to the establishment of "Miss Mary Johnson, Hairdressing and Manicuring, Wigs, Toupees and Marcel Waving," as the gilt lettering on the show window in front announced.

He asked for Miss Johnson, who proved to be a personable light-colored woman in the late thirties, whose abundant straight hair, which she wore long—it was before the day of hair-bobbing—might have been dressed as an advertisement of her trade. Seaton asked for a manicure, and asked to be served by Miss Johnson. She led him into a small room adjoining the main room, and when he was seated and his fingers guided into the bowl of orange-scented warm water, he began his inquiry.

"Pardon me for mentioning the subject—I would never have suspected it and it is difficult to believe—

but I have been told that you are colored. Would you be offended if I should ask you from what source your white blood came?"

The lady, who had obviously been flattered by what he had said about her color, was not backward about replying.

"Not at all," she returned. "I'm not ashamed of my white blood but proud of it. I came by it quite as honestly as I did my black blood—some of my ancestors were slaves, and marriage among slaves had no legal meaning. My mother's grandmother was a favorite servant of Thomas Jefferson. By his will he set her and her children free and gave them property. I am very proud to have his blood in my veins. My mother, when she died, left me a pen and ink drawing of my great-grandfather, signed with his name, and a ring bearing his initials."

She was easily drawn out, and Seaton found her well informed on the race question. But he was interested in it only so far as Donald was concerned, and having learned what he wanted to know, paid the stipulated fee, with a generous gratuity, and returned to his hotel.

His inquiries into Donald's maternity were less exhaustive. His mother was a European white and presumably of pure strain. That she had been born and bred in poverty was no warrant for assuming degeneracy. One of her brothers, he learned, was a lieutenant of police in Cincinnati. She had once been married, a worthless husband had abandoned her, she did not care to live alone, and her church did not recognize divorce. Seaton returned to Cleveland in a depressed frame of mind, to take up the consideration of little Donald's future. He had learned to love the child as though he were his own. He would like to do the ideally fine thing, keep him and give him a white man's chance in life. But he was no radical and that sort of thing simply wasn't done. Moreover, his wife's feelings had to be taken into account, and she would have the last word.

CHAPTER VI

———›—‹———

A MAN destined to play an important part in shaping the destiny of young Donald Seaton was Senator James L. Brown,[1] the leading colored citizen of Cleveland. A member of the legal profession, he had built up such a practice as was open to a lawyer of his race, consisting mainly of criminal and police court work. At that time there was little profitable civil law business to be had from colored people. They were poor and had no large estates or businesses to handle or administer. Then, as to a large extent now, unlike the Jews, the only other differentiated population group with which they might be at all compared, and that only remotely, they had little commercial instinct and no business of any magnitude, nor had they as yet learned to organize and consolidate their small savings into banks, insurance companies and building and loan associations. These, with the great toilet preparations industry, were matters for future development.

An honest politician in an era of graft, when men of his race were subject to even greater temptation than

politicians of lighter hue, Brown had served first as a
justice of the peace, then as state representative for several terms, and now was a member of the State Senate.
No charge of dishonesty had ever been made against
him, and that he stood well in the community was evi-
dent from the fact that he could be elected to an important office in a city where at that time his people constituted an insignificant minority of the population.

He was seated one day at his desk in his office in the
Blackstone Building, when he was called by telephone
and asked if a gentleman could see him at his home
that evening, upon a personal matter, to which he replied in the affirmative.

After dinner that night he sat in his library awaiting
his caller. The walls of his room were hung with photo-
graphic prints of famous paintings—he and his family
had made several trips to Europe, which had been
white lights in their socially somewhat drab and cir-
cumscribed lives, and most of the prints were *souvenirs
de voyage*. There was also an oil painting in vivid col-
ors—a battle piece of some merit, which a stranded
painter of sorts, fallen into evil ways and legal difficul-
ties, had left with the lawyer in pledge for a fee he had
never redeemed.

Of the rows of bookshelves, on one side of the room,
several were filled with books by colored writers. Their
number was surprising—it was long before the day of
the New Negro—though in most cases their literary
value was negligible. With the exception of the three

great Alexanders—two Dumas, and one Pushkin—
they were almost without exception books about the
Negro, his rights and wrongs, his possibilities, his aspirations and his achievements. Colored writers had not
then, nor have they yet, learned to write much about
anything else, perhaps because the subject was so large
and had been so inadequately treated, and because the
race problem was so real and so urgent a factor in their
lives that nothing else seemed to them of even compar-
ative importance. There were thrilling stories of es-
capes from slavery. The life of Frederick Douglass held
a prominent place, George W. Williams's *History of the
Negro* another. They were human documents, material
for the future historian, novelist, essayist and drama-
tist. When the writers of the present day have exhausted the current themes of Negro stories, these earlier literary fumblings of an unlettered people will furnish many a motive for poem or novel or play. Along
with these were the novels of Harriet Beecher Stowe,
Judge Albion W. Tourgee, the speeches of Wendell
Phillips, the poems of Whittier and many another New
England contribution to anti-slavery literature. Fanny
Kemble's *Journal of Life on a South Carolina Plantation*
was an item that Brown valued highly because of its
dispassionate and therefore all the more convincing
description of commercialized slavery.

In the living room adjoining the library were seated
Mrs. Brown and her two daughters. The elder daughter, Esther, was a graduate of Oberlin College and a

teacher in the public schools; the younger, Myrtle, was just ready to enter high school. Mr. Brown himself was a light mulatto, his wife a personable woman of even fairer complexion. The two daughters resembled their mother in the matter of color. Mr. Brown was looking over the evening paper, Mrs. Brown was sewing, Miss Brown was reading a volume of Browning's poems, and Myrtle was studying her Latin lesson.

When the doorbell rang, the ladies escaped with their impedementa, and Mr. Brown went to the door, where he was confronted by a well-dressed white man with the appearance and manners of a gentleman—in other words, our friend Seaton.

"I'm the man," Mr. Seaton explained when he had been ushered into the library and asked to be seated, "who called you up today."

"I had suspected as much," returned Mr. Brown.

"My name is Seaton. I live in the city. I wanted to consult you on a matter of personal interest to me. I came to you because of your reputation for leadership among your people and your well-known interest in whatever concerns them. If you will let me tell my story, and you then feel I am intruding, you have only to say so, and I'll apologize and go away."

Of course Mr. Brown was intrigued by such an introduction and signified his entire willingness to listen. Mr. Seaton then told the story of little Donald as the reader has learned it.

"It's a very interesting story," said Mr. Brown, "but where, may I ask, do I come in on it?"

"My wife and I," replied Seaton, "are very fond of little Donald. He is a dear, bright child, and has entwined himself around our hearts. We should like to keep him, but we have wondered if it wouldn't be better for his and his future happiness if he were brought up among his own people."

"He's your son before the law," returned the lawyer. "You've legally adopted him. If you should be killed in an accident on your way home he would inherit as your son. Why couldn't you bring him up in your own family? I should like to see a white man, by God, who had the courage to bring up a colored child! They have begotten many of them, given them of their blood and brain, and then disowned them and thrown them back on their black cousins, into an infertile soil where their better heritage had no opportunity to direct their lives. In the days of slavery they used their blood to enhance the marketability of their mulatto sons and daughters—they were social cannibals, devouring and battening upon their own flesh."

Senator Brown spoke with some heat.

"I regret the shameful past," agreed Seaton, "quite as much as you. But it was part of an iniquitous system, with which neither you nor I had anything personally to do, and which, thank God, has passed away forever. I should like to keep the baby. I haven't yet decided to let him go, but, if I should, for what I think sufficient reasons, I was wondering if you could suggest or help me find some respectable colored family which would adopt him? I would share the expense of bringing him up, and I should be glad to compensate you for your time and effort."

"The adoption," rejoined Mr. Brown, after a moment of reflection, "might possibly be voided or transferred. I don't know offhand of any family that would adopt a child, but I can inquire. Couldn't he be returned to his own parents?"

"Impossible," said Seaton decisively, "I would rather keep him than expose him to such an environment."

"Well, I don't suppose you could, anyway, for they have parted with their claim and you have assumed their obligations."

"Would you care to see the boy?"

"I should like to very much—I would know what I was talking about."

"He's outside in the car with my wife. I'll bring him in."

"Bring them both in. I should like to meet Mrs. Seaton."

Seaton left the house and in a few seconds returned with his wife and the child.

"This is Mrs. Seaton, Mr. Brown, and this is our dear little Donald."

Brown shook hands with the lady and showed her to a seat in the living room, which opened off the library through a wide door. The boy sat beside her, on the sofa. Mr. Brown extended his forefinger to the little chap, who took it in his chubby fist very amiably.

"What is your name?" asked the lawyer.

"My name," returned the baby, "is Donald Seaton. My papa's name is Angus Seaton, my mama's name is Grace Seaton, and we live on Ethel Avenue, in Lakewood."

He spoke more clearly and intelligibly than would ordinarily a child of his few years—or months.

"We have taught him that formula," explained Mr. Seaton, "so that in case he should get lost he could more easily be recovered."

"Perhaps it was not a wise thing to do," said Mr. Brown. "It might prove a happy solution of your problem if he should be lost and not found."

He spoke with a tinge of cynicism, if not of bitterness, and the lady winced.

Little Donald, after the manner of children, had climbed down from his seat and was exploring the room. At that moment Miss Brown, the elder daughter, appeared.

"Mother and sister and I have been sitting in the dining room. We overheard all you have said, and I just had to come in and see the baby. What a beautiful child he is! Won't you come to me, darling?"

"Yes, go to the lady, Donald," said his mother.

He went willingly enough, and as soon as she took him in her arms and kissed his soft cheek and stroked his curly hair, he piped up in his childish treble: "My name is Donald Seaton, my papa's name is Angus Seaton, my mamma's name is Grace Seaton, and we live on Ethel Avenue, in Lakewood."

"Poor little devil," said Mr. Brown to himself. "He'll have to forget his first lesson almost as soon as he has learned it. However much they may love the baby, they won't keep him, they wouldn't dare to. He'll have to pay dearly for the crime of living, before death exacts the final penalty."

Mrs. Brown and Myrtle came in, and she and her daughters wept over the baby. They knew the fate that awaited him; they too had felt the iron in their souls. They knew what it was to be a Negro in a white world, even amid the most liberal surroundings. Mrs. Seaton joined her tears to theirs and Mr. Seaton's eyes were moist. Only Mr. Brown maintained a grim composure.

"It's an awful mess," he declared. "I'm not as sorry for you as I might be, for after all, it is you and your people who have created the situation. It is the baby that I am concerned about. I should like to see you keep him and bring him up as a white child. But I know you can't, or at least you won't, and I'll see if I can find someone who will take him off your hands."

The Seatons thanked him and took their leave. Mr. Brown and Mr. Seaton went first to the door. The ladies came a little behind.

"Don't you think, Miss Brown," said Mrs. Seaton, "that your father was a little hard on us?"

"He's the kindest man in the world," replied the teacher, "but this awful race problem has embittered him. He used to be an optimist, and believed in the best of all possible worlds, but of late years he has become pessimistic and cynical. We're awfully glad you brought your beautiful baby around. I'm sure father will assist you, and no one could help loving such a little darling. We'll call you up, if we may, from time to time, and ask about him."

"Yes, do," said Mrs. Seaton.

From the front window they watched the Seatons go down the walk to the street and climb into their automobile.

"Quite a tragedy," growled Mr. Brown, as the visitors drove away.

"It would make a theme for a romance," sighed Miss Brown, who was sentimental and had literary aspirations.

"He broke one of the ribs of the fan you bought me in Paris," said Myrtle, the younger girl.

"I think you *were* a little hard on them, Jim," ventured Mrs. Brown mildly. "They were very nice people and very much concerned about the baby. And they *did* adopt him," she added, inconsequently. Logic was not her strong point.

"Yes, they adopted him because they thought he was white, and now they know he isn't they want to throw him out. I don't care a damn about them. It's the baby I'm interested in. They are white people and can take care of themselves. He is a 'nigger,' and God will have to look after him. I hope He'll make a better job of it than He has been doing for the race up to date."

"Don't be profane, Jim," reproved Mrs. Brown, "or sacrilegious. As old Sojourner Truth said to Frederick Douglass in his darkest hour, 'God still lives.'"

Mrs. Brown was a church member and a good Christian. Mr. Brown paid the pew rent, and kept his religion, as he did the titles to his property, in his wife's name.

> "God's in his heaven,
> All's right with the world!"

quoted Miss Brown, who knew her Browning, and loved him all the better because she had read, in an English biography of the famous poet, that some of his friends maintained that because of his dark complexion and curly hair, and the warmth and sensuousness of his poetry, and his West Indian birth and breeding, the probability was that he had some Negro blood.[2] Mr. Browning had replied, smilingly, that there was no record or tradition in his family of any such thing, but if the fact could be established, he would cheerfully admit it, if it would reflect any credit on his darker kinsmen, who certainly needed all the credit they could get. It would require a great deal of proof, Miss Brown was certain, to make Americans admit that the great Victorian could be colored. She recalled an article in a critical review in which the writer, a Southern woman and the leading literary light of Jackson, Mississippi, had maintained that the famous French author Alexander Dumas could not possibly have been colored, for the simple reason that no Negro could have written *Monte Christo*, or *The Three Musketeers*. It was too good to be true about Browning—but the thought was comforting.

CHAPTER VII

———⟫◆⟪———

SEVERAL TIMES during the week following the Seatons'
visit, Mr. Brown mentioned to people of his acquaintance the story of little Donald. He said nothing
about his parentage, except that he was colored, nor
did he name Mr. Seaton, merely mentioning that the
child had been adopted into a white family by mistake,
and that he wished to find a colored family to take him
over. The story spread, and one day a woman's voice
called Mr. Brown on the telephone. The speaker said
that she had heard of Donald's case, that she and her
husband had no children and wished to adopt a child,
and that she would like to get in touch with the man
who had the baby.

Brown had met the lady, who was a Mrs. Glover. Her
husband was a doctor, with a practice among colored
people. At that time the only physician of his race in
the city, he enjoyed a fairly good practice, from the
proceeds of which he and his wife were able to live, not
extravagantly, but comfortably. They were not intimate

friends of the Brown family, though the women had exchanged calls. He was quite sure that should they adopt a child they would be amply able to provide for it.

Senator Brown inquired of Mrs. Glover whether she cared to know the facts about the child's origin. She said no, that the doctrine of heredity did not appeal to her, that she believed in the controlling influence of environment. Colored people, she said, in view of their history, were not in a position to be squeamish about blood and birth. The child, she declared, was a human being. Every human being was entitled to lawful birth, and the fact that he had been robbed of his birthright, if such were the case, ought to make society all the more keen to see that this disadvantage was offset by education and training.

Favorably impressed by these generous sentiments, Mr. Brown volunteered no further information, but gave Mr. Seaton's name and address.

Mrs. Glover called up Seaton and arranged for him and Mrs. Seaton to bring the baby to her home. She would thus be enabled to see the child, and the Seatons could meet her and her husband and form some idea of the child's future home surroundings, should they decide to let him go. They came an evening or two later, and were favorably impressed. Again little Donald was left on approval. If the Glovers, after keeping him a while, should wish to adopt him, the matter could then be arranged. In the meantime the Seatons were to be at entire liberty to see him when they so desired. A day or two later his clothes and toys were carried to the Glovers' home. It was so managed that Donald could be left there while asleep.

When the baby awoke he called for his mama, and for a long time would not be comforted because she did not come. However, by means of a little feminine diplomacy, and a few endearments, he was consoled, and ate his next meal with a very good appetite. For several days he kept asking for his mamma and his papa, but he was told that he now had a new mamma and a new papa.

At the end of the first week the Seatons drove over one evening to see him. Little Donald leaped into Mrs. Seaton's arms and gave every childish expression of delight. A week later Seaton called up on the telephone and wanted to know if they could borrow Donald for a few days.

They kept him for a week and then brought him back. This was repeated several times, at longer intervals, with the idea that they would gradually miss the baby less, and he in turn would become more and more reconciled to their absence.

Mrs. Glover's sister, who lived in Oberlin, came down to Cleveland one day to visit her.

"Where's Donald?" she asked, after she had greeted her sister and taken off her things.

"He's over at the Seatons'," returned Mrs. Glover. "I lent him to them Monday, for three days, and the time is up today. I'm expecting them to bring him back this afternoon."

"You're a funny woman," said her sister, "and a good match for those crazy white people. They want the baby and they don't want him. I'd make 'em either keep him or leave him alone. And the same applies to you—I'd either keep him or let them keep him. It's hard on the boy not to know who are his parents."

Mrs. Glover had felt somewhat the same way about it, and others of her friends had expressed similar sentiments. But she was kindly natured and knew that to give up Donald had been quite an emotional wrench for the Seatons. So she had been willing to let them have him now and then, hoping that Donald and they would gradually become weaned away from each other. But her sister's remark set her to thinking, and as the afternoon wore away and Donald was not returned, she became more and more concerned. He might be sick or something might have happened to him. She rang up the Seatons by telephone but could not get the connection, the operator replying that the line was out of order.

Finally she put on her hat and coat, excused herself to her sister, took a street car downtown, through the heart of the city, across the long river bridge, through the business section of the West Side, which, like that of the East Side, abutted upon the river, to Ethel Avenue, in the residential suburb where the Seatons had their home.

The house, which she knew well, stood near the street, with a small grass plot in front of it. The living room, which faced upon the street, was brilliantly lighted. The opaque shades were up and the interior was plainly visible between the net curtains which were draped on the sides.

As Mrs. Glover stepped on the porch she heard Donald's gleeful shout. It thrilled her through and through and instead of ringing the doorbell she stood a moment looking through the window. Mrs. Seaton and her mother, who was living with the family, were seated on the davenport. The maid, in white cap and apron, was standing by the door leading into the dining room, which was just behind the living room. Seaton was walking around the room on all fours, with Donald astride of his back, kicking his ribs zestfully, and urging him to "Giddap, hossie!" to the plaudits of the rest of the company.

Donald's toys had been brought to her house, but Mrs. Glover saw the floor strewn with new toy cats and dogs, a new rocking horse, and a life-sized indestructible doll in a doll buggy.

Presently the horse bucked and threw the rider, who was laughing in great glee. Mrs. Seaton picked him up and kissed him. He encircled her neck with his little arms, looked up into her eyes with his engaging smile and cried in his sweet childish treble: "Oh, mamma, dear mamma, what a lubly hoss papa makes!"

The watcher outside made an effort to control her feelings. These white people, who had cast him aside, were stealing her beautiful baby's love from her, and she felt all the jealousy of the tigress for her cub. As soon as she felt sufficiently calm to act politely, she rang the doorbell, and the maid admitted her to the vestibule, from which she advanced into the adjoining living room.

"I've come to get Donald," she said in a strained voice, without any preliminary greeting.

"Is there anything wrong?" asked Mrs. Seaton soothingly, noting her emotion.

"No," she replied, "but he's mine, and I want him."

"We meant to take him back today," said Mrs. Seaton, "but he cried to stay, so we thought you wouldn't mind if we kept him another night. I'll have Elsa get his clothes ready, unless you'd rather we sent them over tomorrow."

"No, thank you," said Mrs. Glover. "I'll take them along."

Mrs. Seaton brought Donald's coat and hat from the vestibule and was holding out his coat for him when Mrs. Glover took it from her and put it on the baby.

"I beg your pardon, Mrs. Glover," exclaimed Seaton contritely, "you've been standing ever since you came in. Won't you be seated?" he pushed a chair forward.

"No, thank you," she replied, "I prefer to stand."

By this time Elsa had returned with Donald's suit-case. The baby was somewhat bewildered.

"Am I going with my other mamma?" he asked of Mrs. Seaton.

"Yes," said Mrs. Glover, "you're going with your own mamma, to your own home."

"Can I take Tootsie Wootsie," he asked indicating the big doll, which he had so christened.

"Why, certainly, darling," said Mrs. Seaton, "by all means."

"No," said Mrs. Glover, "it's too large, we can't carry it on the street car."

"You don't need to take the street car," said Seaton. "We'll drive you over in the automobile."

"No," replied Mrs. Glover, "I wouldn't put you to that trouble. Come on, Donald, tell your friends good night."

"Good night, mamma, good night, papa, good night, gramma, good night, Elsa," piped Donald.

"Good night, darling," they chorused but did not dare to kiss him.

Mrs. Glover took the suitcase in one hand and Donald's hand in the other.

"Good night," she said briefly, and went out as Elsa opened the door.

"She seemed offended, as though you had done something to her," said Mrs. Seaton's mother.

"You kicked the milkpail over when you spoke

about Donald crying to stay here," said Seaton to his wife, "I imagine she won't let him come again."

Some months later Mrs. Seaton gave birth to twins, which demanded all her attention. Mr. Seaton called up now and then to inquire about Donald, but did not ask to take him again.

Mrs. Glover, in response to a telephone request, brought Donald one evening some months later to call on the Browns.

"Has he entirely forgotten the Seatons?" asked Miss Brown.

"Yes," was the reply. "Mr. Seaton calls up occasionally to inquire how he is getting along, and has offered to help pay the expense of bringing him up. I thanked him, but told him that I shouldn't have adopted Donald if I hadn't felt able to take care of him. Mrs. Seaton's twins keep her busy, so she'd have no time for Donald. They had the opportunity to bring him up. They might have made a fine white man of him—he looks as white as Mrs. Seaton—but they lost their chance, and I'm going to make a good Negro of him."

In the confusion and delay attendant upon these various happenings, no one looked after the transfer of Donald's adoption, and he still remained of lawful record the son of Angus and Grace Seaton.

CHAPTER VIII

———⟫●⟪———

T HE FIRST FIVE years of Donald Glover's life were
spent in the city of Cleveland, and he was never
conscious during that period that he was in any way
different from any other little boy. His parents lived in
a mixed neighborhood—most of the families were
white, with a few colored people of the better class. It
was a street of young families and Donald played with
the children on the street, in their homes and in his
own. The qualities which were to prove so potent in
molding his future were already in evidence. He was
amiable, truthful, generous and loyal. His parents belonged to a colored church to which they sometimes
took Donald, but he was too young to attend Sunday
school. He heard his parents and their friends at times
talking about white and colored people, but to his
childish mind these were merely terms describing ex-
ternals. No one ever called him "nigger" or "Negro."
Only once could he recall in later years was his race
mentioned. His neighborhood friend, little Jimmie
Jones, said to him one day: "My mamma says you're a

mulatto, Donald, but that you're a nice little boy, and I can invite you to my party."

He repeated the remark to his mother.

"Mamma," he asked, "what is a mulatto?"

Mrs. Glover's first impulse was to tell him, without further parley, that he could not go to Jimmie's party, but on second thought, she reasoned, why should the child be deprived of a harmless pleasure because of a senseless prejudice which had in his case been waived? So she gave him an evasive answer.

"Why didn't Jimmie tell you," she replied, "that it meant a nice little boy?"

Donald's undeveloped mind was already logical enough to sense, obscurely, that his mother was begging the question, and that her answer was neither categorical nor convincing. He was too young to know or foresee the extent to which the little word "but" would confront and baffle him on his way through life, but he accepted her definition, and went to the party and enjoyed it.

But the time was soon to come when a white lie could no longer keep Donald's eyes closed to his real importance—or insignificance—in the scheme of things.

Several other colored physicians had opened offices in Cleveland, and Dr. Glover's practice began to fall off. The newcomers were younger and more energetic— Dr. Glover, if not lazy, was at least none too industrious. Perhaps his competitors were better educated, or

more skillful. When a former classmate of his at Howard University, where he had received his medical education, a dentist practicing in a small Southern city,
wrote him that there was a good opening there for a
colored physician, and offered to share offices and office expenses with him, he closed his office in Cleveland and with his family moved to Booneville, Ken-
nessee.

Little Donald now began, in his new environment, at
the tender age of five, his real training as Negro. Up to
that time he had been merely a small boy, one of a
neighborhood group in what was at that time an unusually liberal Northern community, and not con-
sciously different from any other small boy.

In the first place the Glovers went to live in a Negro
neighborhood. With the exception of a few Jews and
poor white people, a few Syrians, and a lone Chinaman, the neighborhood was solidly black.

The Glovers joined a colored church. The "nigger
heaven" of the white churches had almost disappeared.
With the exception of an occasional old "mammy" or
"uncle," still in the service of or pensioned off by a
white family of which he or she had once been the
chattel, and for whom provision was made in a railed
off corner, the galleries had been turned over to white
people. Negroes no longer contaminated the Lord's
table, even at a second serving or from a different chal-
ice. The church had become a social institution, to
which the strict rules of social intercourse were ap-

plied. Next to intermarriage, which was also a penal offense, the most unforgivable social crime was for white and black to eat together, and the Lord's supper was no exception.

Donald was sent to Sunday school at the Mt. Horeb African Methodist Episcopal Church, of which the pastor was a very black and very eloquent Negro. Despite his degree of Doctor of Divinity from a Negro theological seminary, that he was not very learned was apparent to any educated person who heard him preach. That he was morally unstable had been more than once hinted, sometimes with incriminating details. But he had read enough to quote Shakespeare, and when any such whisper about himself came back to his ears he would reply, in denying the slander: "Be thou as chaste as ice, as pure as snow, thou shalt not escape calumny." But whether he was chaste and pure or not, he certainly did not escape being widely talked about.

Donald's Sunday school teacher, on the other hand, was a very fair young woman. The children ranged in color from black through the many shades of yellow and brown, to apparently white. Little Donald, reacting to his first lesson in color, turned his inquiring mind upon this inconsistency.

"Oh, mamma," he inquired, after his first Sunday school session, "is my teacher white?"

"No, Donald, Miss McRae is a Negro."

"And are the white children in my class Negroes?"

"Yes, my child, they are all Negroes."

"And I," inquired Donald, looking at himself in the mirror, "am I—a Negro?"

"Yes, my darling," she returned sadly, as she clasped him in her arms, "though you are white to look at, you share the blood of a despised race and so are one of them. But don't you worry about it, honey. God made us all, and He'll not forsake us. And when you grow up and become the leader of our people, we'll prove to the white folks that we're just as good as they are."

Despite her zeal for her own people, Mrs. Glover had not yet learned to hate white people. She had her temptations, however, as when Donald came home one day singing, in his childish treble:

> God made the little niggers,
> He made 'em in the night,
> He made 'em in a hurry,
> And didn't make 'em right.

"Why, Donald Glover!" said his mother explosively, "where in the world did you pick up that vile rhyme?"

"Pinky Green and Tommy Blue and I were coming along the sidewalk, when three little white girls, walking arm in arm, crowded us off and sang that song at us."

"Well, you're not to repeat it. It's a vicious slander on your people."

Mrs. Glover had not permitted herself to hate white people because her religion taught her to love her enemies and to pray for them that despitefully used her.

This she tried to do, though it was sometimes difficult. A sensible woman, she adapted herself with as little friction as possible to the customs of the community. If she and her husband chose to live in the South, as they had chosen, they must conform to its customs and adjust themselves to their surroundings, however much they might resent certain things. She must, for instance, be satisfied never to be addressed by a white person, not even a telephone operator or a post office clerk, as "Mrs. Glover." The reference to her personality was generally made in a roundabout way. "Is this Jane Glover?" or "Is your name Glover?" or "Are you Doctor Glover's wife?" Occasionally a white woman as old as she would address her as "Auntie" to her great indignation, which she restrained as well as she could. By custom, a Negro could be addressed by a professional title, as "Reverend," or "Doctor," or "Professor," but the titles, "Mr.," "Mrs.," and "Miss" were reserved exclusively for the superior caste. If she bought shoes or hats or a coat for herself, she must buy them by the size, as Negroes were not permitted to try on things which white people might want to buy. As a result she ordered most of such goods from the mail order houses or through the shopping agents of the dry goods stores in Northern cities. It was only another demonstration that race prejudice was an expensive luxury. The merchants lost much valuable trade, and Mrs. Glover much valuable time.

Much of her explanations to Donald on this and

later occasions were far above his comprehension. But in bringing him up, she had never been afraid of talking over his head. Donald was unusually precocious, with a retentive memory, and a faculty of comparison by which, she argued, in time he would learn to assort and classify the knowledge that he acquired as he was growing up.

When he was six years old, Donald was sent to a Negro public school. The much maligned reconstruction government, which for the first time in the history of the South had established public schools, had in the first instance segregated and classified them as "white" and "colored," but in keeping with the rising tide of prejudice and the consequent tightening of racial lines which was in progress, a later amendment to the statute had denominated the colored schools "Negro" schools. They were inferior to the white schools, as any separate provision for a poorer, a socially inferior and numerically smaller group inevitably is, anywhere, no matter if the laws demand equality, and the laws of the state made no such demand.

A strong characteristic of Mrs. Glover was a passion for justice. But there was, to her mind, so much injustice in the world's dealings with her own people that she had little time or emotional energy left for other causes, although when she witnessed or read of some denial of justice to other men in other lands, or by white men to white men in her own country, her indignation was always aroused. Nor did her compassion stop at human beings. A man beating a horse, a boy torturing a dog or a bird or an insect, would stir her to vigorous expostulation. She came very near rendering life in Booneville impossible for herself and her family, when, one Fourth of July, she saw a white boy tie a pack of fire crackers to a dog's tail and strike a match to set it off. He wasn't much of a dog and would probably have been happier dead, and the world none the worse, but she had read in a Negro newspaper some months before an account of an incident in a small Southern town, where the white young men of the village, bored stiff by the lack of amusement, had found it in pouring kerosene oil on the hair of a half-witted Negro lad and setting fire to it. The sight of the fire-crackers tied to the dog so enraged her that she pulled the boy away none too gently and expressed her opinion of him in terms which were not complimentary. The boy's mother, to whom the incident was reported, was righteously indignant that a Negro woman should have laid hands upon her son, for no matter what reason, and swore out a warrant against Mrs. Glover for assault and battery. It required all the diplomacy of Dr. Glover and his friends among the white physicians to smooth over the incident.

A tall, wiry woman, with brown skin, and sharp clean-cut features only slightly softened by her Negroid strain, Mrs. Glover was a bundle of nerves, but she had inherited a strong constitution and was well-fitted to resist the buffetings of life and adverse circumstance.

Whatever task she undertook, she performed with zeal and enthusiasm. To her the bringing up of Donald to be a leader of his people was no mere fleeting sentimental impulse, but a deep-rooted purpose to which she devoted all her time and energy not demanded by the business of daily life.

CHAPTER IX

—————⊷⊶⊷—————

MRS. GLOVER WAS a dreamer. Like Savanarola and Joan of Arc she had prophetic visions. Whether a dreamer is visionary or prophet is determined by the future. St. Paul was a prophet; his dream of a great church came true. John Brown was a visionary—his scheme for freeing the slaves failed and, like Jesus, Savanarola, Joan of Arc, and all the "the noble army of martyrs," he died for his dream. As Donald Glover, later on, beautifully and forcefully put it in his famous *Essay on the Imagination*, "Dreams are the filmy warp into which the substantial threads of our life are woven."

When Donald, during his career as a writer, was charged with plagiarism, as he sometimes was, he retorted that he wrote to inform and to persuade, and that if another had said perfectly or better than he could, something that would further his purpose, why waste time in seeking a different allocution?

Mrs. Glover's dreams were mostly about the Negro, and while not destined to die for her dreams, she exerted herself to bring about their realization. An ardent "race" woman, as the phrase goes, she believed in the Negro. She had convinced herself, with small evidence at that time upon which to base her belief, that somewhere buried in the sands of Africa were the remains of ancient civilizations which the Negro or Negroid natives had founded and developed until hostile nature and still more hostile man had overwhelmed them. She had been brought up in Oberlin, had attended the college there for two years, before she married Dr. Glover, and was fairly well-educated. She read whatever she could find on the subject of the Negro in history. She subscribed to the current Negro periodicals and bought every new book that was written by a colored man or woman. These were not very numerous during Donald's boyhood and their quality left much to be desired. But they were all inspired by the same motives—resentment for wrongs, mostly real, occasionally fancied, confidence in the race and hope for its future. When a certain mulatto writer published a book[1] in which he postulated the inferiority of the Negro and the degeneracy of mixed blood and claimed to prove it by the time-worn arguments of failure and inadequacy of achievement, she was furiously indignant, wrote a letter to the author in which she stated her opinion of him in no uncertain language and another to the publishers, in which she expressed her surprise and grief that so old and honorable a house should lend itself to the defamation of an oppressed and struggling people; and when it was later announced that the publishers, in view of the storm of protest which the work had elicited, had suspended its sale, she was correspondingly elated, and sent them a letter of thanks.

She believed that the Negro had a future, and a worthy one. She anticipated the scientists of our day in maintaining that there is no essential intellectual difference in races, any apparent variation being merely a matter of development; that the backwardness of the Negro was due to his historical environment and to the restrictions with which he had always been surrounded and the repressions and inhibitions to which he was still subject. She dreamed of a future in which her people should be adequately and personally represented in lawmaking bodies, in the courts, and in all branches of the public service. She dreamed of the day when they should produce great healers, lawyers, writers, artists, thinkers—great men in every walk of life. She had dreamed, when a young woman, that she might have a son who would help this splendid vision to fulfillment. When she had been forced, sadly, to relinquish this hope and had taken little Donald to rear, she transferred her dreams to him. She had found him abandoned by his natural parents, and by his adopted parents, as, in the days of the Pharaohs, a little Hebrew boy had been found floating among the reeds of the ancient Nile, and carrying out the Scripture analogy, she thought of him as the Moses who should lead his people, her people, out of the wilderness of poverty and ignorance and low estate which the abolition of slavery had not yet dissipated, and "unto the land of the Canaanites, and the Amorites, and the Perizzites, and the Hivites and the Jebusites, unto a land flowing with milk and honey"—a land of opportunity and achievement—a trite but always vital figure.

She saw him as one who would take hold of this inchoate, mixed mass of people, held together loosely by the dark blood which they shared in varying degree and which, had they been permitted, many of them would willingly have forgotten, but because of which they were forced back upon one another—to take this mass of people, in the second generation of their nominal freedom, still slaves to ignorance and superstition, still exploited and robbed and scorned by the children of their former masters, and weld them into a racial solidarity that could resist and overcome the powers of oppression, and prove to a skeptical world that Negroes, as Negroes, could contribute to the best things of that world; that would make of their color, hitherto a badge of inferiority, no longer something to be ashamed of but a mark of distinction and a source of pride; that would repudiate the white man's condescending patronage, and repay his scorn with scorn or, by preference, transmute it into friendly cooperation. It was a dream that seemed unlikely of fulfillment, but the Lord had helped the children of Israel, and He would help his Negro children. For Mrs. Glover, though she had been to college and had read much, had not yet abandoned her belief in God, but had merely transferred the tribal deity of the Hebrews over to the sons of Ham. When downcast and disheartened, as she sometimes was, she remained loyal to her faith. "Though He slay me," she would quote, "yet will I trust in Him."

Her dreams, like all dreams, were more or less vague and disconnected. Some capable colored men and women were already reaching out and groping for solutions to these problems. Of these leaders the most conspicuous one of the day would attain the desired result by emphasizing the more elementary social virtues—industry, patience, application to the simpler forms of labor—agriculture and the trades, "casting down their buckets where they were," and building up in the South, or in whatever environment fate had placed them, a community within a community, "separate as the fingers but one as the hand," which in due course would flower into the better things. Another, a man of high culture and far-reaching vision, maintained that it was unjust and wicked to ask the colored people to wait several generations before they could enjoy the rights and liberties which were freely open on equal terms to all white men and guaranteed to themselves under the Constitution of their country and the doctrine of the Rights of Man from which the Constitution drew its inspiration.

The first of these leaders, the opportunist, in his

public utterances and writings, preached patience and forbearance and the importance of winning, by whatever temporary compromise or concession might seem necessary or expedient, the friendship and good will of the white people among whom they lived. The other, the idealist, buckled on his armor, grasped his sword and set out to slay with the weapons of knowledge and reason and ridicule and sarcasm the flaming dragon of race prejudice. That cynics might sneer and declare that he was merely a futile Don Quixote tilting at windmills did not disturb him nor deflect him in the least from his steadfast purpose.

Mrs. Glover was a follower of the crusader, but she dreamed of Donald as a Messiah of whom these smaller men were merely the forerunners. He would find the key to the puzzle. He would solve this modern riddle of the sphinx, and it would prove as easy to him as the solution of that ancient puzzle was to Oedipus.

Mrs. Glover directed Donald's education and reading along these lines, so far as she could, but his expanding intelligence reached out beyond the limits of the instruction imparted at the high school and by his mother, and explored the whole field of knowledge so far as it was open to him. He had a passion for learning, and especially for the study of languages, which he found it somewhat difficult to indulge. For example, Latin, Greek and the modern languages were not taught in the local colored high school. The Negro could have no possible use for them, in the opinion of the public school authorities, who were all white, but Donald's father had studied Latin in his preparation for medicine, and his mother rudimentary Latin and a little French in her brief college career, but they had learned neither language at all thoroughly and had forgotten most of what they had learned, so neither was of much assistance to Donald, though his mother helped him to some extent. He exhumed his father's and mother's old text books and procured through the local bookstore some of the elementary manuals by the aid of which a bright student could learn French, German and Italian without a teacher. To get the German pronunciation, he cultivated the acquaintance of the German Jewish merchants of the town who sought the Negro trade. If the accent was more or less Yiddish, Donald did not know it, and it was not long before he could make himself understood and could understand his interlocutors.

In French he was less fortunate. There were no Frenchmen that he knew of in the city, and he would have had a very nebulous notion of spoken French had it not been for an Alsatian Jew, a Professor Adolph Neuman,[2] who came to the city and opened classes in French and German for the white young people. At Donald's request, Mrs. Glover sought out Professor Neuman and engaged him to give her boy lessons. Donald would go to the professor's room at the hotel in the evening, and was making very good headway in his French, until one of the teacher's white pupils called on him one night without an appointment and found that he was teaching a Negro, and the professor was obliged to discontinue Donald's instruction. The matter would probably have stopped right there, had not the teacher, with very poor judgment, and to the discomfiture of his other pupils, remarked that Donald was the brightest of them all. The professor's popularity fell off, and he soon had to leave Booneville and seek some other place to earn a living.

None of his teachers in the high school, not even the principal, had studied Latin or Greek. Donald in his thirst for knowledge must learn them both. The Greek, perhaps because of the unfamiliar letters, did not at first especially appeal to him. He was to learn its beauty and flexibility in later years, when he was able to read and appreciate the intellectual treasures handed down in that ancient tongue. Latin, on the other hand, he simply ate up, so to speak. When he had learned enough of the language to begin to read it, someone gave him an old copy of Anthon's edition of the *Aeneid*,[3] with its copious notes and commentaries, and in six weeks, during a summer vacation, he read the whole twelve books of Virgil's masterpiece—twice as much as demanded in most college courses in a year.

Thus Donald Glover, with limited opportunities, was able, mainly through his own efforts, to acquire the beginnings of a liberal education. Even at the age of fifteen he had begun to explore the wilderness of philosophy. He had the run of the books of all the colored people in the city. These were not numerous, but there had sifted down into the Negro homes, from the libraries of white people, some of the classics of literature. The high school had a copy of an old edition of the *Encyclopædia Britannica*, which some visiting Northerner had presented to it. From this he read the articles of Plato, Aristotle, Kant, Schopenhauer, Bacon, Rousseau, Goethe, Spencer, Mill and Comte. Among the books of the Reverend Ebenezer M. Jones, his pastor, he found Josiah Royce's *Philosophy*, Paley's *Evidences of Christianity* and Drummond's *Natural Law in the Spiritual World*. He did not, of course, understand it all, but he assimilated enough to make him wish to learn the rest.

His appetite for learning grew by what it fed upon and clamored constantly for more. There was a public library in the town, to the support of which Dr. Glover contributed through his taxes, but which was not open to colored readers. Donald, with the friendly aid of the white pharmacist from whom Dr. Glover rented his office and to whom he sent his prescriptions to be filled, was able to circumvent in large measure this discriminative regulation. He would give the pharmacist a list of the books he wanted, and the pharmacist would draw them in his own name and turn them over to Donald. Works on evolution were carefully excluded from the library, but he ordered through the local bookstore Darwin's *Descent of Man* and *Origin of Species*. He did not learn of Frazer's *Golden Bough* until he went to college. The boy could not know the joy of browsing over the shelves of the library and discovering their hidden treasures, and he had access to no catalogue from which he could select; but in this indirect manner much of the best English literature was available to him. His reading, of course, was undirected and therefore desultory, but he carried into these early studies the same inquiring habit of mind which he had evinced when a small child. He never at any time in his life, after he became old enough to think, believed anything simply because someone else said it. Anything not obvious he had to verify. He was a born rebel, in the sense that instinctively he had no respect for authority which was not founded on reason, and he early discovered that a large part of life was hedged around by inhibitions, sounding in prejudice, selfishness and greed, and having no warrant whatever except that of superior force.

CHAPTER X

—————➤●◄—————

WHEN DONALD, who played the organ for the church choir, went to choir practice one Thursday evening in June, he found another member of the choir present in the Sunday school room, where there was a reed organ and where the choir practice was conducted. The usual hour for beginning was eight o'clock, but Donald as a rule went half an hour earlier, so as to get in some preliminary practice of his own. Upon this occasion he found another member of the choir present ahead of him.

"Good evening, Mamie," said Donald, "you're early tonight."

"Yes," she said, "I knew you always came early, and I had a song which I thought you might play over for me before the others came."

Mamie Wilson was a dark brown young woman, with pronounced but agreeable Negroid features, and abundant, shining, crinkly hair, which she knew how to arrange attractively. Indeed, to make herself attractive was Mamie's chief preoccupation in life. She was very popular with men, but not nearly so well liked by those of her own sex. In fact, more than one woman had suggested that Mamie was no better than she should be, and it was hinted that at least one wife had laid violent hands upon her. But she was amiable and, if not good, reasonably careful. Moral standards among her people were none too high, and her friends and acquaintances were in the main charitable. She had a beautiful though untrained voice, and was easily the best singer in the choir.

Donald sat down at the organ and ran over the accompaniment of the piece of music which she had brought with her. It was a lyric by Ernest Hogan,[1] at that time a popular Negro song writer, whose song "All Coons Look Alike to Me," had been a musical best seller which had broken all preexisting records. The term "blues" had not yet been invented, but the song she brought with her this evening was something along the same line, and as Donald played the plaintive minor chords of the accompaniment, Mamie sang it very effectively. She could control her really fine contralto voice to make it ring clear and trumpet-like for "Adeste Fidelis" or "Onward, Christian Soldiers," or low and husky for "In the Gloaming" or "Auld Lang Syne," or soft and crooning for "Swing Low Sweet Chariot" or "The Gypsy's Lament."

She stood to the left of Donald at the end of the organ, where he could see her distinctly while she followed the notes. In fact, such was his ear for music and

the ease with which he played, that he required
scarcely more than one glance at the score to be able to
play it through. He had "picked up" music as easily as
languages. He had met Mamie at all rehearsals, and he
had never paid more than casual attention to her, but
tonight he was conscious of her sex allure. Indeed she
radiated sex. Every line of her lithe and shapely body,
the liquid glance which she bent upon him from her
large dark eyes, and, when she leaned over occasionally to read the music, the seemingly accidental, but
really carefully calculated pressure of her firm young
breast upon his shoulder, produced upon him an effect
to which he had hitherto been a stranger, and stirred
within him primal emotions which had as yet been un-
disturbed. From his wide but desultory reading he was
mentally familiar with the sexual side of life as portrayed in books, but emotionally and physically it was
to him unexplored territory.

Very soon the other members of the choir began to
come in and their private session was ended. They ran
through the hymns for the next Sunday's service, and
indulged in the usual gossip and badinage. At the close
of the rehearsal, when the rest were leaving and Donald
was gathering up his music preparatory to his own departure, Mamie lingered behind the others and, when
they were all gone, remarked to him: "Since we are
going the same way, Donald, s'pose we walk along
together."

They left the church, Donald closing and locking the

door, and strolled slowly along the brick sidewalk, shaded by spreading elms and maples. There was little said between them. Donald felt the stirring of strange impulses, and Mamie, who knew her business, left Donald to himself, merely pressing lightly the arm she had taken.

It was a beautiful summer night. The gibbous moon, visible through the branches of the overhanging trees, was riding high, and the glory of the stars filled the firmament. It was an ideal night for love, of whatever sort.

It was about a half a mile from the church to Mamie's home. A little more than half way thither, on a quiet street, there was a large vacant lot, in the rear of which stood a group of shade trees. As they reached this space, Mamie turned into the vacant lot with Donald. He went with her as the pale knight at arms with the *Belle Dame Sans Merci*, impelled by unknown or unfamiliar forces. And there, in a leafy temple, on a grassy altar, by the immemorial rite this dusky siren sacrificed him to her god, Priapus, a divinity whose name she never in all her life heard, but of whom she was none the less a devout and zealous worshipper. She was young in years—not much older than Donald in fact—but she was as old as humanity. She had been born with more knowledge about the basic concern of life than Donald ever acquired.

Such was Donald's introduction to the simplest form of the riddle of sex. There was no element of romance or sentiment about it, and no intellectual complications, and yet it was a natural and almost an inevitable awakening, though a moralist might wish it had taken place under different conditions. Nature, however, has little concern for morals; they are, as the word implies, merely the established customs of society, which may, from an ideally ethical standpoint, be either right or wrong. And aside from a certain feeling of shame and later of disgust with himself, it made no lasting impression upon Donald. Indeed once satisfied, the primal urge subsided for a long time.

Mamie's deeper emotions, if she had any, were no more involved than those of Donald. To Mamie a man was only a man, after all, and in her world there were many men, not all as desirable as Donald, but all male.

As in this first instance, Donald, all through his young manhood, was destined to be the quarry and not the hawk, the sought and not the seeker, the hunted and not the hunter—this partly because of his own nature and in part because of his environment.

Donald's conscience troubled him about Mamie. His views concerning women were founded on what he had read about them and that mostly in mid-Victorian novels—Dickens, Thackeray, Bulwer-Lytton, George Eliot, Thomas Hardy—which he had read for the stories, with an instinctive appreciation for purity of style and beauty of language. A fine word aptly employed always struck him like a note of music. But until just now, when he had reached the age of puberty, incidents and situations involving tense and vital sexual problems had made no emotional appeal to him, however much he might sense their dramatic value. He was familiar with the poetry of Tennyson and Longfellow, with their reticence in regard to sex. Of the more sensuous poets, such as Browning and Swinburne and their school, he had read nothing except the excerpts published in school readers, always selected *virginibus puerisque.*

It is not astonishing, therefore, that he should be disturbed by his fleeting amour with Mamie. His fine mind had held him more or less aloof, intellectually, from the colored lads who made up his associates. They were, like most growing boys, lively, fond of horseplay, some of them precociously sexed and given to lewd conversation, but Donald's studious habits had protected him from any lasting impression from their crude and cubbish nastiness.

The affair weighed on his mind. No one had ever given him any advice on sexual matters. His mother, after the fashion of her day, would have considered it indecent to discuss the subject with any male person except her husband, and that very delicately. Perhaps the fact that she was herself of the virginal type had had something to do with her not having children of her own.

Dr. Glover, who had sincere respect for Donald's intellect—he admitted to himself that he could never have sired[2] such a son—and though among his cronies he was not averse to a "good story" and indeed had quite a line of them—also respected the essential purity of Donald's mind, and in the effort not to soil it had left unsaid some of the things an adolescent ought to know.

Donald met Mamie several times, and though she more than once led up to their affair, he always turned the subject and escaped as quickly as possible. Finally, one day, she managed to encounter him on the street, face to face, so that he could not evade her.

"Donald," she said, softly and with a note of pathos, falling into step behind him, "you don't love me no mo', but I gotta talk to you seriously. You took advantage of my youth and innocence, an' I'm in trouble, I'm goin' to have a baby. What is a' hones' man's duty in such a case and what are you goin' to do about it? Mus' I go through life wearin' the badge of shame or are you goin' to ac' like a gentleman and make me a' hones' woman?"

"I suppose," said Donald, as soon as he had recovered from the shock, "you think I ought to marry you."

"Don't *you* think so?" she returned.

"I suppose," he said, weakly, "I ought to, but am I old enough?"

"You was old enough to get me into trouble and oughta be old enough to get me out."

"I'll have to tell my mother," he said, after a moment.

"No," said Mamie, quickly, "that wouldn' do a-tall. She's a hard woman and would say it served me right.

She'd have no mercy. The only way, Donald, for you to make it right for me is for us to go right to a preacher without tellin' anybody first, an' the sooner the better. Right now would be as good a time as any; Rev'en' Williams, of the Free Will Baptis' Church, lives right aroun' the corner, I saw him at the winder as I come by there just now, and he'll marry us right away. He won' charge but a dollah, and I got the money with me."

But Donald, perturbed as he was, would not permit himself to be stampeded. He ought, he felt, to marry Mamie, according to the best literary traditions. True, she had tempted him, as woman had tempted man since the episode in Eden, but he had been most to blame. It was the duty of a real, strong man to protect the woman in such a case against even her own weaknesses, not to take advantage of them.

"I won't tell my mother," he said, "but I've got to find out what the law is about marriage, and I'll see you in a day or two and tell you how we'll do it."

At table that evening Donald seemed preoccupied. He ate little, he put salt on the stewed peaches and stirred his coffee with a fork.

"What's the matter, Donald?" asked his mother. "You're not eating anything. Aren't you feeling well?"

Donald was decidedly not feeling well, even from a physical point of view, though he was in perfect health—so much does the mind affect the body—but he dissembled. His mother had not pampered him, in the ordinary acceptance of the word, but she had always looked carefully after his health. He was her paschal lamb, and she wanted him kept clean and healthy for the sacrifice on the altar of her race. He made a noncommittal answer, and after reading for a while went to his room and to bed.

He passed a sleepless night considering what it would mean to marry Mamie. He would have to work to support her. No gentleman would permit his wife to support herself. Mamie was a good dressmaker and would willingly have worked to keep him, but he did not know that, nor would he have permitted it. He could not ask his parents to support Mamie; it was quite enough that they should provide for him. To marry would interfere with his education. Of course he could keep on studying, but he had shared his mother's wish that he have a college education and training. He could find work at something; he was strong and capable. If the worst came to the worst, he could get a job as waiter or porter and earn a living for himself and his wife.

When he finished his breakfast next morning he accompanied his father to his office downtown, upstairs over Pemberton's drug store.

"Dad," he said, while the doctor was running over the advertising circulars which mainly constituted his morning mail, "I've got something very important to say to you."

"All right, Don, shoot," returned his father lightly. "Do you need a new suit, or a new book, or a new fiddle, or what?"

"No, Dad," he said, going directly to the subject, as was his habit, "but I feel that I ought to tell you that I've taken advantage of Mamie Wilson. She's going to become a mother and I'm going to marry her."

"The hell you are!" exploded the doctor, startled out of his usual composure. Naturally of placid temperament he could be vehemently profane upon a suitable occasion. There was nothing absurd about the proposition, for Donald was as tall and well-grown as many an adult man. The marriage laws of the state were very liberal, not to say loose, and such a marriage, provided the male were physically capable of performing his marital duties would probably be good if consummated, especially if no one questioned it. The authorities were not at all particular about the personal morals of colored people. To white people, moral turpitude among Negroes, outside of murder, applied chiefly to offenses against property or to breaches of caste. A Negro would be sent to jail for stealing, or for riding in the white coach on a railroad, but such petty misdemeanors as adultery or bigamy were beneath judicial observation, unless the municipal treasury were running low, in which case crapshooting or a poker game became, for the purposes of revenue, a serious offense.

"By the way, Don," asked his father after a pause, "when was it that you plucked this modest violet?"

"Two weeks ago Thursday," replied the boy, to whom a figure of speech never presented any difficulty. Much of his own speech was in tropes and similes.

"And where?"

"On the way home from choir practice."

"'Umph," growled the doctor, "and I suppose she asked you to make her an honest woman, and not condemn her to wear the badge of shame all her life?"

"Something like that," replied Donald, wondering how his father could know.

"And I suppose she suggested that you ought to marry her right away, to protect her reputation, without telling your mother or me about it?"

Donald had to admit it.

"And no doubt she had a preacher all picked out, and he not your own pastor?"

Donald was beginning to feel very foolish.

"That girl has the devil's own nerve," said Dr. Glover as he shook the ash from the end of his cigar into a cuspidor.

"Donald," he continued calmly, "you're the brightest boy in town, as everybody, both colored and white, agrees, but in some ways you're the biggest fool I know, in fact, just plain damn fool. Mamie Wilson is a patient of mine, and some of the things I know about her I learned under the seal of professional confidence. But I can say this much, that if she married every man that has taken advantage of her as you say you have, and the laws were enforced, she would be forcibly retired from society for a long, long time. Now, you run along. Don't tell your mother, stick to your books and your music, and keep away from the women, especially Mamie Wilson. It'll be time enough for you to begin to play around with the girls when you're grown, and even then you'll probably have your hands full shooing them away. Don't worry about Mamie, I'll put the fear of God into her."

Donald had no further trouble with Mamie. Dr. Glover discovered that she had a weakness of the throat which made it necessary for her to retire from the choir until fall, by which time Donald had gone away to college. He was to meet her some years later, in a vastly different environment, long after the colored promoter of a musical show had discovered her voice and taken her into his company.

CHAPTER XI

⸺⸺⸺

IT WAS THE year before the United States declared war on Germany. Donald had finished high school, and the question in Mrs. Glover's mind was where and how she should send him to college. In the late spring of that year an easy solution of this difficult problem presented itself.

Mr. Seaton had not lost his interest in the little colored boy who had smiled his way into his heart. He kept in touch with Mrs. Glover through an occasional letter, inquiring about the boy's growth, his health and his progress in school, to all of which questions Mrs. Glover made satisfactory answers. After her definite refusal of his offer of financial help in Donald's upbringing, Seaton had made no direct pecuniary proffer, but always let it be understood that he could be called upon if need be. When Donald was about ten years old, in reply to one of Seaton's letters, Mr. Glover sent him a photograph of the boy. It was none too good an example of the photographer's art, but not even the artist's indifferent skill could disguise the image of the

tall, upstanding, clear-eyed, curly-haired lad who
looked at him out of the picture so fearlessly. He compared it mentally with his own rather scrawny, sickly
looking children whom not even the lavish expenditure of his now large income had been able to do much
more than keep alive, and he wished more than once
that he had kept the little waif for his own.

The Seaton carburetor, invented early in the automobile game, had become one of the basic patents of
the modern structure. It was used in practically every
internal combustion engine manufactured. By its aid
men rode the air, plowed the waters and devoured the
highways, not to mention the growing place of the gas
engine in the industrial arts. The stock of the Seaton
Carburetor, Inc., until it was absorbed by General Mo-
tors, was one of the favorites traded on the New York
Stock Exchange, and its bonds had always sold above
par. The war in Europe had vastly increased the demand for the device, and the company had prospered
amazingly.

Although a man of simple tastes, as Mr. Seaton grew
into the ranks of the multimillionaires, his habits of
living changed correspondingly. The modest cottage
on the West Side had long since given way to a magnificent stone building on Lake Avenue, from the rear of
which one could look out, over the broad bosom of
Lake Erie, at the great steel freighters which carried the
iron ore of Michigan and Wisconsin to meet the coal of
Ohio and Pennsylvania at the blast furnaces of Cleve-

land. He owned a lake in Canada, a salmon run and a hunting lodge, where he spent part of the year, and a house at Pinehurst for the winter.

In Donald's fifteenth summer, when the Glovers were considering ways and means to send him to college in the fall, Mr. Seaton, going north from Pinehurst, where he had taken part in a golf tournament, made a detour and stopped at Booneville. He called on Dr. Glover at his office, and, after they had exchanged greetings, expressed a desire to see Mrs. Glover and Donald. He walked with Dr. Glover to his home, which was only a short distance away. The boy was not in the house at the moment, but Mrs. Glover sent for him and he soon appeared. He was carrying under his arm a copy of Macaulay's *Essays*, which he admired for their verve and brilliancy.

Mr. Seaton was introduced to Donald as an old friend from Cleveland who had known him in his infancy, and who had stopped off on his way north to see his former acquaintances the Glovers. He conversed with the boy and drew him out skillfully. He was struck by Donald's unusual intelligence and rare physical beauty—there is no other word which would aptly describe, and that with no suggestion of weakness, the impression which Donald Glover made, from infancy, upon those who met him. His shapely head with its curly thatch suggested the portrait of Shelley or of Lord Byron in their young manhood. Whatever diverse strains may have mingled in his blood, they had seemingly combined the best of each into a physically perfect whole.

Mr. Seaton talked with Donald about his studies, and his choice of reading. The conversation, which lasted an hour, impinged now and then upon topics of current interest, concerning which Seaton was surprised at the grasp and clearness of Donald's views. He had never met a boy of his age with so mature a mind. Upon leaving, he stated that he would remain in town overnight and would call again the following day.

He had not mentioned the hour at which he would call, and when he came the next day about eleven o'clock, Dr. Glover was absent visiting a patient.

"Mrs. Glover," he said, when she had shown him into the living room, "I'm sorry that I ever let Donald go."

Mrs. Glover scented trouble and braced herself to meet it.

"You had him once," she said, "by your own choice, and by the law, and you let him go."

"Had I known that he would turn out to be the boy he is, I'd not have permitted myself to be stampeded by my wife's foolish fears. My own sons haven't proved any too satisfactory, and I'm sure I'd have enjoyed the society of this bright lad. In fact, I should like to take him now, and I stayed over in this deadly dump merely to thresh the matter out with you. I should like to have him back. I should love to have him in my home. I would send him to a good college and give him all the advantages which money could provide. He is worthy of the best."

Mrs. Glover knew that Mrs. Seaton was dead and that there could be no objection from her.

"I suppose you'd make him white?" she said.

"So far as anyone can see," returned Mr. Seaton, "God has done that already. If an invisible drop of Negro blood always produced a Donald, it might perhaps be well to distribute it a little more widely."

Mrs. Glover was thinking very rapidly. If Donald were taken away from her by this rich white man, he would be lost to her and to her people. He was still at the impressionable age, and the training which she had been giving him for a special purpose would soon be overlaid by the veneer of wealth and luxury which would surround him. He would learn to despise or at least ignore his people, and all her dreams of his future leadership would be dissipated. He might distinguish himself in some field of effort, but it would be as a white man and would reflect no credit upon her people. She had brought up this boy. She had done everything for him that a mother could do, except bring him into the world, and she did not want to let this white man steal him away from her and her race.

And yet she realized that it was a great opportunity for Donald, and that he was worthy of the opportunity, and she hesitated to assume the responsibility of an answer.

"I'd rather not say until I've consulted my husband. What time does your train leave?"

"The best train leaves at three o'clock this afternoon," he answered. "There's another at six, but my
heart is in this thing and I can wait for the later train."

"If you want to go back to the hotel," she said, "I'll
telephone you when Dr. Glover comes in. He went out
into the country to see a patient, but I expect him back
around one o'clock."

So it was arranged. About one o'clock Mrs. Glover
called the hotel, got Mr. Seaton on the telephone, and
said that Dr. Glover would be glad to see him. Mr. Seaton came to their house.

"My wife has been telling me," said Dr. Glover, after
they had shaken hands, "of your plans for Donald. Of
course, it would be a wonderful opportunity for him.
Whether it would be for his ultimate good is an open
question. He has been brought up so far as a colored
person—a Negro, as our Southern white friends say,
and my wife insists. He has ideas and ideals, and he has
been trying to be loyal to his race. I fear the black has
struck in too deep to be easily dislodged."

"We mean to send him to college," he went on. "It
may not be Yale or Harvard, but some colored school
where he can remain in touch with his own people and
still acquire a liberal education."

"I love him," interjected Mrs. Glover passionately, if
somewhat inconsecutively, "and I don't want to let him
go."

"I think we'd better leave it to Donald," said Dr.

Glover. "He's upstairs in his room and we'll have him down."

"I've never told him," explained Mrs. Glover, "that I'm not his real mother. No mother could have loved him better or done more for him than I have. I've been so jealous of his affection that I tried every means to make it secure."

"Of course," said Dr. Glover, "if we put Mr. Seaton's proposition up to Donald, it will be necessary to give him some explanation which would make our letting him go seem natural. Sometime or other perhaps we would have told him, so it might as well be now."

Mrs. Glover went to the stair in the hall and called, "Donald, oh Donald, son, come on down. Mr. Seaton is here and wishes to see you."

When Donald had descended and had taken a seat in the living room, Dr. Glover undertook the somewhat difficult task of explanation.

"Donald," he said, "we have brought you up as our own dear child. Neither your mother nor I could have loved you more nor could you have been a better son had we been your real parents. But you are an adopted child, and before we adopted you, you had been adopted by Mr. Seaton, in your early infancy. He kept you several years, and then, for reasons which seemed sufficient to us all, he gave you up and we took you into our own home and our own hearts."

At this point Donald noticed the tenseness of his

mother's expression and that her fingers were tightly clasped upon the handkerchief at which she was pulling nervously.

"Mr. Seaton," continued Dr. Glover, "who is a gentleman of great wealth and high social standing, is sorry that he ever let you go, and would like to take charge of your future. He can give you everything that money can buy—education, luxury, travel, society. He will take you into his home, and the freedom and opportunity that is open to a white man will all be yours. We would be glad to have you stay with us, for I love you as a son, and it would break your mother's heart to have you go away. But we both realize that it is your own future that is at stake, and that you are old enough to make your own decision."

Donald observed, with concern, that his mother was weeping softly. Mr. Seaton was listening gravely, without volunteering any remarks.

"It isn't altogether news to me," said Donald, "to learn that I'm an adopted child. I've sometimes suspected it, not from any lack of affection on your part or on Mother's, but from things that Mother has unconsciously dropped from time to time, or things she hasn't said. I'm not foolish enough not to see that I am offered a great opportunity. But, if I may ask, why did Mr. Seaton give me up after he adopted me?"

"Because he found out that you were a Negro," said his mother, explosively.

Donald frowned, and even a frown was becoming to his perfectly molded features.

"Am I not still a Negro?" he asked reflectively.

"I don't think," said Mr. Seaton, "that in your case it is a matter of much importance. Indeed, it was against my own instincts and feelings that I let you go in the first place. I don't want to coerce you, Donald, but I'll make it worth your while to come to me."

By this time Mrs. Glover was sobbing, openly and unashamed. Donald stepped over and put his arm around her shoulder.

"Mother," he said gently, "do you want me to go?"

"Oh, my God, no! No! No!" she cried, drawing him to her fiercely. "I'd die if you left me."

Donald patted her arm reassuringly.

"There, there, Mother," he said, "I'll not leave you. I thank Mr. Seaton very much indeed for his kind and generous offer, but not for the whole world would I do anything that would hurt you the least bit. I'll get my own education, if I have to work for it. I'll make my own way in the world, and perhaps can get for myself most of the things, at least those that are really worthwhile, that Mr. Seaton wants to give me."

Mr. Seaton accepted his defeat gracefully, like a wise man.

"I've not the slightest doubt," he said, as he rose to his feet, "that you'll make good on your own, and I admire you all the more for the stand you have taken.

I'd be glad to take care of your future, but, as your mother told me, I had my chance once, and threw it away. I shall keep informed of your progress and every good thing I hear of you will make me happy. Perhaps in the future I can be of service to you in some way. Certainly I could give you no more love than these good people have lavished upon you. Goodbye, my boy, and good luck."

CHAPTER XII

———⟫●⟪———

AFTER THE refusal of Mr. Seaton's generous offer, Mrs. Glover realized that she must make up to Donald, as far as possible, for his lost opportunity. This meant that she must earn money. Her husband had a fair practice, entirely among his own people except for an occasional furtive white patient afflicted with an ailment he wished to keep a secret and shrank from making known to physicians of his own race or caste, or some shiftless poor white who had neither money nor credit. He provided adequately for his family, but the money to give Donald such an education as his mother desired was quite beyond his ability to procure.

Mrs. Glover looked over the economic field for some means of earning money, and discussed the matter with her husband, who had no concrete suggestion to make, except that she had perhaps been unwise in rejecting Mr. Seaton's offer, without knowing in advance what she herself could do.

She took up the subject one evening with Donald.

"Donald," she said, "I want you to go to college, but I haven't figured out yet how we can afford it."

"I'm quite willing to work my way through college, Mother," he said. "I can get a job on the railroad or at a hotel during the summer vacation and earn enough to pay my way. Lots of our boys do."

"I'd rather you wouldn't," she said. "You'll have a hard enough time, even with plenty of money, and I'd prefer that you put in your time studying. Youth is so short and there is so much to learn."

Donald was reading the advertisements in a colored weekly paper. They comprised a very narrow scope, being at that epoch mainly devoted to patent medicines, cheap jewelry, brass watches, fortune tellers and hair straighteners and face bleaches.

"There is an idea, Mother," exclaimed Donald. "Get up some really good, scientific toilet preparations, especially adapted to the Negro, things that will promote cleanliness, health and beauty. Put them on the market, advertise them intelligently, and you'll not only make money but render a service to the race. Some very rich men have made their fortunes out of soaps and perfumery."

This idea appealed to Mrs. Glover, for she had learned hairdressing when a young woman and had paid her expenses in college by the practice of her art among the students. It might prove an easy and practical solution of her problem.

Thus was sown the seed of an enterprise which was

destined to develop, in the hands of Mrs. Glover and her imitators, into a great industry and give employment to many thousands of people.[1] As Donald afterwards pointed out, it was a natural business development, along the line of least resistance. Colored barbers and hairdressers had had for a long time a practical monopoly of the entire business among both white and colored people, but the tightening of race lines and the competition of whites, often of greater energy and enterprise, who no longer scorned these humble pursuits, had cut into the Negro barber's white patronage disastrously. The commercialization and extension of the hairdressing business among colored people offered a promising way of escape from economic disaster.

With the aid and advice of her husband, Mrs. Glover conducted experiments and devised several formulas which she tried out among her personal acquaintances. Finding the results satisfactory, she established a laboratory in her own home and began manufacturing in good earnest her "Creole" creams and soaps and lotions, which she advertised, first in one and later on, as the business developed, in most of the Negro and many of the white newspapers, varying the wording of the advertisement to suit the trade sought. And while she never made a million dollars, and several other manufacturers outstripped her in volume of business, her product remained the most select of all such preparations, and its sale supplied the wherewithal to pay for Donald's education.

CHAPTER XIII

⟶≫●≪⟵

As DR. GLOVER had intimated to Mr. Seaton, Mrs. Glover had decided that to train Donald for effective leadership, it was better that he be educated among his own people. She would have liked to send him to school in New England, but she was afraid that, with his personality, the obvious advantages of being white, in a community where race lines were less tightly drawn than in the South, might pull him away from the Negro. She never lost sight of the Biblical parallel between Donald and Moses. Moses, though of an enslaved race, was never himself a slave; he did not sweat under the lash to help build the pyramids or other monuments of old Egypt. He had been the adopted son of the king's daughter, the pet of the harem, instructed from infancy in the learning of the priests and the manners of the court. Most Negro leaders of the past had been born in slavery, and those who had come to the front since emancipation, had almost all done some sort of menial work in their upward struggle. The ranks of colored teachers and preachers and doctors and lawyers were full of former porters and waiters—her own husband had worked on a Pullman dining car. It was one way for them to spoil the Egyptians and prepare for their Exodus to the promised land of freedom and opportunity. Some of the older leaders were in the habit of boasting about their small beginnings. She had heard a Negro orator, addressing a white audience, and playing for sympathy, declare that he had been born in slavery, when she knew perfectly well that his mother was a free woman. When she charged him with imposture, he replied that well, he was born during slavery, which meant about the same thing. But Mrs. Glover could see no merit in having been a servant; though nothing to be ashamed of, it was nothing of which to boast. She not only wanted Donald to be as well-educated as any white man, but wished to save him from the inferiority complex which might result from servile employment. She decided finally to send him to Bethany College[1] in the adjoining state, where he would be in a measure among his own people and at the same time in contact with others who had had superior opportunities.

This institution had been established by a wealthy Quaker, a follower of Garrison and Sumner, who in witness of his belief in the brotherhood of man, had built and endowed, in the mountain region of the state, a school open to all young people without regard to race or color. It was in a Southern state, but in a section where there had been few slaves and where there were therefore relatively few Negroes, and the school had prospered. For many years the white and colored pupils had enjoyed in common, in entire harmony, the advantages offered to them.

Though Donald had accumulated a large amount of general and unrelated knowledge, he had not acquired it in the conventional way. For example, he had read a great deal of Latin but knew nothing whatever of scansion. He could read French, and while he learned the rules of pronunciation in grammars and tried to apply them, he had no means of finding out whether his pronunciation was anywhere near the real thing, and such lessons as he had had for a brief period were from a German-speaking teacher whose accent was obviously far from impeccable. He had a logical mind, but had never been taught the rules of logic, while of the higher mathematics he knew nothing beyond the elements of algebra. And he had yet to learn how to express himself clearly and concisely in writing.

One of the teachers in the high school had studied at Bethany College, and with his advice and assistance the preliminary steps were taken to have Donald admitted as a pupil of that institution. At the beginning of the fall term he entered the preparatory department, a year or two of which would fit him for matriculation in the college proper. He was given a comfortable though plainly furnished room in one of the dormitories, and assigned a roommate whom he liked very much. Henry White was a very dark youth, with an intelligent, open countenance and an engaging smile. When he learned that Donald was colored, he warmed to him at once, insisted on his having the best corner of the room, and constituted himself his mentor and guide, and faithful henchman. While Bethany College was founded on the principle of human equality, and the students fraternized in class and in chapel and in the dining rooms, white and colored were not mixed in the dormitories unless by special request.

Donald found it easy to study, and when he had been examined and graded, plunged eagerly into the work. His Latin teacher, Professor Dean, who also taught logic, took a liking to Donald from the moment they met, for Donald's personal and intellectual charm was equally potent with men, as with women—with perhaps a difference, as between the sexes, in the nature of the appeal. Professor Dean invited Donald to his rooms, gave him the run of his personal library, discussed history, literature and race questions with him on a footing of intellectual equality. Professor Dean had written several books on various phases of the race problem. His theories and beliefs were profoundly impressed on Donald's mind and were destined to influence deeply his intellectual development.

Professor Dean, like Rousseau, believed in the equality of man as a philosophical concept. He did not maintain that every man was the equal of every other man in gifts or attainments—the contrary was too obvious. But he believed in humanity, and therefore in democracy, and that every man should have the fullest opportunity to develop what was best in himself, so that he might render to society the highest service of which he was capable. As to the Negro specifically, he did not care whether or not he was the equal of the white man—it was beside the question. If he were not, he needed opportunity all the more. The question could never be settled in the abstract. It was easy to find Negroes who were intellectually the superiors of many white men, but as to the mass, it could never be proven except by a test under equal conditions.

"And I'm glad, Glover," he said, "to be able to participate in such a test. This school is a laboratory in which, in time, a great many hoary prejudices face extinction. It is proving that white and black can live together on terms of equality and friendship even in the South."

Donald warmed to this liberal and generous spirit. Professor Dean was by all odds the best of his teachers. For it was by no means easy to get good teachers for a small college in the Southern "hinterland" with little outlook for the ambitious educator, and running counter to the settled convictions of the people at large. Some of the teachers were in poor or at least uncertain health. Some of them had proved failures at other institutions. Most of them were attracted by the ample salaries which the foundation provided. But only now and then did a man like Arthur Dean, who believed in a just and benevolent God—in spite of reason and experience—find himself in that galley. There had been more of them just after the Civil War, when the missionary spirit was strong, but in the gradual social readjustment which followed the emancipation of the slaves, the flame of self-sacrifice had more or less subsided.

But neither Professor Dean nor Donald was destined to see what the outcome of this particular experiment might prove to be. The state legislature, foreseeing danger to the purity and prestige of the dominant race by this vicious example of social equality in their very midst, enacted a law forbidding the instruction of white and colored pupils in the same school, and to make sure that no contaminating influence could get over, under or through this dam, making it equally unlawful for any person to give instruction in both a white and a Negro school which were less than a hundred miles apart.

This drastic measure terminated for the time being the friendship between Donald and Professor Dean. They were to meet later on, in a field which gave a wider scope to Professor Dean's talent for teaching on the one hand, and on the other hand to Donald's talent for learning. It is only just to the trustees and officers of Bethany College to say that they protested against the change, but the protest was rather half-hearted and wholly ineffectual, and it was an open secret that most of them welcomed the new order of things. The college continued to function, for white students only, thus defeating the chief purpose of the founder and adding another chapter to the long and shameful record of spoiliation and exploitation of the Negro by the white South.

Some effort was later made to provide similar education for Negroes in another institution, but the spirit of Bethany College was lost and the intention of the founder nullified.

In Donald's case it interrupted his education at a critical point, robbed him of a good friend—indeed of a number of good friends, for he was popular with teachers and pupils alike—and added to his growing embitterment at the treatment accorded his race.

Henry White and he went to the railroad station together. Donald had two suitcases, one of which Henry insisted upon carrying in addition to his own. "And thus endeth the first chapter," sighed Donald, as they stood on the platform awaiting the train. "I'm sorry, Henry, for we've been good friends."

"And we'll remain good friends, Donald. Let me know where you go next year, and if I can possibly make it, I'll come to the same school. I had a scholarship here, which I can't take with me, but I'll find something to do for part of the year so I won't lose you."

But Henry was just one of the ships that pass in the night, and Donald and he were never again schoolmates, for Henry, no longer a student exempt, was drafted into the army during the summer, and assigned to a labor battalion at Brest, later transferred to a fighting regiment, and laid down his life in the fighting near Metz, to make the world safe for a democracy which had meant little to him.

CHAPTER XIV

——⟫●⟪——

DURING THE summer following his enforced with-drawal from Bethany College, Donald taught the eight-weeks colored school in a rural school district not many miles from his home, and in the fall went to Athena University, one of a group of Negro schools situated on the hills outside the thriving metropolis of what was claimed to be the most progressive of the Southern states. There was no colored public school in the city above the eighth grade, but Northern philan-thropy and Negro church enterprise had established four or five schools of secondary and college education in the environments of the city.

Having registered in the dean's office, Donald was assigned a room and a roommate. He had a janitor carry up his trunk and other things and put them in his room. He followed the man, and when he reached his room, opened his trunk, and a little later, leaving it unlocked, stepped out into the hall to find a wash-room. Upon his return after several minutes, he found a well-dressed, light brown young man just closing down the lid of his trunk.

"Ah," said the stranger, easily, with no sign of embarrassment, "I presume you are my new roommate. I found your trunk open and took the liberty of putting the lid down. It's a rather mixed crowd around here, and it's a good idea to keep valuables locked up. My name is Lincoln Dixon—Link to my friends—at your service."

"And mine is Donald Glover," said the other. "I'm glad to know you."

"If I can tell you anything or do anything for you, you have only to ask me," replied Dixon. "I'll introduce you to everybody and show you all the ropes."

Donald would have liked to ask him what he was doing in his trunk, for he was quite sure he had closed the lid down before he went out, although he had not locked it. In spite of Dixon's seeming frankness and *bonhomie*, he conceived a prejudice against his roommate which not all of his friendliness, and, to a newcomer, really valuable assistance could entirely eradicate. For while he learned to like Dixon, and saw much of him in later years, he never entirely trusted him.

Of course, he might have been mistaken about having closed the trunk, or Dixon might have been moved merely by idle curiosity. But thereafter he strictly followed his roommate's advice and looked after his valuables very carefully.

Donald remained at Athena University[1] three years. These three years were pregnant with great world events, which only indirectly affected him. America entered and came out of the World War, but Donald, unlike Henry White, was under military age and therefore exempt from conscription, though even had he been old enough he could have claimed exemption as a student.

He had formed many friendships in the university, the most outstanding of which was that with Dr. Lebrun,[2] professor of history and dean of the university, and the leader of the radical wing of national Negro thought. Donald had read and admired his books, and was prepared to sit at his feet, as Paul at Gamaliel's. He had echoed in his own mind all the crusader's protests against racial intolerance of every kind, and his demand for equality for the Negro—not one kind of equality or another, but *equality*, which, he maintained, as soon as it was limited or confined, became something less than equality. Dr. Lebrun recognized Donald's intellectual brilliancy and concerned himself to so direct it as to prepare Donald for the greatest usefulness to his people.

Donald attracted the attention of the president of the university, the successor of the devoted missionary who had headed the school in pre-Reconstruction days, when it was an American Missionary Association school, and who had devoted his life to it. He made many friends among the teachers and among the students, some of whom were destined to play a large part in the future life of their people.

He learned from statistics compiled by the university the extent to which the Negroes were growing in numbers, and in social efficiency. The demand for labor during the war had drawn and was still drawing many thousands of them to the North, where they earned larger wages and their children had better opportunities for education. They were beginning to develop financial institutions—building and loan societies, banks and insurance companies. Until quite recently their principal investments had been in churches, which, however valuable they might be in preparation for the next world, were a source of expense rather than of income in this one. On the whole, the colored people seemed to Donald to be doing very well.

But there were countervailing influences. The pseudo-scientific Nordic propagandists[3] had, by their pontifical announcements, prepared the soil for the Ku Klux Klan, which was organizing the ignorance, the race prejudice and religious bigotry of the South and other parts of the country at ten dollars a head and extra for the nightgowns. The baleful glare of the fiery cross had displaced the gentle radiance of the Cross of Christ.

There had been in the past a number of race disturbances in Athena, but none since the riot of 1905.[4] In Donald's third year at the university, an incident occurred which stirred the sleeping dogs of race hatred into activity, and sent him farther afield for the rest of his education. A young white girl was murdered in the city, under circumstances of peculiar atrocity. As was usual in such cases, it was at first assumed that the murderer was a Negro. But very soon suspicion fell upon the girl's employer, a Jewish merchant of good standing.[5] Race feeling ran beyond the Negro, and in the confusion of opinions the colored suspect got a fair chance and escaped by the skin of his teeth. The Jew was not so fortunate; he was tried, convicted, and after numerous appeals and a legal battle which stirred the nation, sentenced to the penitentiary for life. While under the protection of the state, he was taken forcibly from the prison by a mob, and the majesty of lynch law was again vindicated by another brutal murder.

These events had brought about a rather strained race feeling in the community, and Jews and colored people had to walk warily. And it was during this time that Donald had his first and worst personal experience of racial bigotry. His complexion, which in the case of a dark man was an invitation to insult, had hitherto protected him to some extent, but was in this instance to operate to his disadvantage.

When he shaved on the morning of a certain fine day in early spring, his razor had pulled a little, and when he had finished shaving he stuck it into his inside vest pocket, which he rarely used, intending to leave it at the barber shop downtown later in the day, to be honed. It was an old-fashioned folding razor which his father had given him, and he had lost the case. In a free period during the early afternoon he started down the hill for this purpose.

As he left the campus, a pretty brown girl, one of the students, was leaving the grounds. He knew her as a student—the university was coeducational—from seeing her on the campus and at chapel and in the student social activities. She was Bertha Lawrence, the daughter of Archdeacon Lawrence of the Protestant Episcopal Church, who was a principal of a church school in North Carolina.

"Where are you going, my pretty maid?" quoted Donald, as he fell into step beside her.

"I'm going a-shopping, sir," she came back, "down to the Emporium," a large drygoods store on Plumtree Street.

"May I go with you, my pretty maid?" continued Donald, frivolously.

"Thank you, kind sir, you may," she replied, with equal lightness.

Bertha Lawrence, of course, had no objection to being seen with the handsomest and the best-dressed of her fellow pupils. Donald always wore good clothes and had an air of distinction. More than one young woman would have envied Bertha the opportunity.

They walked along and presently found themselves on Plumtree Street. Donald noticed white people looking at them closely as they passed, but paid no especial attention to them. He was accustomed to being looked at by women, and few men would pass Bertha Lawrence without a second glance, so they did not perceive that some of the looks directed at them were unfriendly. Just as they paused a moment before the drygoods store into which Miss Lawrence wished to go, he noticed a white man speaking excitedly to a policeman a few yards down the street. Donald was lifting his hat to his companion before starting on alone, when the policeman stepped forward.

"Wait a minute," he ordered, gruffly, "both of you. You're pinched."

"Pinched?" returned Donald, astounded.

"Yes, pinched, you and the nigger woman. You're under arrest, if you know what that means."

"And why in hell are we under arrest?" demanded Donald, boldly, conscious of his rectitude.

"Because I say so," retorted the Law, "and don't give me any of your lip. Stand here quiet till I call the wagon, or I'll put the bracelets on you."

Miss Lawrence had turned pale with embarrassment and shame.

"It's all some dreadful mistake," said Donald, seeking to console her. "It's a damned outrage, but we'll soon know what it's all about. We haven't done anything to be arrested for, and I'll have the dean or the president take it up with the magistrate."

In a few moments the patrol wagon drew up in front of the police station. The prisoners were told to alight and ordered into the station. While they stood waiting, the arresting officer stepped up to the sergeant's desk and spoke to him in a low tone, inaudible to Donald and his companion.

"Step forward to the desk, you there," barked the sergeant. "Turn out your pockets."

Donald drew out his purse, his keys, his pocket knife and his fountain pen, and laid them down upon the desk.

"Got a gun?" demanded the sergeant.

"No," said Donald.

"Frisk him," the sergeant ordered the officer.

It only took a moment to locate the overlooked razor in Donald's vest pocket.

"But what are we charged with?" demanded Donald.

"You're charged with disorderly conduct," returned the sergeant, "an offense against the peace and dignity of the state, against an ordinance of the city, and against the unwritten law of the South."

"But we want to know what all that means," insisted Donald, "and we demand an immediate hearing."

"You'll get a hearing when the judge comes back from lunch," replied the officer, "which will be about three o'clock, unless he gets tied up in a poker game or an argument at his club. Meanwhile you can roost in the cooler, along with your nigger woman. You're a disgrace to your race."

Donald was at a loss to know what he meant. "I should like to use the telephone," he said. "There's some mistake here which can be cleared up. May I use the telephone?"

"The telephone is out of order, but there is no mistake. And if there is, you can clear it up with the judge, and believe me, it'll take some clearing."

Donald was hustled with scant ceremony into a large and badly lighted, barred cell where he found himself in company with a half-dozen white men, most of them obviously common drunks, unwashed, unshaved, unkempt and redolent of bad whiskey, stale tobacco and unpleasant bodily odors. Several of them were smoking rank cigars, one or two were puffing cheap cigarettes. They looked sneeringly—or suspiciously, or enviously, or indifferently, as dictated by their several dispositions—at Donald's good clothes, but made no audible comment; and Donald, who was not disposed for conversation, held his own tongue. In an adjoining room, separated by a grill from the one in which he found himself, he saw a number of male Negro prisoners, most of them black and ragged, seemingly not quite so dirty as the white men, perhaps because the dirt didn't show so much, and unbroken sartorial continuity was hardly to be expected of the average low class Negro, and a breach of it not so conspicuous. They were more cheerful, on the whole, than the white prisoners, and were laughing and joking boisterously, whereas their paleface neighbors gloomed and grouched and growled.

Miss Lawrence was shown into a cell on the same

floor, similar to the others, where there were no white women and only a few colored women. They crowded around her and manifested considerable curiosity.

"What yuh in fuh, honey?" demanded a full-breasted huzzy with a strip of court plaster across her brown cheek. "Shopliftin' or street s'licitin'?"

If a look could have withered, the one Miss Lawrence directed at the woman would have blasted her on the spot. Absolutely rigid with indignation at the insult, added to what she was already bearing, she with difficulty restrained herself and going over to the hard backless wooden bench next to the wall, with its shiny patina of grease and dirt, sat there until her mood changed and she bowed her head in her hands and burst into tears. As she wept unrestrainedly, the sobs shaking her shapely shoulders, an elderly dark woman with wooly grey hair came forward and sat beside her.

"Doan' cry, honey," she crooned. "You sho' ain' done nuthin' so awful bad."

"Thank you for your confidence," rejoined Miss Lawrence, by way of expressing her appreciation of the old woman's sympathy. "I haven't done anything at all."

"Niggers doan' hafter do nuthin' to git in jail right now," returned the old woman, "'cep'n' jus' ter be colored."

This remark was, of course, not true, in every instance, but it was perfectly accurate as applied to this particular case. It was a decided disadvantage to be a

Negro in Athena at any time, and particularly so at this juncture.

By ill luck, the day's police cases were being heard in Police Courtroom Number Two, before Judge Stonewall Jackson Steele, a creature of the political boss who held both city and state in the hollow of his hand. The judge's reputation for harshness toward colored prisoners was well known to the habitual Negro miscreants. His court was the chief source of supply for the chain gang, and if wishes were effective he would spend a long eternity in a very hot hell. But Donald had never heard of Judge Steele or his idiosyncracy, or he might not have felt so confident of immediate release when he should have explained his case to a learned and just judge.

The judge returned from his club, and the afternoon session of the court began at about three o'clock. The prisoners were brought into the courtroom and seated on two long benches, one for the whites and one for the Negroes. Donald was placed on the white bench and Miss Lawrence on the colored. The cases were heard in their order, and as Donald and his companion were the last charged, it was after four o'clock before their cases were reached. In spite of his indignation, Donald found the proceedings very interesting. The white prisoners were tried first. Several were charged with drunkenness or fighting and were fined or sent to the chain gang. One, charged with violating the Mann

Act, was ordered turned over to the federal authorities. Others, charged with different felonies, were bound over to the grand jury.

The old black woman was charged with intoxication.

"Well, Sally," said the judge, with grim jocularity, "drunk again. Where'd you get it?"

"I disremembuh, yo' honah. It wuz so strong it jes nach'ly 'stroyed my recomembance."

"I'll commit you to the workhouse for ninety days, and give you a chance to stay sober. The warden sends me word that they need a good cook."

The young woman who had talked to Miss Lawrence in the detention cell was next called to the bar. She gave her name as Roseola Benson, and was charged with being a common prostitute. The policeman who had arrested her told his story, which the prisoner denied volubly, but not convincingly. The judge asked her how much she earned at her ancient profession.

"Well, suh, yo' honah, dat 'pens on how good or how po' business is—sometimes two dollahs, three dollahs, five dollahs, and once in a long while ten dollahs a day."

"I'll fine you twenty-five dollars and costs, and thirty days in the workhouse. I'll suspend the days and give you time to pay the fine and costs, which will amount to twenty-nine dollars and seventy-five cents. The city treasury needs the money. How long will it take you to make it?"

"Lemme see, yo' honah. Dis is Friday. I c'n pay it by nex' Chuesday."

"All right, see that you do, or you won't fare so well next time you're brought in."

"Thank you, yo' honah," said the poor wretch, who had just been dispatched to pursue her vile trade for the financial benefit of the cultural center of the South.

The Negro men, whose cases were called next, were charged with gambling, drinking, petty larceny or cutting to wound. There was one case of possessing cocaine. They pleaded guilty as a rule, and their cases were disposed of rapidly enough, most of them by sentence to the chain gang. Some of the sentences seemed to Donald rather severe, and the manner of the judge, in spite of his attempts at humor, was far from encouraging, and Donald was wondering what he and his companion might expect. He had not yet been informed what they were charged with, nor had he been permitted to use the telephone.

"Call the next case, Mr. Clerk," said the judge.

"Donald Glover," replied the clerk.

"Step forward, Glover," said the judge. "What is he charged with, Mr. Clerk?"

Donald rose from the bench where he had taken his seat when the prisoners had been brought into the courtroom.

The clerk read from the docket, "You are charged with disorderly conduct in consorting with a nigger woman in public, carrying a concealed weapon and resisting an officer. How do you plead, guilty or not guilty?"

"Not guilty," said Donald. "I am—"

"That'll do," said his honor. "You'll have a chance to be heard when the state has put its case. Call the arresting officer."

The officer, Patrolman John Creel, of the Fourth Precinct, testified that his attention was called to the prisoner Glover who had been walking down Plumtree Street with a young nigger woman, and was lifting his hat to her in front of Marvin's Emporium. That he had placed them under arrest, brought them to the station in the police emergency, where they were booked, searched and locked up. That he had taken from the prisoner's person a razor which he carried, without a case, in his vest pocket, within easy reach, and that the prisoner had used profane language when arrested. The razor was identified by the witness and received in evidence as State's Exhibit A.

"The State rests," barked the prosecutor.

"Take the stand," the court ordered Donald.

"What's your name?"

"Donald Glover."

"Where do you live?"

"Athena University."

"Oh, you live at the nigger school. What do you do there?"

"I'm a student."

"Who's the woman?"

"The lady is—"

"I'm not asking you about a lady, but about the nigger woman that was brought in with you?"

"She's a student of the university also."

"What sort of white man are you, anyway?"

"I'm not a white man. I'm a Negro."

"You're damn' white for a nigger. I suppose we can't hold him on the consorting count, your honor, but there's the razor. He probably *is* a nigger—the razor proves it. And he used profane language to the officer."

Donald explained his possession of the razor.

"That's old stuff," said the judge. "They all say that. Fifty dollars and costs or sixty days in the chain gang. Call the next case."

"Bertha Lawrence."

Miss Lawrence came forward forlornly.

"She was arrested with Glover," said the prosecutor.

"Unmph! I guess you may *nolle* her case. You may go, young woman, but next time you walk downtown with a man, see that he's a real nigger, the blacker the better, or you're likely to get into more trouble."

Donald, in default of cash to pay his fine, was returned to the bull pen. Miss Lawrence hurried back to the university, and to the dean's office. The dean took her to the president, to whom she related the events of the afternoon. The president expressed his feelings in as vigorous language as his official dignity would permit in the presence of a pupil, got former Judge Graves, the school's white lawyer, on the telephone, and made an appointment with him—fortunately he was still at his office—summoned the school automobile, and hurried downtown. They tried to find the police judge, but he had left for the night.

"Well," said Judge Graves, "I don't think we better bother him. Besides, while the arrest was a mistake, Glover *was* carrying a razor, and swore when arrested, as any man in such a case would have felt like doing, so technically he was guilty of a misdemeanor. It was unfortunate that the charge was heard before Steele, and it wouldn't be worthwhile to file a motion for a new trial, because he wouldn't grant it. I think he'd better pay the fine and let it go at that. And I shouldn't make any public comment on it, if I were you. It wouldn't accomplish any good and would only stir up more bad feeling."

The clerk fortunately was still at the police station, and somewhat ungraciously, since it was after hours, consented to receive the fine and costs, which amounted to fifty-four dollars and seventy-five cents, for which the dean gave a check, and Donald was released. He asked for his razor, and was told that he could not have it, that it was part of the court records. It was a piece of fine cutlery, as the clerk discovered when, after sterilizing it, he used it the next morning to shave himself.

The incident gave rise to great excitement on the hill. Donald was looked upon as a hero who had suffered for principle's sake, and Miss Lawrence took on the halo of martyrdom. Dr. Lebrun was coldly furious, and declared that he was tempted to hate the whole white race, with a few honorable exceptions, and that at the end of the year he would shake the dust of the South from his feet and devote his life to fighting race prejudice, in an atmosphere where he could speak his mind. And he thanked God that he had no drop of American white blood in his veins. Whatever other than Negro blood he had—and he was of a light brown complexion—was of other strains.

But things were not quite as they were before. Miss Lawrence had been arrested and had been in jail with thieves and prostitutes. And Donald had been fined for a misdemeanor. When the first glamour or romance began to fade, the odium of these things persisted in some envious or malicious minds, of which there naturally would be a few among so large a number of people.

Donald wrote the story home to his mother. A brief correspondence between them resulted in the decision that Donald should leave the university at the end of the school year and finish his education in a Northern institution.

Donald and his partner in crime, Bertha Lawrence, were bracketed together in the school mind. They often met and spoke of their harsh experience. But neither they nor any one else ever joked about it. It was too serious a matter, and it was a long time, indeed not until the excitement following the murder had entirely subsided and the public sentiment of the city had resumed its normal attitude of calm contempt or cold indifference toward the Negroes, that the venom ceased to rankle among the college people.

CHAPTER XV

———⟫●⟪———

I N COLUMBIA University, where Donald entered the College of Arts as a sophomore, he found a seat of learning comparable in spirit with the great universities of Paris and Bologna, which during the Middle Ages kept alive the flickering torch of learning, and to which during the Renaissance students of all nations and all races flocked to study the humanities, philosophy, theology, rhetoric, mathematics and dialectics. The advance of science, of course, had widened the scope of the modern university. Philosophy had become only one and not the greatest of many subjects, and dialectics had yielded to the test tube and the microscope. There was little room for disputation about the natural sciences, and religion, while still studied comparatively, was no longer taught as a cult nor the chief concern of intellectual people. Greek and Latin had not yet been banished, but the practical school was lifting its head and preparing to lay impious hands on those ancient idols.

The student body was a lesson in democracy. The

largest group of students was, of course, American white, of the Nordic or Mediterranean types. The Jews were a close second. In fact, they were so numerous that a professor, voicing a feeling which he shared with others, once made the remark in the company of teachers that the Jews were swamping the university and ought to be gotten rid of. To which indiscreet utterance one of his hearers replied that if he were not more careful of his speech the Jews might get rid of him.

The other elements of New York's cosmopolitan population were well-represented, as well as many foreign nationalities directly. There were native colored students of all shades, including a few American Indians, and foreign Negroes and mulattoes from the West Indies, Brazil, Central America and a few from continental Africa; Hindus, Chinamen, Siamese, Hawaiians—an intellectual melting pot which, to the glory of its management, took no account of race or color or religion, and demanded only the desire for learning, the mental equipment to acquire it, the ability to pay the fees, and a standard of personal decency which fitted the student for association in school with ladies and gentlemen.

The university was like a new world to Donald. Coming from a section of the Union where, except during his brief sojourn at Bethany College, he had been held almost as far away from white people as the untouchables of India from the Brahmins, it was a novel and not unpleasant experience to find himself rooming in the same dormitory with white young men, and sitting in a classroom side by side with white men and women. He had been trained to class consciousness and despite the freedom of the Columbia atmosphere and the conviction that he was "as good as anybody else" it took him some time to get over a certain feeling of constraint; indeed he never entirely lost it. However, he plunged into his studies and soon attracted the attention of the professors by the brilliancy of his recitations and the comment he had occasion to make. The quality of a natural born student, which he had displayed at Athena University, showed no sign of slipping in the new arena. True, the conditions were somewhat different, the standards somewhat higher and the tests more severe. He had to work harder, at least until he found himself, but he was not afraid of work, and soon succeeded in distinguishing himself among a brilliant student body of several thousand.

Social conditions he found not quite so ideal. The native and foreign colored students, he soon learned, were not invited to join the fraternities and sororities—the Greek letters, except the Phi Beta Kappa, like the common courtesy titles in the South, were reserved for white people. There were colored and white students in every class, and their relations as a whole were pleasant, though an occasional class conscious student of one race or the other might be guilty of what a sensitive person could construe as rudeness. Between the white men and the colored men there was little or none of that friendly personal familiarity which finds expression in walking arm in arm, clapping each other on the back or accosting each other in language not exactly adapted to Sunday school instruction or parlor conversation. The same was even more true of the women students, and there was no more mingling of the sexes, outside the classroom, than there was in the outer world. An occasional near white might constitute a rare exception, but black or brown and white were seldom seen together.

Of course, a man of Donald's virile beauty and charm could not pass through his young manhood without love affairs. He was of a physical type rather similar to that of a famous screen actor, though better looking, and wore his hair in its natural loose glossy curls rather than plastered to the scalp like that of the movie sheik. It was beautiful hair, and he had no desire to have it different. His handsome, somewhat Italianate features, his erect and manly form—he stood just two inches under six feet in his stockings—made him a noticeable figure in any company. His naturally graceful bearing, the gleam in his eyes, the friendly smile which was his characteristic expression, were irresistible to women and attracted them without conscious effort on his part.

For example, there was Amelia Parker, a tall, fair girl with corn yellow hair and turquoise blue eyes, who sat next to him in Dr. Boaz's[1] class on ethnology. She always spoke to Donald and sometimes congratulated him on his recitations. The subject was his major study, and one in which he was thoroughly informed.

One day at noon, as the class adjourned, she walked beside him out upon the campus.

"Mr. Glover," she said, "can't we study together? I'm sure I'd profit by it, and I'd hope that in some degree I could reciprocate. Why can't we do our reading together in the library?"

Donald reflected. Such a proposition from such a girl would have been unthinkable in his Southern *alma mater*. He would love to study with Miss Parker. She was a New Englander and bore the name of a famous preacher who had been a great friend of his race[2]—perhaps she was related to him. And she was a beautiful and gracious young woman who was doing him, unconsciously to herself, a signal honor. Yet he hesitated.

"Well, Miss Parker," he said finally, "I should love it. But you know, my race is not socially popular. People who know us would see us together and there might be unpleasant comment. In the Southern city I came from such a thing couldn't by any possibility happen. First, I wouldn't be admitted to any college or university which you might attend, nor to any library you might frequent. If I were seen in public with you more than once I would be warned, and if I repeated the offense would be ordered out of town—if I escaped arrest or personal violence. Of course, none of those things could happen in New York, but I like you too much to expose you to unpleasant comment. Professor Boaz may postulate and demonstrate that by way of race I am as good as you—I couldn't be in any other way—but, except in theory, few other white people feel that way, and some of our own most loyal leaders sometimes wonder. So I think it would be safer for us not to be seen together."

"I'm my own mistress," she replied, "'free, white and twenty-one,' and can choose my own associates. If you're afraid on your own account, that ends it; I wouldn't urge you for the world. But if you'd like us to study together, I live off the campus, on Riverside Drive at 140th Street, and we can study at my home. I'm sure my mother and sister will not object to any friend of mine."

It was so arranged. Several evenings a week he called at the house where the Parkers had a handsome apartment, and read the class assignment with her, and they quizzed each other. She admired his keen and crystal intellect. He took pleasure in the manner in which she grasped an abstract proposition. She was that rare bird, a woman with a logical mind, to which was principally due the manner in which, as will be seen, their later more intimate friendship terminated.

Propinquity had the usual result. Insidiously their intercourse broadened beyond the purely scholastic. One evening she had not warned him that she had a theater engagement until he came as usual, and when she told him, he would have retired.

"Why not come along with us?" she said. "I can easily change the tickets and get four seats together."

He yielded to temptation and spent a delightful evening, listening to a great actor in a great role. Upon two other occasions he accompanied her to the opera, alone, and from rear seats in the dress circle they watched and listened, once to *Aida* and once to *Otello*, two moving and melodious tragedies of love and death, which appealed to Donald not only for their superb music but also for the element of race involved in both.

One evening they were talking about religion.

"What church do you attend?" she asked.

"I was brought up in my mother's church, the Methodist Church," he answered, "but I confess that I haven't attended it often since I've been in New York. There are too many other distractions."

"Come with me to my church some Sunday," she said. "I'm sure you'll like it."

So the following Sunday morning he called at her apartment and accompanied her to a Unitarian Church, on Cathedral Parkway, which was in the neighborhood. The service was simple and dignified. There were hymns, carefully selected, responsive readings, a sermon and of course a collection. The subject of the sermon was "Where is Heaven?" The preacher very gracefully but convincingly disposed of all the existing conceptions of paradise and argued that no heaven was needed and that a hell was equally superfluous.

"Well," commented Donald as they rose to go, "it was quite an interesting lecture, with none of the fervor or joyousness which mark a Methodist or Baptist service. The preacher very reverently, and at times it seemed regretfully, as if mourning the loss of a beautiful illusion, discarded revelation, the divinity of Christ, and the life hereafter. I wonder he let God escape!"

But he did not wonder long, for, on the way out, in the lobby, where they were exposed for sale, he purchased copies of other sermons by the pastor, which negatived the existence of a personal God. The only worthwhile religion was Humanism, the cult of the good, the true and the beautiful, without illusion, or supernaturalism or superstition of any kind. This, Miss Parker maintained, was her religion, which she considered sufficient for any intelligent person. Donald did not argue with her. Although he had never until then formulated his views upon religion, they were, he felt, too nearly her own to admit of much argument. It was a long way from the Methodist faith and doctrine, but, logically, he had to admit that the minister had made a *prima facie* case.

Miss Parker had read about a certain Negro café in Harlem, and asked Donald to take her to visit it.

"You wouldn't like it," he said. "It's out of your class."

"It's life," she replied, "and the functioning of a race. As a student of sociology and ethnology I ought to see all phases of their life."

He could not argue with her literally, but he finally consented to accompany her. One evening after finishing their reading they took a taxi to a place on Lenox Avenue in Harlem. It was a fairly large hall, in a converted basement, with a jazz orchestra, small tables, a good dancing floor and a very mixed audience. They found a table for two a little to one side, ordered sandwiches and coffee, and as they ate and drank, studied the company. There were many dark men, but if any of the women were black, it could not be detected under their makeup. The Negro had not yet become quite the fashion among the liberal white intellectuals, but there was an occasional white man or woman who visited the Negro cafés as a sort of slumming stunt, much as the rubberneck wagons carried people to the faked opium dens of Chinatown, and there was a table here and there at which a couple of strongly contrasting complexions, might be seen—whether the white one was all white or not would require an expert to determine.

Amelia had visited night clubs before, once with Donald, but the racial element lent this one an exotic flavor even more interesting than that of a Russian or Hungarian cabaret. The music was good, as in most places in New York, where the competition is so keen that music must be good in order to exist at all. The horns pealed, the saxophones sobbed, the drums rattled and the cymbals clanged. The program dances were more athletic than graceful.

A dancing waiter brought their order. They ate their sandwiches and drank their coffee. There was no cover charge.

"Well," asked Donald, as they were leaving in a taxi-cab, "how did you like it?"

"It was different," she replied, "from the white places. With an occasional exception the girls were not as well-formed as the white girls."

Donald had noticed the same thing, that as a rule the Negro dancing woman ran to heavy hips and slender calves.

"But what they lacked in pulchritude," added the lady, "they made up in ease and agility. They have a marvelous sense of rhythm. They're light as a feather and never miss a step."

In the intervals of her studies, Amelia was writing a play which she meant to submit to the Little Theater. It was somewhat on the order of *Hedda Gabler*, dealing with an unhappy marriage and the best way to terminate it. In it she revealed that instinctive knowledge of the human heart which many women writers, young or old, seem to have, regardless of experience, a point which Donald dwelt upon in the *Essay on the Imagination*, which he had chosen as the title for his doctoral thesis. She read the play to him as she went along with it, and asked for his advice and criticism.

"I'm using you for my hero, Don," she said one evening. "I wish you were the actor and could play the role."

But Donald was not an actor. "It will be interesting," he said, "to have a play with a Negro hero. I'm sure you'll be just to my people."

"Don't be silly, Donald," she replied. "Of course you're not a Negro in the play, any more than you are when you go around with me. I'm not interested in your race, except as human beings, and ethnological and sociological subjects. You're the only one of them I know at all well, except George, the elevator man in our building. I believe you're a white man, just passing for a Negro for some dark and sinister reason which you dare not disclose."

Donald repelled the insinuation with a laugh. With all her philosophy, Donald had never been able to make her consider him a Negro. The play, it may be said in passing, was accepted and produced the following season. It was well received, and while it made no such disgustingly large sums of money as *Abie's Irish Rose*, it won the Pulitzer Prize for that year, played to good houses, and was the first step in Miss Parker's career as a successful playwright. She had been preparing herself to teach in a woman's college, but soon found that Pallas could not compete with Euphrosyne in the age of jazz.

One evening they sat in her study before a grate fire. The reading went rather slowly. She left the table, sat down on the davenport and motioned for Donald to sit beside her. A spark flashed between them. A moment later they were in each other's arms.

"I love you, Don," she said, sealing the statement with a kiss. "Do you love me?"

He answered her with another kiss and other appropriate endearments.

"Let's get married, Don," she said a little later.

"I'd love to," he replied, "but I couldn't. I'm a Negro and you are white."

"I felt you might think something like that, so I took the initiative—this is leap year anyway, I believe. Of course if you don't love me, that's that; but if you do, as you say you do, I think the objection on the grounds of your race ought to come from me. If you have any other reason—if you are married already, or you don't think I'm good enough for you—"

"My dear, I'm not married and you are far too good to spoil your life for me. I'm classed as a Negro, and you couldn't be a Negro, and there is no comfortable social plane for a marriage between us."

"But there are such marriages?"

"Yes, and most of them turn out unhappily. Marriage is not merely a personal affair. It's a social matter, and in this country at this time such a marriage is a misfit and condemns the contracting parties to social odium. Your people wouldn't accept a Negro, and you wouldn't be happy among my people, even if they were friendly, and some of them wouldn't be."

They argued the point.

"Why be a Negro?" she asked finally. "In your case it is merely a name after all. You are far more white than

Negro, and more entitled to call yourself a white man. You are young, you haven't really started your life yet, and few people know you. Forget it and come with me. Why should our love be denied for a mere sentiment?"

"Need our love be denied?" he insinuated. "I beg your pardon," he added a second later, contritely. "I don't mean what you might think. I— I—"

"Oh, yes, you do," she returned, "so you needn't mind explaining. But I'm not a bohemian nor a bolshevist, and free love wouldn't appeal to me. I'm liberal enough, God knows—I have no prejudices, I sometimes doubt if I have any principles, which, after all, in most cases are only inverted prejudices—but I have decent instincts and a certain degree of respect for the traditions of my ancestors. No, Donald, I'd love to marry you, but you won't have me. I'd love to be yours without marriage, but I can't. So I guess there's nothing left for us but to kiss and say goodbye."

They performed the sacramental rite of renunciation with the solemnity due to its importance, and he went away sadly. He met her afterwards in classes, and they spoke as casual acquaintances, but he went no more to her home.

CHAPTER XVI

—————⇒►●◄⇐—————

DONALD'S VIVID and striking personality broke through, to a great extent, the crust of constraint which is seldom absent anywhere in America when white and colored people meet on any plane but that of master and servant. He occupied a room in Livingston Hall, looking out on the Van Am Quad. A used piano of excellent tone, purchased outright at a bargain, constituted one article of his furniture. He had a good, though not robust tenor voice, and could play his own accompaniments. He had taken piano lessons from time to time, had learned music without effort and sang almost as he breathed, intuitively. Indeed, music came to him so easily that he rather looked down upon it as unintellectual and therefore negligible. His taste was for the better class of music. He would play and sing from the scores of operas. He knew the songs of Brahms and Schumann and Schubert. Later on, when recounting the achievements of his people, he would, of course, mention jazz music and the Negro spirituals as creations of theirs. But in his heart, or rather in his mind, which always took precedence, except in some emotional crisis, these forms of musical expression were essentially primitive—a survival of the tom-tom, the war chant, and the moaning of the slave coffle. They might, at the hands of genius, like that of Dvorak or Coleridge-Taylor,[1] furnish themes or *motifs* for finished work; when harmonized by competent musicians like Johnson[2] and Burleigh,[3] they made admirable music for choral singing; but musically, like other folk songs, they were only raw material. He felt, when later on he heard Roland Hayes[4] sing "Steal Away to Jesus," as he had felt when he had heard the world's greatest soprano sing "Home, Sweet Home." They were pretty and appealing pieces and rendered with superb artistry, but why waste a rare voice on something within the range of barbershop or Sunday school harmony when there was so much fine music that was rarely performed for lack of competent executants?

Among the young men in the same dormitory was a young Russian Jew, Isador Rovelsky by name. He heard Donald playing one day, waylaid him in the corridor, and introduced himself. They proved to be kindred spirits and soon became fast friends. Rovelsky was fond of music, played both violin and piano, and was better taught than Donald. They played and sang together. Other young men would come in, and Donald's room became a place of popular resort for the house.

Rovelsky was an ardent Jew and proud of his ancient race and its history. He expressed a profound contempt for those of his people who for social or business gain changed their Russian or German names and or denied their race—sold their birthright, as he put it, for a mess of pottage. He regarded Jewry more as a race than as a religion. A liberal thinker, like so many educated Jews, he considered the rabbinical faith valuable chiefly as a means for keeping the race together. He had no prejudice against other races. His parents had fled from a pogrom and made their way from Russia to New York during his infancy. His father, a talented physician, had built up a lucrative practice on the East Side, and in time, by virtue of some special research work in zymotic diseases, had become attached to the staff of Bellevue Hospital.

Like many of his race, Isador had a fellow feeling with Donald as a victim of social proscription. He spoke of it more freely than most Jews—many of whom seldom discuss with gentiles the social disadvantages to which their race is subjected, and still more rarely compare them with those of the Negro, due to an instinctive feeling that to admit they are discriminated against at all is to acknowledge their social inferiority, and that to compare themselves with colored people is to put themselves upon a level with them. But Isador was not of this type. He would condemn a lynching or any other outrage or indignity against a Negro or the race as fiercely as he would the persecution or scorn of his own people.

Their friendship was not limited to intellectual

bounds. Of like tastes, they often sought their pleas-
ures together—a concert or a lecture at Carnegie Hall,
an opera from the cheaper seats at the Metropolitan, an
occasional leg show at some roof garden—these were
among the diversions they shared. They saw Eugene
O'Neill's *The Emperor Jones*, with Gilpin[5] in the title
role, and agreed that he had the finest speaking voice of
any actor on the stage. There were quite a few colored
people in the house, and Donald was much annoyed
when some of them laughed noisily at the most tragic
emotional crises. Izzy and he, in trying to account for
this demonstration, while discussing the play afterwards, ascribed it not to lack of feeling but to limited
experience in play going, and therefore to an imperfect
appreciation of the finer shades of emotional reaction.
And Donald made a note that this was one of the things
he would write about.

Now and then Donald and his friend would go together to visit Greenwich Village, which still retained
some of its earlier vogue.

"Don," said Isador one evening, several weeks after
the termination of Donald's intimacy with Amelia
Parker, "let's go down to the Dead Horse, the new joint
on Eighth Street. It isn't quite as macabre or putrid as
its name, and they have a fine Hungarian orchestra and
good eats."

Donald was quite willing and the subway soon
landed them near their destination.

The café was housed in the converted stable of a once handsome residence now used as a rooming house. It was reached by an alley leading from Eighth Street. The interior was fitted up with various equine suggestions. The tables were designed to represent mangers. The chairs were fitted with saddles. There were racks attached to the walls and filled with hay— purely for effect, since the hay was never used for anything, but merely changed now and then for sanitary reasons. There were pictures of famous race horses hanging between the racks, and the waiters were attired like jockeys, in top boots, white breeches and jackets with numbers on the backs.

The head waiter had stepped out and they looked around for a table, but found none unoccupied. Finally, toward the rear, partially screened by an artificial palm in a tub, they discovered a table at which was seated a young woman.

"Oh," exclaimed Isador, "there's Mitzi Cohn, all by herself. We'll go over and join her."

Donald observed, as they drew near, that the girl was a pronouncedly Jewish type. With her red hair, vivid dark eyes, slender form and well-molded arms and legs, generously displayed according to the mode, she was decidedly attractive to Donald in a novel and exotic fashion.

"*Bon soir*, Mitzi," Isador greeted her, "*comment ça va?*"

"Speak Yiddish, Izzy, don't be ashamed of your race. You couldn't get away from it if you tried. Your face is a map of Jerusalem."

"So's your old man," retorted Isador. "Meet my friend Donald Glover. He's a student, a philosopher, a gentleman and a judge of good music. His taste in women is as yet unformed. He's a golden opportunity for you."

"He *is* a pretty boy," returned Mitzi, as she eyed Donald appraisingly, and gave him her hand. "Is he one of us? He's dark enough to be."

"He's one of the elect, but not one of the Chosen People. He's an American."

"An American Negro,"[6] supplemented Donald, conscientiously.

"He has an ingrowing conscience," scoffed Isador, "and feels it only honest to explain. We pure bloods don't need explanation. Our faces speak for us."

"Sit down, both of you," said Mitzi, "and order me something to eat. I've just been marking time with a ginger ale until some boy friend should blow in and feed me."

One of the jockeys was summoned and Mitzi ordered a raw beef sandwich, Isador a ham sandwich, and Donald a Welsh rarebit. They were all young and had perfect digestions.

"And say, Mike," said Mitzi to the attendant jockey, "bring three cups of—you know what I mean."

"Nothin' doin', Miss, the lid's on tonight."

"Oh, hell," sighed Mitzi, plaintively. "But bring the cups and some orange juice."

When the cups were brought, Mitzi, under cover of the table produced from some esoteric cache about her person a small, flat silver flask of synthetic gin, and with the orange juice and some water from the carafe on the table, concocted a passable cocktail. While they were waiting for the rest of their order, Donald learned more about Mitzi.

"Mitzi," continued Isador, "is an illustrator for *Modesty*, a sex magazine which specializes in adultery, and she also writes lurid tales for its columns, illustrated with bedroom scenes from life by her own brush or crayon."

"Don't be so crude, Izzy. You make me blush. A poor woiking goil has got to earn her living—or ought to."

They talked about the music, which was excellent of its kind. At Mitzi's request, one of the waiters asked the orchestra leader to play a Russian dance, based on the "Volga Boat Song," which she and Isador went through quite skillfully while Donald looked on. As they were returning to the table, a young man came up and spoke to Isador.

"Izzy," he explained, "Mannie Einstein, Abie Rosenbaum and I are the nominating committee of the Zebes, and we're meeting over at the Brevoort to fix up a slate for the fraternity election Monday night. Can't you come over?"

"Will you excuse me, Don," asked Isador, "if I leave you to Mitzi's tender mercies?"

"I can protect myself," countered Donald. "She doesn't look very formidable."

Mitzi's eyes narrowed craftily over a cryptic smile. She had a wide mouth with full red lips.

"Appearances are deceitful," returned Isador. "She's a vamp of the first order. You can report to me tomorrow, if you're in condition to. Knock on my door in the morning."

Mitzi and Donald listened to the music and danced together for an hour, except when an acquaintance of Mitzi's, to whom she introduced Donald, came up and carried her off for a fox trot.

"I'd like to show you some of my sketches," she said, about ten o'clock. "Come with me over to my studio; it's only a couple of blocks away."

Donald paid the bill and went with her. Since his split-up with Amelia, he had had little female society and was beginning to feel lonesome for it. They walked past the Washington Arch and diagonally across the square to one of the streets running into it from the south. Mitzi had a latch key—there was no janitor in evidence—and they reached her flat after climbing two flights of stairs. It was a common type of studio apartment—one large room with a kitchenette, and a bathroom. There were a few bright but inexpensive rugs on the floor, an easel, a model's throne and several chairs. A sofa bed, draped with an artistically faded cover, served as a sofa by day and sleeping place at night. A row of Mitzi's drawings in charcoal were tacked to the walls, along with some signed photographs of actors and movie stars. There was a short shelf of yellow-back French novels, and a file of the magazine *Modesty*, to which Mitzi contributed. An easel with palette hanging on it, a couple of figure models, one male and one female, and a box of crayons on the table helped make up the tale of the tools of Mitzi's trade.

She showed Donald some of her work, of which he expressed an honest appreciation. It was really clever, in a bizarre sort of way, and quite daring. Some of her sketches would not have been out of place in *La Rire* or *La Vie Parisienne*, either for subject or for treatment. They were seated on the couch, and as she turned over the sheets of the album, her arm touched Donald's shoulder, and her hand strayed to his hair.

"What lovely curls you have!" she said.

Donald did not leave the studio until nine the next morning. It was Sunday and there were no lectures at the university. He did not knock at Izzy's door, and when Izzy came to his room later and asked for a report, Donald's description was discreetly edited, and Izzy, with characteristic delicacy, did not press him for details. For however far the conduct of these young men might fall below the strictest standard of morals, their speech was always clean. According to their code, a gentleman might sin, but never with his lips.

Several weeks later Donald was dining with Mitzi

one evening at a new Russian restaurant on Seventh Avenue near Fourteenth Street.

"Don," said the girl over their *borscht*, "you'd make a stunning movie sheik. Moe Silberstein, a friend of mine, director of the Interplanetary Studios of Long Island, is getting ready to produce a new picture. He's looking for a man to play the leading part. From what he told me I'm quite sure you could fill the role perfectly."

Donald laughed. "But I'm no actor," he said, "and absolutely without stage experience."

"It doesn't require an actor, and you could soon learn all that is necessary. You're as handsome as any movie actor now on the screen."

"But I'm in school," returned Donald, "and couldn't find the time."

"He'll not be ready to start until the end of June, and by that time your school year will be over. I'll arrange for you to meet him."

He met the director at Mitzi's studio one evening. Silberstein was an affable person and very cordial. He sized Donald up with an expert eye and was enthusiastic. He was looking for a man, he said, and a novice, if promising, would be less expensive. The business was not a very large one, in spite of its name, and was really in the experimental stage.

"You'd make an ideal male lead for my picture," he said.

"It's entirely out of my line," returned Donald. "I'm

studying philosophy, and mean to devote myself to literature."

"This needn't interfere at all with such pursuits," rejoined the producer. "It would be a great card to have a philosopher in a picture. You'll be well paid and there may be a future in it for you which will make philosophy look like thirty cents. The women would simply eat the picture up. Let Mitzi bring you over to the studio, and we'll give you a screen test."

Donald was young and adventurous. He went with Mitzi one Sunday to the studio and looked it over, and he posed before the camera. He had made no plans for the summer, and to take the leading part in a good picture might be a pleasant interlude for part of his vacation. And if he should make good it would be a fine thing for his race. There were many Negro movie actors, but they played nothing but servants' parts and comic roles, at many of which, even when amused, he had been disgusted. He had seen Gilpin and Paul Robeson in *The Emperor Jones* and other Eugene O'Neill plays,[7] and had admired their superb acting but no Negro to his knowledge had ever played a serious or a dignified role in any moving picture. Such rare parts were always played by white actors blacked up for the occasion.

"If my success would reflect any credit on my people," he said at last, "I might be willing to try it."

"What do you mean—your people?" inquired the producer.

"The colored people," replied Donald. "Didn't Mitzi tell you I'm a Negro?"

"She did intimate something of the sort, but after seeing you I forgot all about it. No, we'd have to keep that dark. You'd be billed under a French or Spanish or Italian name. As a Negro you wouldn't do at all. The principal girl in the picture is a Southern woman and wouldn't play opposite a colored man, in the first place. You're just the man for the part, but much of the success of an actor, on the screen or off, is due to his personality.

"If we keep your racial identity dark," he added, unconscious of the inverted pun, "the ladies can admire you and run after you, all of which makes for the success of the picture. You're as handsome or handsomer than Valentino, or Eugene O'Brien or Ramon Navarro or any other film actor. Neither Mitzi nor I will ever give you away. You're just exactly what I need for the role, so far as looks are concerned, and after talking with you, I'm convinced you can act. I'd like to have you, and I'm sure you'd be doing a good thing for yourself."

Donald said he would think the matter over and promised to let Silberstein know in ample time to find someone else in case he declined the offer. Mitzi urged him to accept it. She herself was cast for a small part in the picture.

Donald considered the proposition, but not for long. He had always known that he could easily pass for white, and that so far as the laws of any state touched upon the question of race admixture, he was legally a white man. But while he had never hesitated to take advantage of his complexion in any public place or relation where his dark strain was not known, he would have scorned to deny it. In private life he did not seek any privilege that his darkest friend might not share, or at least anything that was not freely accorded with full knowledge of what he was. This was not, perhaps, good sense or sound philosophy, but it was in tune with good manners and the sentimental side of his nature.

"I guess I'll pass it up," he told Mitzi.

"I'm disappointed in you, Don," she declared. "Here I go out of my way to get you a chance that any sensible man in your place would jump at, and you turn it down cold. I think you're a damn fool!"

Her friendship began to cool, and before long a Hindu swami replaced Donald in her vagrant affections, and thus ended this chapter of his amorous experiences. He had liked Mitzi and had found her good company, but had never loved her and had never even thought of marriage in connection with her.

CHAPTER XVII

—————➤●◄—————

DONALD WAS strolling along Seventh Avenue one afternoon on his way to make a social call. He always found it interesting to walk through Harlem. The dark faces, the little black babies in their carriages, the black policemen, the dandy in high hat and spats, the pretty brown girls dressed cheaply but effectively in the latest styles, the self-possessed, not to say impudent Jamaicans, the crude and as yet bewildered recent importations from the far South, even the occasional old mammy in a head handkerchief, all appealed pleasantly to his race consciousness. They were his people, in their own milieu, where they were not overshadowed and dwarfed into insignificance by the white man. He had stopped on the curb to watch a passing parade of some secret society, with a blatant brass band, resplendent banners and gaudy uniforms, when he felt himself clapped familiarly on the shoulder and heard a familiar voice saying: "Why, hello, Don, old son, how's tricks? I heard you was in town, but this is the first time I've run across you."

Donald looked down into the smiling face of his old roommate at Athena, Abraham Lincoln Dixon—"Link" for short. Dixon showed all the signs of prosperity. He wore a light brown suit, of good cloth and good fit. His tan shoes and socks and brown silk necktie matched his suit perfectly. His complexion was lighter than Donald remembered it to have been and his kinky reddish brown hair was plastered down on his scalp to a glassy smoothness. He wore a pince-nez, secured by a black ribbon, and a large ruby seal ring—though whether the stone was real or synthetic Donald was not sufficiently expert in gems to determine; it was at least a very good imitation.

"Well, Don," Link went on, "I'm sure glad to see you again. The sight of you is good for sore eyes. Whatcha doin'?"

Donald replied that he was studying at Columbia, and inquired as to Link's place of residence and occupation.

"I'm livin' here," replied the other, "and I'm a' orator by profession."

"Oh," returned Donald, "you mean a lecturer?"

"No, I mean a' orator. Here's my card."

He handed Donald an engraved square of cardboard which read:

Dr. A. Lincoln Dixon, A.B., LL.D.

Orator

New York address — 1627 West 135th Street,

Chicago address — 3799 South Clark Street,
Washington address — 2123 K St., N.W.

"The A.B. is from Athena?" asked Donald.

"Yes," replied Link, "you left there before I gradu-ated."

"Where'd you get the LL.D., Link?"

"Oh, I delivered a commencement oration for Sumner University last spring, and they offered either to pay my traveling expenses or give me a degree. I happened to be in funds at the moment, and could use the degree in my business, so I'm now Dr. Dixon. It looks better on a card or in a newspaper item."

"What's your principal subject, Link?" asked Donald. "On what do you speak?"

"Oh, I don't need any subject," returned the orator. "People come just to hear me talk. Usually I speak on the Race Problem—it's a live topic and easy to talk on. You don't need any preparation. If you're a pessimist, every number of *The Climax* will give you a text and an argument. For the optimistic, Pollyanna speech, every issue of *The Opening Door*[1] will suggest a subject and a line of talk."

The two magazines named, in the order of their mention, were respectively the radical and conserva-tive organs of Negro thought. Donald read both of them every month from cover to cover, and had con-tributed several articles to *The Climax*.

"Are you an optimist or a pessimist," asked Donald, "a radical or a conservative?"

"Depending entirely on the company or the occasion. To a NAACP or a UNPA audience I'm a militant radical. To an Interracial League audience I am conservative. I tickle the vanity of the white folks by telling 'em how glad we are to cooperate with 'em, when they know and we know, and they know that we know that our cooperation will consist of merely doing what they tell us."

"You have quite a wide field to range over," suggested Donald. "Don't you ever get tangled up or called down?"

"Oh, yes," returned Link. "There are skeptics and cynics everywhere, and there's where the art of the orator comes in. If someone in the audience should ask if you didn't say so-and-so on such-and-such an occasion, you can shut him up by a flat denial, or by claiming that his memory is at fault, or by quoting Lincoln's famous statement—I guess it was Lincoln's, and nobody in the audience would know if it wasn't—that 'only a fool never changes his mind'—or if you think the audience will stand for it—and almost any one of my audiences will stand for anything I say—once I grip 'em I can hold 'em—by asking whether he has stopped bootlegging, or sniffing coke, or beating his wife, or some such little thing, as he promised to do at such-and-such a time. Yes, old son, oratory is my long suit.

William Jennings Bryan ain't got nothin' on me. If I was white, like he is, I'd make a fortune."

"But meanwhile?" asked Donald.

"I'm under temporary contract, just at present with the Universal Negro Progress Association.[2] Part of the time I'm on the road, organizing new branches, and part of the time here in New York, performing secretarial duties at the main headquarters. The pay's not very big just now, but there are chances for a smart man, and I reckon I can qualify in that class. When I'm entirely on my own, I get from one hundred to five hundred dollars for a speech. It's a great racket, Donald. Have you seen our new building? I'm going up there now; come along with me."

Donald excused himself on account of his engagement, but agreed to dine with Dixon at a certain restaurant in Harlem at seven o'clock, and then to accompany him to a meeting at the UNPA Hall, at which Dixon and the head of the organization, the President of the African Empire,[3] were to speak.

Donald was well-informed of the fantastic enterprise on which this new black Napoleon—the first Negro since Toussaint L'Ouverture to be so denominated—was embarked. He sympathized with its underlying purpose—the uplift of the Negro, and the administration of Africa by and for the Africans. He had no illusions about the mandatory powers among which the Treaty of Versailles had partitioned the territory of the darker races of the world. They would be false to every experience and tradition of European overlordship if they did not administer their mandated colonies, as they had always administered their outlying possessions—for the interest and profit, first, of themselves. If, by spending a little of their revenues on the natives, or leaving them a little to spend on themselves, they could increase the efficiency of their labor, or their trading value, they might do it, but little more need be expected. And so Donald sympathized in theory with any project which looked toward saving Africa for the Africans. It was something to dream about, as his mother had always dreamed; it was something to write about, as Dr. Lebrun was already doing, and as Donald himself was to do at great length in later years; it furnished a stirring theme for a lecture and an interesting topic of discussion, but from a practical standpoint it was as yet a mere chimera.

But he wished to hear from the mouth of the propagandist himself a statement of his scheme, so he said he would be glad to go with Dixon.

CHAPTER XVIII

⟶⟶❖⟵⟵

THE HOUSE at which Donald was going to call in Harlem was that of Senator James F. Brown—the title had long survived the office and had become a mere term of courtesy—the Cleveland lawyer who had played a part in the adoption of Donald by the Glovers. Mr. Brown had made money in Cleveland real estate, had invested it in a promising Negro life insurance company and had moved to New York to take charge of the legal work of the company at its New York office. He had also bought some property in Harlem, and, with the astuteness derived from experience and good judgment, was adding to his real estate holdings from year to year.

In one of her letters to Donald, Mrs. Glover had suggested that he call on Senator Brown and his family, and Donald was carrying out the suggestion. The Browns, he had learned, lived on what was called Striver's Row, a block of good houses on 137th Street, affected by well-to-do colored people. The family occupied the ten-room second-floor apartment of a handsome brick house owned by Mr. Brown himself. Donald ascended to the apartment by an automatic elevator. His ring at the doorbell brought a servant who stated in answer to Donald's question that Mr. Brown was at home and showed him into the library. Mr. Brown came in a moment later and Donald introduced himself.

"I'm awfully glad you came to see me," Mr. Brown said after he had shaken his visitor's hand cordially. "You don't remember it, but you came to see me one night over twenty years ago. I was thinking about you only the other day when I saw you named in *The Climax* as one of our most brilliant young intellectuals. And how are your mother and father?"

"They were well," said Donald, "when I heard from Mother the other day. She asked me to call on you."

"I first met you in my library in Cleveland," continued Mr. Brown, motioning toward his well-filled bookshelves. "I had quite a few books then, but have been adding to them as the years have gone by. My first idea was to have every book that was written about the Negro or by a Negro. I found it too large an order for any one man, so of late years I've been restricting my acquisitions to books by colored authors, and these are becoming so numerous that it keeps me putting my hand in my pocket all the time to keep up with them."

He asked Donald about his work and his plans and expressed his pleasure at learning what Donald was doing.

"It's a great opportunity our young men have in these days," he continued. "When I was young, no colored man had ever attended Columbia University, and colored college graduates were as scarce as hen's teeth, while now they are taking degrees there and elsewhere and making their contributions to literature and education. My eldest daughter graduated from Oberlin College when you were an infant, and is now teaching French and Latin in one of the New York high schools. My younger daughter went to Howard University and then married. Her husband is a dentist with an office over on Lennox Avenue, and they are living here with us."

Mrs. Brown came in at this point and proved to be a motherly amiable woman in the fifties. She was not the mother of Esther, the elder Miss Brown, but was a second wife. She greeted Donald cordially and referred to their first meeting and his adoption by the Glovers. Since they had moved away from Cleveland, she had met them rarely, but she inquired about Donald's mother and father and hoped they were well.

While they were talking, Mr. Brown's younger daughter, Myrtle, now Mrs. Morgan, came in from her work—she had no children and was employed in the Harlem branch of the public library. She was a handsome young woman, thoroughly up-to-date both in dress and manner.

"You're the little boy who came to see us one night,"

she said, after they had shaken hands, "and who broke my Paris fan."

"I don't recall it," said Donald, "but I'll take your word for it and replace it with another just as good."

"Thank you," said the lady. "I'll hold you to that. I saw some nice ones at Wanamaker's yesterday. I told my sister when you went away that night that I meant to marry you, when you grew up, but you took too long, and a nice boy wanted me and we were married. As I look at you, I could almost wish I had waited, but I'd be too old for you now and you probably have another girl anyway."

Donald made the obvious reply, that she didn't look a day over twenty-five, which was his own age, that he had no girl, and that it was his misfortune that she hadn't waited.

Mr. Brown mentioned that Mr. Seaton, Donald's first father by adoption, had written him several times about Donald and had called on him once to make inquiries. Mr. Seaton, he said, spent much of his time in New York, where he lived at the Waldorf. He was taking marked interest in Negro education, and had made large contributions to several of the colored institutions of learning.

Donald told him of Mr. Seaton's visit to Booneville and his offer to take him back.

"Yes," said Mr. Brown, "he told me about it. I thought it very fine of him to make the offer and finer still of you to refuse it. He still retains a deep interest in you."

Donald spent a pleasant hour and departed with the cheerful farewells of the whole family and an invitation to call often. He went several times and at their house met a number of the better colored people of New York—not the blatant pleasure-seeking jazz hounds who wasted their substance in dissipation and riotous living, but the self-respecting business and professional men, writers, artists, musicians, actors, teachers and editors who constituted the worthwhile Negro people of Harlem.

———➤●◄———

CHAPTER XIX

DONALD MET Link, pursuant to their agreement, at Martin's restaurant on Lennox Avenue. The dining room was clean and attractive and the food excellent. They had a small table to themselves, a little to one side, where they could eat their chicken à la Maryland and talk freely without disturbing others or being themselves disturbed. Most of the guests were talking and laughing, more or less noisily, and there was little likelihood of their being overheard, though several men came over and spoke to Link and several of the women looked at Donald with interest. Had Donald been at all conceited, he would long ago have been utterly spoiled. But being modest and self-contained he was not at all disturbed by this sort of attention and preserved his usual philosophic calm.

Dixon was good company for a taciturn companion. He did most of the talking, and did it well, and Donald listened with interest to his frank characterization of New York Negroes and their activities, and his naive, shameless and unconscious revelation of his own character. Speaking in confidence, as to a friend, he was more or less skeptical about the progress of the Negro.

"There's supposed to be about two hundred and fifty thousand of these Harlem niggers," he said. "They have the ballot, and they can't pull together long enough to elect a man to Congress or any other important office. Many of 'em are doctors and lawyers and preachers and editors and undertakers, and they haven't got a single bank of their own. They haven't one real hotel. The butcher shops, grocery and drygoods stores, with rare and insignificant exceptions, are all run by Jews. There are even Greek shoeshining parlors and restaurants for them. Some of these places employ black waiters or bootblacks, but most of the owners are Italians or Greeks."

"Perhaps they're handicapped by lack of capital," suggested Donald, willing to find an excuse for his people's apparent lack of enterprise.

"They've as much capital as the Jews have when they start. It takes only a few dollars to buy a pushcart and a stock of street merchandise. No, Donald, it's simply not in 'em. Instead of saving their money, like Jews and Greeks and Syrians, until they have a little working capital, they squander it on craps and 'numbers' and women and gin. Instead of going to night school, they go to cabarets and gambling joints and blow in the tips they have groveled and grinned for all day on the railroads or in the elevators. I don't think a great deal of our race, Donald. Between you and I and the gate-post,

it's not our race, anyway; we're more white than black.
I'm a Negro for revenue only. I could pass for white,
but it pays better to be a big Negro than just one of the
common or garden variety of white men. You get more
credit for what you accomplish and less criticism for
your failures. A few big niggers are making money
rackrenting the poor jaspers up here in Harlem, but the
majority of them ain't worth a tinker's damn."

They ate leisurely, Donald with a hearty appetite,
though he was not a gross feeder, and Link with the
reputed racial appreciation for good food, for which
the restaurant was famous. Dixon asked Donald if he
cared for a drink, but Donald declined. He had no
more scruples about violating the Volstead law than a
congressman, a judge, a policeman or a prohibition en-
forcement agent. He had drunk in the homes of
preachers and teachers, but he valued his health and
did not care to risk it by experimenting with casual
Harlem bootleg.

Donald had his doubts as to how far or for how long
or in what sort of light Link could pass for white, but,
naturally, he did not raise the issue. He had heard the
same argument, less crudely expressed, from lips of
whiter and brighter men than Link Dixon, and as a
philosopher he could see the force of it. He had heard
Dr. Jefferson, the conservative Negro leader, say once
from the platform that if he could be reincarnated after
death and were given his choice of races, he thought he
would choose to be born an American Negro; that the

hill of difficulty was so high and the upward climb so hard for one of that race that the effort to reach the top would bring out the best in him, and that those who survived would have proved their equality with the world's best and get credit accordingly. It was a safe bet, since it could not happen, but it was a good talking point. Donald did not go quite so far. It might be very well for a man like Jefferson, but except for the especially gifted or fortunate, to be a Negro, in America, was a serious handicap in the race of life. A philosopher, however, must, as Goethe said, "accept the universe," bow to the inevitable and make the best of it, and try to help forward the day when it would be no disadvantage not to be white.

And all thinking Negroes, he reasoned, were philosophers perforce, even if unconsciously. That they were not all pessimists was due to their keen love of life, which was also the main source of their improvidence, and, in their dealings with white people, to a somewhat ironic sense of humor like that of the philosophic rabbit that Aesop—himself a slave and an Ethiopian, as well as a very profound and cunning philosopher—might have written about, who, when a wolf was tearing him to pieces, accepted his fate as a matter of course, but made fun of the wolf's atrocious table manners.

"And now, Donald," said Dixon, as they left the restaurant, "we'll take a taxi and go around to my rooms a few blocks away where I'll change and get ready for my speech."

Link's apartment was a one-room bachelor suite, consisting of a living room with an in-a-door bed, a bathroom, and a kitchenette with a Pullman breakfast nook. There was a davenport, a victrola, and several easy chairs in the living room, where Donald sat while the orator made his toilet in the adjoining bathroom, the door of which remained open. First he washed the sheik paste from his hair with hot water, which, when he had dried it with a coarse towel, restored its natural roughness. Then he powdered his face with dark brown powder, and changed his clothes to a black frock coat with gray striped trousers.

The hall to which they directed their course proved to be a large, pretentious but not impressive, and as yet unfinished brick building, containing on the ground floor the administration offices and a printing plant where the newspaper organ and other literature of the society was printed, and on the second floor, approached from an entrance lobby by two broad flights of stairs, a large auditorium with a seating capacity of twelve or fifteen hundred people. The walls were decorated with lithographs of famous Negroes, among them Toussaint L'Ouverture, the Haitian liberator; his successor Desalines; General Antonio Maceo, the Cuban patriot; Frederick Douglass, the abolition orator; Senator Blanche K. Bruce, John M. Langston, Booker T.

Washington,[1] and several Negro bishops whose fame did not extend beyond the confines of their own race. Curiously enough, though Donald knew that many of these men were mulattoes or nearly white, they were all pictured as deep black. Donald thought this a childish performance. He called himself, it was true, an "American Negro," but this did not mean at all a black man, but one of the group in all shades which used the designation sociologically and for convenience's sake. A portrait of the President of the African Empire, draped with the flag of his mythical government, occupied the place of honor over the platform.

The program began with a complicated ritual like that of a secret order. The participants, male and female, were in white uniforms decorated with crosses and other insignia in black. There was marching and countermarching in the aisles. Special hymns, in verse even more unspeakably bad than that in which such special hymns are usually written, were sung to stale old tunes which even the mellow Negro voices could not rescue from banality. The constitution of the society was read, with a preamble suggesting the Declaration of Independence, followed by an antiphonal recital in which the leader read a sentence and the audience responded.

The audience was almost unrelievedly black. Donald learned later that white people were not wanted at the meetings and that persons suspected of being white were sometimes refused admittance or even ejected.

There were few present besides Donald who showed signs of any corrupting white blood. The President introduced Dixon as "one of us," an eloquent advocate of the principles for which the association stood. He hoped ere long to add him to their permanent staff. He would now address them on the greatness of the Negro race, once the rulers of Africa, now struggling to recover their place in the sun and destined in the near future to regain their ancient power and to dominate at least Africa, South America and the West Indies, if not the whole world.

Dixon was proud, he asserted, after loud applause following the introduction, to belong to this great race, and he hated the little white blood in his veins. He envied the President his purity of race. As a matter of fact, as Donald could but notice, the President was of chocolate brown complexion and not entirely Negroid of features, nor was his hair kinky.

Dixon proved an eloquent speaker, with a ready flow of fine words and flamboyant phrases employed with excellent rhetorical effect, though his arguments and his conclusions made no intellectual impression on Donald, and were so overdrawn as to make their emotional appeal negligible. The rest of the audience, however, swallowed them with avidity. When he led up to a point and paused for effect, the hall rang with vociferous applause. The meeting assumed the fervor of an old-time camp meeting, with cries of "Amen," "Atta boy" and "That's right, brother," certain self-appointed cheer leaders directing the applause and drawing it out like a well-organized claque.

The greatest excitement ensued when the orator declared that when the Almighty had created the heavens and the earth, had divided the sea from the land, had set the sun, moon and stars in the heavens, had created the birds and the beasts and the fishes, he made man, first the red, white and brown races, and later on, when these races fell short of his expectations, to correct his mistakes and as the capstone of the structure, the crowning glory of creation, he made the black race. If this great race had not yet attained the rulership of the world to which it was destined, his hearers must remember that it was young yet, and that with the virility and strength of youth it was bound to forge ahead, and if they would all stand together, under the leadership of that great man, their president, in due time they would prevail against the effete races which were already morally and intellectually bankrupt and merely marking time to save the expense of liquidation.

The President followed Dixon. It was a principle with this remarkable man, before he was sent to federal prison for misuse of the mails, and afterwards deported from the country, to keep the spotlight upon himself all the time. He spoke, somewhat vaguely, about negotiations in progress to secure territory for an American Negro colony in Africa, and asked very definitely for contributions to send a commission to the Dark Continent to secure concessions in Liberia and Abyssinia, the only two independent black nations in the world. This would involve a quite large expense, since these envoys must travel first class on the best boats and stop at the best hotels in order to make a good impression and maintain the dignity of the organization. In the western continent, he maintained, Haiti had been occupied by the whites and could never be redeemed until the future African super government should assume the task. He advised his followers to save their money and to keep their money and their property in the form of liquid assets which could be promptly realized to take up homesteads and form mining and manufacturing companies to develop the vast mineral resources of the African continent. He predicted black Carnegies and Rockefellers and Fords in the future industrial development of his African Empire.

A good part of the address was devoted to abuse of the mulattoes, who, he declared, with Dr. Lebrun at their head, had conspired to defeat his plans. They posed as Negroes, but were really hand-in-glove with the whites, who in the West Indies had enticed them away from the blacks by conceding them a certain degree of political and social recognition which was denied the darker people. But when the black empire was once established and its supremacy secure, there would be no more mulattoes. Since he did not mention any particular time for their disappearance, Donald wondered whether they were to be eliminated by massacre, like the whites in the Haitian and the aristocrats in the French and Russian Revolutions, or whether they were to be sterilized so that the black race would be relieved of the fear of contamination by white blood. Donald could see no other way to dispense with mulattoes, unless it could be accomplished by rigid laws forbidding the intermarriage of persons of pure black blood and those of any degree of white blood whatever—and similar laws to preserve the purity of any race or caste had ultimately proved ineffective wherever in history they had been enacted.

Donald was unable, at the close of the speech, to decide whether the President was fool, fanatic, self-deluded visionary, crook, or a more or less unconscious combination of them all. His fundamental proposition, that Africa should belong to the Africans, was philosophically and ethically sound, but his plan of bringing it about was the wildest of fantasies. That he could secure for his projected colony any of the European African territory, out of the lust for which had grown the bloodiest and most costly war of all history, was palpably absurd, and that the governments of Liberia or Abyssinia would abdicate in favor of a foreign power of their own blood was equally unthinkable.

At the close of the meeting, while the audience was dispersing, Dixon came down from the platform and led Donald forward to meet the President.

"Your Excellency," he said, "I want my young friend, Mr. Glover, to meet the greatest Negro in the world. My friend Glover has a white skin, but he's got a black heart. He's a graduate of Columbia University, a writer of talent, and means to devote his life to the service of our race."

The President gave Donald a small, cold, podgy hand, and eyed him appraisingly. Donald found him in the brief conversation that followed, as pompous, vain and egotistical as he had seemed from the audience. But Donald knew that men accepted by the world as great and given a prominent place in history had been vain, pompous and egotistical, and he was still unable to determine to what extent the President was sincere, or in what degree he was honest. Donald left the hall with Dixon, who suggested a visit to a Negro cabaret on Seventh Avenue.

"It's Saturday night," said Dixon, "which is the big night for the jaspers. We'll go by my rooms again for a minute, while I get into my glad rags."

As they sat side by side in the Negro taxicab they had summoned, Dixon continued to talk. Talking was his business. He loved to hear himself talk, and seldom neglected a favorable opportunity.

"Well, boy," he queried, "whatja think of my speech?"

"It was very eloquent," Donald conceded, "and seemed to make a hit."

"It was a cuckoo, a knockout!" exulted the orator. "It takes me to handle them niggers." Dixon, when off the platform, often reverted to the vernacular of his youth. "That black baboon that calls hisself the President of

Africa is jus' clay in my hands, and I can flatter them tar babies till they can't see straight. That's the art of the orator, Donald. You've got to adapt yourself and your viewpoint to your audience. When I'm out socializing among the highbrows and the high yellows, I look like 'em and I talk like 'em. When I go among black people, I try to look and talk black. That's one advantage in our being light mulattoes—we can fraternize with people of any color."

Donald waited until Link had washed off the brown powder, reanointed his hair and changed to a dinner jacket and dancing pumps. Then they hailed another taxi.

"I'm taking you," said Link, "to the Golden Slipper, which is the finest Negro amusement place in New York. It belongs to Mamie Wilson, caters to the dickties and the ofays, and is a regular gold mine. I'm engaged to Mamie, by the way, and when I'm ready to marry, I'll foreclose my matrimonial lien and take the business over. I want you to meet Mamie. She's a lula, and a knockout, and the berries."

CHAPTER XX

———⟫●⟪———

M AMIE WILSON,[1] like so many of her race, had suc-
cumbed to the lure of Harlem. She had left
Booneville, shortly after Donald had gone away to college, to join the Creole Belles, a troupe of colored entertainers. She had become, very soon, a popular singer
and dancer, and later, though she had not yet reached
Broadway, had formed and headed The Ravens, a
Negro company which had played their revue in the
Lafayette Theater in New York, and in the Negro thea-
ters of Chicago, Washington, Philadelphia, Baltimore
and other cities. Though she was fond of pleasure and
absolutely without sex morals, she was capable in business and thrifty. She had never squandered her money
on lovers or in expensive forms of dissipation, but with
the prudence which had marked her youth in Booneville, when Donald had known her, had been reasonably careful of her good name. When The Ravens
finished their flight, Mamie's nest was well-feathered.
She invested part of her capital in a lease and the neces-

sary furniture and appointments and opened The Golden Slipper in a basement on Lennox Avenue near 140th Street.

Donald had never visited the cabaret, though he had more than once heard of it. It was a spacious room, with tables and chairs for four or five hundred. The walls were divided into panels, decorated for the most part with rather decent nudes of fairly artistic quality, without anything suggestive about them except the nudity, which in this enlightened age seems to have lost its erotic appeal. There was a good dancing floor and a good Negro orchestra, of which the acrobatic drummer was a whole show in himself. The corybantes were or were made up light-colored and personable, and were only less undressed than they might have been. The male dancers were cyclones in ebony and bronze. The audience was in large part white, and Dixon pointed out to Donald several literary and theatrical celebrities at the tables. It was after theater hours, and a constant stream of taxicabs delivered new guests at the door.

When they had checked their hats and started from the lobby, a handsome golden brown woman with straight bobbed hair came forward to meet them. Donald had known Mamie as a dark brown girl with crisp, crinkly hair, but time and money and art and a measure of taste had softened her bad points and emphasized her good ones, and practically made her over. In spite of the metamorphosis and the lapse of years, Donald recognized her at once.

"Hello, Mamie," cried Link, as he put out his hand, "*comment ça va?*"

"*Très bien, cheri, et vous le même, j'espère?*" returned Mamie, who had picked up a little colloquial French from returned Negro soldiers, and as Link knew, liked to show it off, in which respects they were sympathetic souls.

Link introduced his companion.

"This is my friend Donald Glover. I wanted him to see the handsomest woman and the finest cabaret in Harlem—I mean in New York, I beg your pardon—so I brought him around. Miss Wilson, Mr. Glover."

"I've met Miss Wilson before," said Donald, "when we were younger."

"Yes," returned Mamie, "we're old friends. I used to know Donald as well as I knew myself, didn't I, Donald?"

"Yes," rejoined Donald, "we were close friends. We belonged to the same Methodist church choir."

"Say no more," Link chuckled, unctuously, "say no more! I used to belong to a Baptist choir, and you can't tell me nothin'. How's the show tonight? I see you've got a good house."

"The show's fine, and we've seated four hundred people. Last Saturday night we crowded six hundred in."

"Whoo-pee!" exclaimed Link. "Six hundred at a dollar cover charge, besides the eats! I guess we better sign up our partnership articles."

"There'll be no cover charge for either of you tonight, nor any other charge," declared Mamie. "You'll be my guests," and she added in her low throaty voice, with a sentimental glance at Donald, "for Auld Lang Syne. Here's a good table, and I'll tell the waiter to serve anything you want—don't forget now, *anything*."

They had something to eat, the best the house afforded, washed down with a bottle of "the widow," which appeared on ice in a silver-plated pail, and was kept discretely under the table. The singing and dancing numbers were the best of their kind and the acrobatic drummer performed feats which would have qualified him for the part of a conjurer or a contortionist on the vaudeville stage. Mamie did a solo dance which brought out vividly the feline sinuosity of movement which Donald marked as one of her new acquirements. In the social dancing between the professional stunts, she danced, once with a white writer who specialized in Negro stuff, and afterwards with Link, and a little later, at her own invitation, with Donald.

"You were a good looking girl, Mamie," he remarked, as they swam through "The Merry Widow Waltz, "but you've become a beautiful woman."

"I'm glad you like me," replied Mamie, softly. "Your mother is partly responsible. I've used her toilet preparations ever since she started making them, and have never found any better, not even Madame Walker's."

When the waltz was finished they saw Link at a table with a handsome fair girl. They seemed to be enjoying themselves immensely.

"Come into my office," said Mamie. "I'd like to talk to you about the old times."

Donald was not anxious to talk with Mamie about old times, but she was his hostess, and the benign influence of the champagne, though he had indulged but lightly, had made him feel at peace and harmony with all the world, so he was willing to humor her. They weaved their way through the dancing waiters and the lightly clad dancers who were moving toward the platform for the next number on the program. As they were leaving the room, Mamie called another young woman and asked her to be hostess until her return.

She led him, not to a leafy glade, as she had in their youth, but to an urban substitute in the shape of a handsomely decorated small room with a desk, a table, a telephone and several chairs. When she had shown Donald to a comfortable armchair, upholstered in rose-colored tapestry, she sat on a low stool in front of him and began to talk about old times. She spoke of his father and mother, of the church, of Elder Jones; he had turned out to be a sort of black Elmer Gantry, had become pastor of a large Negro church in Harlem, and was spoken of as in line for a bishopric in the next general conference. Then she mentioned the choir.

"Those were good old times, Donald," she went on, softly. "You taught me to love good music, and helped to make me what I am."

Donald recognized this as the rankest flattery, for Mamie had sung like a bird, instinctively and without apparent effort. He had never attempted to give her any special instruction in music, and his contribution toward making her what she was in other respects had been limited to one lesson, in which she had been the teacher and he the pupil.

"I asked you to marry me once," she continued, pensively, "and gave you a good reason. It turned out that I was mistaken; and anyway, when your folks found it out they wouldn't let you. But I've always remembered you, Donald, and I'm still of the same mind. You might do worse than to marry me. I'm a rich woman already. I own an apartment house, have money in the bank, and this place is a gold mine."

"Link says you're engaged to him."

"Link's just bluffing. He doesn't want to marry, and I certainly wouldn't marry him. And I couldn't trust him, anyway. He'd run through all I have and then work me to death to keep him. I could trust you, Donald, and you might do worse. You're probably thinking of those dickty girls up on Striver's Row, who'd only marry you for your good looks and would expect you to work for them."

"Thank you for the compliment, Mamie, and though you're a beautiful woman, I couldn't let a woman keep me, not even my wife. Besides, I've been reared and educated for a definite purpose, and a rich wife would spoil my career."

"Well, I'm sorry, Donald. I didn't suppose you would, but I mean every word of it, and if you should change your mind, you'll always find me here. Come around as often as you like, and bring your friends, or call at my flat some afternoon, and I'll sing for you."

She gave him a number, which he carefully and ostentatiously jotted down in his pocket memorandum book, but which he never made use of. In spite of his philosophy, he was an incurable sentimentalist and could never have forgotten a woman who had been kind or more than kind to him—fortunately their number did not overburden his memory—but he was not of Mamie's world and would never be. Their meeting was but a passing episode.

———⟶◆⟵———

CHAPTER XXI

DONALD'S THESIS for his master's degree, like most of those by Negro candidates, dealt with the race question. There is so much to be said on the subject in its various aspects, so much that has not been presented intelligently from the Negro's side, that the intellectual student of that group invariably turns to the problem always foremost in his mind; or should he not, his professor or student advisor is sure to suggest it. Donald's thesis presented a simple, clear, rational and humane solution of this vexed question. Of course, to make it practicable would have required the scrapping of many cherished taboos, and the frank acceptance and cooperation of the entire American public, which it was hopeless to expect from a people still intermittently addicted to witchcraft, heresy hunting, and under different names, the *Vehm-gericht* and the *auto-da-fé*; by whom war was glorified and men kept in prison for opinion's sake. Later on, in the light of further experience, he was inclined to believe that white people, generally speaking, did not want to get rid of the race problem, that they found it less irksome and more profitable to label it insoluble and let it ride, than to make any genuine effort to settle it. However, the style and reasoning and intellectual appeal of his paper were such that it attracted attention beyond university circles, and an enterprising publisher offered to bring it out in book form. Permission was secured from the authorities of the university, and the volume appeared in the publisher's list for the ensuing fall.

In the summer Donald went to visit his mother at Booneville and accompanied her to Atlantic City to attend a convention of the National Federation of Colored Women's Clubs, to which she was a delegate, and following that, a convention of the Alpha Sigma Phi, a Negro Greek letter sorority.[1] The cleavage between white and colored had gone so far in the country that there seemed no place anywhere for them to meet in friendly intercourse. The natural rapprochement between the two races which the advancement of the Negro might have been expected to bring about was conspicuous by its absence. There were Negro associations of all kinds—bar associations, medical societies, chambers of commerce, YMCAs and YWCAs, to say nothing of churches and benefit societies. They had not yet risen to the height of Rotary or Civitan.

Donald was not long in discovering the underlying reason for this wasteful and antisocial situation. Many of such associations were nationwide, and they all held conventions at which the social side was very prominent. Each of them had its annual banquet, which all members were privileged to attend, and at which colored members, if there were any, would be entitled, by virtue of their membership, to sit and eat. In the eyes of many white people, especially the Southern members, no community of interest, no intellectual or social gain from the exchange of views or from personal contacts could possibly offset the breach of caste. And so in self-defense, the colored people, barred from fellowship in these bodies, had organized themselves into as many societies of their own. Naturally a light-hearted people and fond of travel and change of scenery, they spent far more than they could afford on long journeys in special cars to distant points, to attend conventions from many of which one could discover no gain except "a good time." The same might be said of the whites, but they were, presumably, better able to afford it.

Mrs. Glover had had in mind for some time the removal of her business headquarters from Booneville to New York or Chicago, as a more convenient center from which to operate, but had not yet reached a decision. Dr. Glover had given up most of his practice and was mainly occupied in helping his wife in her business, at which he turned out to be very competent.

For his last year at Columbia, Donald left Livingston Hall and took a flat in a Harlem apartment house where he could meet and fraternize more freely with the young colored men of his acquaintance, among whom he formed some warm friendships. He and others whom he had met at Senator Brown's and elsewhere, organized the New Negro Club,[2] which met once a week to discuss literature, music and art. The discussions proved to be almost entirely on Negro music, literature and art, varied by causerie on different phases of the race problem.

They discussed many subjects, with an unanimity of opinion on what they regarded as fundamentals, but with considerable diversity on points of minor importance. For instance, they believed in the right of the Negro to absolute equality in the social organism, but differed as to methods of securing its recognition. There was the old cleavage between the radicals and the conservatives, with the radicals strongly in the ascendant.

There was the much mooted question of how their people should be designated, whether as Negro, Colored American, Aframerican, or Negro American. The majority favored the word Negro. One or two of the fairer ones shied at it as not ethnologically accurate, and as connotating so many unpleasant things in their history—barbarism, slavery and all its indignities, ignorance and social inferiority—and thought the word "colored" more comprehensive and better descriptive of their mixed group; but the prevailing opinion was that they should call themselves Negroes. Donald had no quarrel with them—the name was less an ethnological distinction than a group designation. His mother used it and he had been content to follow her example, notwithstanding, the word might seem incongruous when applied without explanation to men like himself.

The discussions covered the whole field of race and race relations and helped to fix Donald's determination to devote his life to the advancement of his people. There was some loose thinking, as was inevitable in any human group, but this only strengthened Donald's belief that to think logically was the highest function of the mind and to inculcate it the *raison d'être* of philosophy.

The club often invited distinguished liberals to address them. Dr. Lebrun was a frequent guest. Dr. Boaz and Dr. Dean, both of Columbia, spoke to them at Donald's request, and the club became a forum for free and informal discussion to which Donald contributed his share.

This particular year was barren of amatory experiences. Donald's mind was fully occupied with his studies and the development of a new theory of philosophy which he meant to make the subject of his doctoral thesis. He met girls from time to time, some of them "real ladies," some "perfect ladies," but most of them simply ladies, danced with them, or took them out to dinner or to shows; but they did not interest him unduly or interfere with the mental serenity which the study of philosophy demanded.

He called his paper "An Essay on the Imagination." In it he compared reason with imagination, which he declared to be the initial source of human progress.

Reason, he argued, is a cold and chaste deity, who denies her favors to all except the choicest spirits. Imagination, on the other hand, is a warm and voluptuous goddess, who lavishes her favors impartially upon all, in proportion to their receptivity. To the ambitious she gives dreams of power and glory, to the avaricious visions of great wealth. To the poor and oppressed she gives heaven as a place where they shall be compensated for their sufferings here below, and hell as place of punishment for their oppressors. To genius she gives poetry, music, art and letters.

To all she gives hope, but her greatest gift is that of faith; faith in our fellow men, often misplaced, but without which we could not live together. It gives us love, the mainspring of society, from which come alike the belief in marital fidelity and its concomitant, green-eyed jealousy. To imagination we owe both Romeo and Juliet, and Othello.

Imagination inspires scientific research. If the hypotheses of imagination are verified by experience, they become part of the data of reason which thus in the last analysis is itself the product of imagination.

Religion is entirely the child of the imagination. It had its beginnings in the dim gropings of the human mind from savagery toward civilization, the ever existing, though sometimes flagging and at times scarcely recognizable upward reach of humanity. Men made their own gods out of sticks, or stones, fed them on flesh and blood, decked them with dead men's bones, and ascribed to them the hatreds and fears of savage men—made them, in fact, in their own image. Afterwards, with advancing civilization, the bones gave place to precious jewels, the blood to wine, and hatred and fear to gentler attributes. The idol became a spirit enthroned in heaven or on Olympus. Always the deity came down to earth, consorted with the daughters of men and on them begat demigods. In thirty ancient religions the god descended from heaven, became incarnate by a virgin, prophesied, died a shameful death for the salvation of the people, was buried and rose again, generally within three days, and ascended into heaven.

Reason does not recognize the supernatural, which is contrary to the ascertained laws of nature and insusceptible of proof. To reconcile science with supernatural religion is impossible without the abrogation of reason. They exist upon two different planes. The laws of birth, life, death and corruption can no more be changed than the multiplication table. Man cannot by taking thought add one cubit to his stature, nor one ounce to his weight. Imagination's handmaid, faith, makes these and all other things possible.

Imagination does not concern itself with denials. It is the great inspirer, the primal incentive, the "ultimate force" of Herbert Spencer, the "life force" of Bernard Shaw, the *élan vital* of Bergson.

Reason is static, imagination is fluid. Reason deals with facts. Imagination overleaps the boundaries of the known and soars into the empyrean of conjecture. A religion thus derived may be vital and appealing and its ethics just as sound, as though it were founded upon pure reason. A strong soul might not need it, but to the weak and wavering it might prove a welcome support and solace.

Donald won his doctorate with the highest honors. His essay was published and recognized as a new note in philosophy. His friend and mentor Professor Dean, while he did not agree with Donald in all his conclusions, complimented him on the development of his theme and predicted for him a brilliant future.

"If you were white," he said, "or our people were broader, you could find a place in one of the great universities. But the colored schools need good teachers, and the one that can secure your services will be fortunate."

Donald thanked him, and replied that he had not yet decided what he should do; that he meant to serve his people, but they needed service in so many fields that he would have to look the ground over carefully before making a choice.

CHAPTER XXII

⟞⟞●⟞⟞

THE *Essay on the Imagination* was published in a popular series of works on philosophy, and welcomed among discerning scholars as a real contribution to realistic, or idealistic philosophy, both schools claiming it. Following their lead, the Negro press acclaimed Donald as the brightest intellect of the race and clearly predestined to leadership. The Negro, it was asserted, had proven his quality in music, art, and polite literature, to the confusion of his detractors, and it had only remained for him to establish his equality on the highest intellectual plane.

Donald's fitness having thus been squared with his ambition, he set about seriously considering the immediate field in which he should seek to lead. His education, his mentality and his inclination indicated intellectual leadership. He had realized instinctively, early in his scholastic career, that the chief end of the higher education, as he had maintained in his *Essay on the Imagination*, was to teach the student to think correctly. A career, a movement, founded on false premises, was a house built upon the sand and foredoomed to disaster. He realized also that in the modern world leadership in any field must be achieved against fierce competition, that its achievement is easier for some than for others, and that the path to success is strewn with the dry bones of failure, and haunted by the pale ghosts of frustrated hopes.

With his two books Donald had made a fair start toward the intellectual leadership to which he aspired. But with a people in the condition of his, it was not enough to think, even correctly. Thought must be transmuted into action. To square the circle, to discover the fourth dimension, to solve the riddle of the universe would be great achievements, but to know how to conform one's life, however derived, to the three known dimensions and to the multifarious aspects of the complicated social mechanism of modern life was vastly more important. And an intellectual leader, like any other, must have a background of experience upon which to base his teachings. Donald had not yet decided upon a profession or a calling when events took a turn which opened a way to him.

The able man who presided over the destinies of the great Negro industrial school at Tuscaloosa, in the heart of the black belt of the South, was always seeking to strengthen his executive and teaching forces and to this end kept his eyes constantly open for bright young colored graduates from the Northern colleges and universities. Added to his teaching staff, they would pre-

serve or raise the level of instruction, repel adverse criticism of its quality, and incidentally reflect credit upon
the institution and its head.

Thus when Donald's name began to appear with
laudatory comment, Principal Jefferson took note of it,
and even before Donald received his doctor's degree,
invited him to call at the Manhattan Hotel, which he
made his headquarters while in New York, and at the
interview which ensued suggested that when Donald
was ready to work he might be able to find a place for
him in his school; this would give him an opportunity
to study at first hand the needs and aptitudes of his
people, and thus better prepare himself for the intellectual leadership for which Dr. Jefferson declared he was
obviously fitted.

Donald consulted his mother, and though she
leaned toward the left or radical wing of race opinion,
thought it well that Donald should study every phase
of Negro life. Therefore when, upon leaving Columbia,
he was offered a place as assistant secretary to the principal of Tuscaloosa, he accepted it and entered upon
the discharge of its duties.

These, at first, were not very onerous. Dr. Jefferson,[1]
like the heads of most modern educational institutions,
spent much of his time traveling and soliciting dona-
tions for his school. He needed someone to make hotel
reservations, buy railroad tickets and arrange confer-
ences, and he had learned from experience that these
things could be done to better advantage by one whose

appearance did not challenge race prejudice. From this point of view Donald was ideal, and for a large part of a year he travelled all over the country with his chief, meeting the colored people of prominence and many leading white men with whom his employment brought him in contact. He often had to explain that he was a Negro—he soon found out that most white people preferred the word to any designation that suggested or assumed blood kinship with themselves, though it was quite obvious that he got along better with them than a darker man would have done, and in this way they acknowledged in practice what they rigorously ignored in theory.

Donald from the beginning had the intellectual respect of his employer. Dr. Jefferson was a man of great native ability, but he had only the education of a normal and agricultural school, reinforced by wide reading and experience of the world. Harvard University had given him an honorary degree, not for learning but for achievement. He wrote many books, and had a simple and virile style, but he wanted someone to read over his manuscripts and see that their English was impeccable. Like Rubens and Dumas *père*, he welcomed cooperation. Had the great Flemish artist not availed himself of the time and talent of his pupils, he could never have signed his name to the acres of canvas which bear his signature and which he informed with his genius. It was said of the elder Dumas that he could take the first draft of a novel of poor or doubtful merit,

add a character here, an incident there, and turn out a
Dumas romance, not as good as his best, but good
enough to get by. Otherwise he would hardly have put
out the hundreds of novels and plays issued under his
name. Dr. Jefferson reversed the process—he wrote the
book, and the other fellow edited it.

Donald did this work to the author's entire satisfac-
tion. He was wise enough not to try to alter or modify
Dr. Jefferson's style, which was marked by simplicity
and force, but merely smoothed out rough places, adjusted carelessly misplaced clauses, reunited split in-
finitives and occasionally hunted down an elusive par-
ticiple. His duties were similar to those of a congressman's secretary, indeed somewhat less onerous, as he
never wrote any of his employer's speeches. He never
obtruded his advice or indulged in any adverse criticism. For, although Dr. Jefferson was regarded as a
wise and reasonable man, Donald had read his *Gil Blas*,
and kept the bishop's case in mind. Fortunately, the
principal's writings needed nothing more than Donald
could safely give and the author graciously accept.

One day in spring, Dr. Jefferson received a letter
from Mr. John Culver Bascomb, an English gentleman
who was visiting America, recalling the fact that he had
once heard Dr. Jefferson lecture in London in Exeter
Hall, before the World War, and had sought an introduction to him after the meeting. He had, he said, interests in British West Africa, and was at that time considering the promotion of the Tuscaloosa type of in-

struction for the education of the natives. The war had turned his mind to other matters, but his sister, Lady Merrivale, and he were now traveling in America and wished to visit Tuscaloosa and see with their own eyes the work of which they had read such glowing accounts.

Dr. Jefferson replied that he would be honored to have them visit the school. He suggested that his private secretary, Mr. Glover, a young colored man, was in New York, and if Mr. Bascomb would communicate with him at the Manhattan Hotel, he would arrange to accompany Mr. Bascomb and the lady to the school at their convenience.

Mr. Bascomb got Donald on the telephone and asked him to come see him at the Ambassador. Donald called at this hotel, at that time the latest and most magnificent of metropolitan hostelries, and was shown up to the handsome suite occupied by the English lady and gentleman. Mr. Bascomb turned out to be a sturdily built man of about forty-five, with a slightly graying beard and a monocle—which, by the way, is not worn exclusively by morons. His sister, who was introduced as Lady Merrivale, was a handsome fresh-colored woman in the late thirties, at the point "where brook and river meet"—where what remained of the lithe slenderness of youth was passing into the solidity of approaching middle age.

They seemed slightly surprised when Donald came in, but gave him a cordial welcome.

"Dr. Jefferson's letter described his secretary as a colored man, but that was obviously a mistake, or else he had sent someone else," said Mr. Bascomb.

"No," said Donald, "I'm the secretary, and I'm a colored man—an American Negro."

"Oh, yes," returned the Englishman, "I believe you do have some such curious classification in this country. In Europe, in Africa, or in the West Indies you would rank as a white or at least as a near white, even if your origin were known. My sister there—she really is my half-sister—has some dark blood, and many of our friends know it, but no one would dream of calling her a Negress."

"It's different here," returned Donald. "If one is known to have a drop of Negro blood and admits it, he or she is a Negro. But we never say 'Negress.'"

"Why not? There is 'Jewess.'"

"Well, I can't explain it," returned Donald. "Perhaps it's because it sounds so—biological, so to speak—or zoological—suggestive of the big cats."

"That's quite clever, Glover," chuckled Mr. Bascomb.

"I'm a woman," said Lady Merrivale, ignoring the pleasantry, "and I understand it perfectly, though I can't explain it, any more than Mr. Glover can."

The conversation continued along the same line. The race question was Donald's specialty, and the others found it interesting. The lady had been struck by the young man's virile beauty and charm, the gentleman by his intelligence. They inquired about Donald's education and plans for the future. Mr. Bascomb, who, besides being a man of affairs, was a public school man and a Cambridge graduate, with a taste for serious reading, had read and admired Donald's *Essay on the Imagination*. Lady Merrivale was well read in English literature, and Donald discovered during the conversation that their tastes were quite similar. Among the Victorian novelists she was most fond of Thackeray.

"I ought to be," she said, "for one of my ancestors appears in *Vanity Fair*. She was the original of Miss Schwartz, the West Indian fellow pupil of Becky Sharp at Miss Wilkinson's Academy."

As Donald learned by reference to a copy of Debrett, which he found in the public library, this ancestress of Lady Merrivale, whose English father had left her a large estate in British funds and Jamaican lands, had married an English gentleman of good family who had been knighted for distinguished services to the government—the fact being that he had made a large contribution, out of his wife's fortune, to the campaign committee of the Whig party on the eve of the general election. Lady Merrivale had been a widow now for several years, and was visiting America for the first time to see what it was like. She learned during the interview that Donald was unmarried.

Donald found the visit very pleasant. Mr. Bascomb had come over in connection with some unsettled war

claims for cocoa and other West African products supplied to the AEF during the World War, and wanted to
remain in New York the next day to wind up his business. It was arranged that Donald should call at the
hotel for them late the following afternoon, and that
they would take the six o'clock Southern Express.

"I'll have the head porter make the Pullman reservations," said Mr. Bascomb, "so that we may be together."

"If Mr. Glover has no evening engagement," suggested Lady Merrivale, "perhaps he would dine with us
here at seven."

"Yes," Mr. Bascomb concurred. "We shall be glad to
have you. We can continue our interesting conversation."

Donald thanked them and said he would come. He
had no other engagement, he was a judge of good food
and good company, and the hotel's cuisine was famous.
He dined and spent a couple of hours with his hosts
and then went to his hotel and to bed.

"What a beautiful boy!" said Lady Merrivale pensively, after Donald had gone. "Why didn't I meet him
when I was young?"

"He would have been too young for you then, sis.
But he's a handsome youth, and as bright as he is good
looking. Perhaps it isn't too late yet."

Though her brother spoke jestingly, the lady was
half in earnest. In England there was no incongruity in
a wealthy woman's marrying a poor young man. The
happy union of Lady Burdett-Coutts, the head of the

great banking house, at the age of sixty, to young Armisted Bartlett, at twenty-eight, was a classical example.

CHAPTER XXIII

———

DONALD CALLED at the Ambassador shortly before six the next evening, and a taxicab delivered them at the Grand Central Terminal in a few minutes. They checked their luggage and found their places in the car, and at seven o'clock went into the dining car for dinner. The journey through the night was uneventful, and when they got up in the morning they were in the South. As the train rolled through the countryside, Donald indicated occasionally points of interest—universities, Civil War battlefields, and as they would whirl through some town, a public building of some sort.

"I like your Pullman porters," said the lady. "They are courteous and deferential, yet not quite so obsequious as some of our English servants."

Donald was glad to hear her say this. He always took an interest in the porters because they were of his own race, and, but for his mother's devotion, he might have been one himself. Their politeness and deference were, of course, more or less interested, as good business demanded, but they were naturally amiable and reacted immediately to courtesy or consideration. He knew many of them on the trains running north and south. There was a prevailing superstition among colored people that the Pullman porters were made up of supermen whom race prejudice had condemned to menial servitude. Donald had not found it so. Most of them were stodgy, middle-aged black men, and though poorly paid, their work as porters was, as a rule, at just about the level of their intelligence. The dining room waiters, on the other hand, were mostly mulattoes, and many of them were students earning the money to put them through college or professional school.

The trip had promised to be quite ordinary, until a typically Southern incident occurred as they were nearing the far South. A well-dressed dark brown woman got on the train at a junction point and sat down in the front end of the car. Donald and his party were a few seats nearer the rear. As the conductor was going through, taking up the tickets of the new passengers, a white man who had gotten on with a female companion at the same stop as the colored woman, spoke to the conductor, who thereupon returned to the passenger.

"You can't ride in this car," he said. "You'll have to get off at the next stop and wait for the local, which has a Negro car."

"But this is my car," returned the woman, indignantly. "I've paid for my ticket and I'll not get off unless you put me off."

The conductor, who was a man of peace and not looking for trouble, went back and spoke to the white man, evidently arguing with him successfully, for he returned and collected the woman's ticket, and nothing more was said, much to Donald's relief. He had read in the *Chicago Crusader*[1] an account of a similar case on the same railroad a few months before, in which, when the colored woman passenger had refused to leave the car, a white passenger had sent a wire to a station ahead, and a local constable with a "posse" had stopped the train, taken the passenger off and hailed her before a magistrate, who had fined her five hundred dollars and costs for violation of the separate car law.

"Is this sort of thing common, Glover?" asked Mr. Bascomb, who had overheard the conductor's conversation with the woman.

"I'm ashamed to say, sir," replied Donald, whose Northern training had not broken him of the pleasant Southern habit of saying "sir" to older men or men of superior position—it never occurred to him as connotating anything more than respect for age or authority—"I've never seen it before, but I've heard and read enough to know that it might happen anywhere in the South at any time."

Mr. Bascomb had noticed and liked this use by

Donald of the deferential particle. Young Englishmen showed their respect for their seniors in the same way.

"I think it is an outrage," said Lady Merrivale, indignantly. "Why do they sell them tickets if they can't use them?"

"Well," said Donald, "the 'Jim Crow' car law, as it is called, is one of the greatest grievances of the race. They regard it as unfair discrimination, meant to degrade them, and will evade it if possible. Very likely she got some light-colored friend or relative to buy the ticket, thinking she might be able to put it across, as she seems to have done."

A little later Mr. Bascomb, going back in the car for a drink from the ice water tank, saw the conductor sitting in an empty drawing room, assorting his tickets.

"Conductor," he said, "I just witnessed the incident with the colored woman just now. I suppose the white couple complained?"

"Yes."

"Did they relent when you went back to them?"

"Yes, at my request."

"I suppose it's the law?"

"Well, yes—and no. If it was just an ordinary passenger train the law would compel the separation. But the company embarrasses us conductors by selling niggers Pullman tickets. If we honor the tickets the white passengers kick. If we don't, the ticket-holders sue the company."

"The colored people, I notice, are of many shades. Do you ever have difficulty in classifying them?"

"Oh, yes," replied the conductor, "everyday."

"What do you do in such a case?" asked the Englishman.

"Well," returned the conductor, "if the passenger comes into the white coach and sits down as though he or she belongs there, and the color is not obvious and nobody complains, I let 'em stay."

"Suppose you should go into the Negro car—the Jim Crow car you call it, I believe?"

"*I* don't—the niggers do."

"Suppose you were going through the car and saw a person sitting there, like say the lady with me or our young friend who is with us, what would you do?"

"I'd ask 'em to go into the white coach."

"But suppose, for the sake of the argument, he or she should claim the right, as a Negro, to sit there?"

"Oh, well," returned the conductor, "he or she could stay there, as far as I'm concerned, till the next snowstorm in hell. Anybody that would rather be a nigger than white is welcome to the privilege."

Along toward evening of the second day Donald and his friends left the express at the nearest station to the school, which was located some miles back from the railroad. Lady Merrivale and Mr. Bascomb stood on the platform while Donald went to look for the school automobile which he had expected to meet the train. No other passengers got off and there was no business to occupy the station agent, who strolled over and accosted them, genially.

"Good evenin'," he said, "I s'pose you all are goin' over to visit the Institute?"

"Yes, thank you," returned Mr. Bascomb.

"Well, I reckon you'll find it int'restin'. We all like Jefferson down here. He's a good nigger, knows his place, teaches the niggers how to work, and don't preach social equality. The school automobile generally meets this train, and I guess it must have blowed a tire, or something."

Which proved to be the case. Donald got another car from the only garage in the town, and on their way to the school they met the school automobile. They changed cars, Donald told the driver of the hired car to charge it to the school, and they soon arrived at the end of their journey. The car drew up in front of the administration building. Donald ushered them into the principal's office and introduced them to Dr. Jefferson.

Dr. Jefferson welcomed the visitors cordially. He had met many great and famous and powerful people, and was entirely at his ease in any society. He led the way over to his own house, where they were assigned to pleasant and comfortable rooms and given the opportunity to refresh themselves after the strain of their long journey. Mrs. Jefferson, who had traveled with her husband in England and Scotland, where they had been entertained at nice houses, designated a special maid for Lady Merrivale's service.

After dinner some of the officers and teachers came in and were introduced to the visitors. They were all educated people, and some of them had visited England. Dr. Jefferson, in the good days before the war which had depleted the purse, decimated the young manhood and well-nigh broken the heart of England, had taken a group of singers with him on a foreign speaking tour. They had sung themselves into the hearts of the English people and sold them the Tuscaloosa idea. Some of the singers were still connected with the school and had come in with the others. At Lady Merrivale's request, they rendered very effectively "Deep River," "Steal Away to Jesus," and several other well-known Negro spirituals, in which Donald joined with his clear, sweet tenor. The conversation was general, as Dr. Jefferson feared the travelers might be tired and would prefer deferring anything serious until the next day.

Donald, at the principal's invitation, joined the guests at breakfast the following morning—he usually took his meals in the school dining hall—after which Dr. Jefferson took them on a tour of the grounds and buildings— the schoolrooms, workshops and dormitories. They saw blacksmithing, carpentry, brickmasonry, tailoring and shoemaking in process. They visited the brick kilns, where all the brick had been made for the buildings. They drove through the farms and saw crops of cotton and corn and field vegetables in growth.

Then, while Mr. Bascomb and Dr. Jefferson went

back to the office to talk over Mr. Bascomb's plans, Donald, by the principal's orders, devoted himself to the entertainment of Lady Merrivale. He took her through the laundry, the millinery and dressmaking departments, the kitchens and the girls' dormitories, and then to some class recitations. She was immensely interested and expressed her surprise and pleasure unstintedly. Donald did not notice, as they went along, though some sharp-eyed young women did, that she kept her eyes quite as much on him as on what he was showing her.

In the evening there was a concert in the capacious chapel, where there was a fine pipe organ. Donald sang a tenor solo, and a quartet rendered a number of spirituals, the audience joining in the chorus.

"You didn't tell us you could sing," said Lady Merrivale to Donald, who sat beside her on the platform. "You've a grand opera voice, if it were only trained."

"Thank you," said Donald, with the blush which is so charming in a young man.

"And the choral singing is simply wonderful. I'm awfully glad we came here. It gives me a higher opinion of our dark ancestors—yours and mine. I've never been ashamed of them, but from what I've seen in this wonderful place today, I'm almost proud of them."

"I feel that you may well be, dear lady, when they have had their innings. They have a long, hard hill to climb, and with wise leadership, and with courage and encouragement, they will make the grade."

"Oh, I'm sure of it, Mr. Glover," replied the lady with enthusiasm.

The visitors left the next afternoon. Mr. Bascomb had suggested a plan for introducing industrial education into the West African colony where he had cocoa plantations, and had asked Dr. Jefferson to work it out, and when it was completed to send it to England by Donald, whose pleasing personality and unusual intelligence had impressed him very much, so that they might work out further details. He would pay his traveling expenses and entertain him while in England.

Dr. Jefferson would have preferred to go himself, but since they wanted Donald, it would give the young man an opportunity to make friends for the school. His pleasing appearance would enable him to penetrate circles and make contacts which one less gifted, physically and mentally, might not be able to do.

CHAPTER XXIV

━━━━━➤●◄━━━━━

Several months after the visit of Mr. Bascomb to Tuscaloosa Institute, Dr. Dean of Columbia and Donald's friends among the Negro intelligentsia in New York were instrumental in securing for him a Morganheim fellowship. The founder of this fund had made an immense fortune in lead mines and the manipulation of their stocks. When merely being a multimillionaire had ceased to be interesting, he sought relief from the monotony of simply watching his money grow and acquired a United States senatorship. When this was no longer exciting, he looked over the field of philanthropy and established the Morganheim Foundation, with an endowment of several million dollars, for providing talented and ambitious young people with the opportunity to do creative work in literature, science, music, art and historical research—a subsidization of intellect often suggested as desirable, but now for the first time carried out on an extended scale. Donald was awarded one of these fellowships, which carried with it a sum of money sufficient to pay his expenses in Europe for a year or two while he wrote or studied.

He consulted with Dr. Jefferson, who was, of course, delighted at the honor reflected upon the school by this noteworthy recognition of one of its staff. Donald wanted to go at an early date. He was writing a new book, and would now have leisure to complete it without having to burden his mother with his support.

Dr. Jefferson suggested that he had about formulated his plan for the kind of industrial training best adapted to tropical West Africa, and arranged with Donald, when he reached Europe, to call upon Mr. Bascomb, in accordance with the original arrangement, submit and elaborate the plan and discuss it with him, and then report to Dr. Jefferson.

A few weeks later Donald sailed for Liverpool upon the *Campania*.

Mrs. Glover came to New York to see him off. He met her at the Pennsylvania Station in the morning and took a taxi out to his apartment, which he had given up, but was not leaving until the last day. When she had washed and refreshed herself after her journey, they went out to breakfast at Martin's, the restaurant where he had dined with Link Dixon, and where he took most of his meals since he had changed his living quarters. He could have eaten anywhere, but as a rule he preferred the company of his own people.

Mrs. Glover had not yet decided, she said, whether to move to New York or to Chicago. New York had a

large colored population, but Chicago was more cosmopolitan and more centrally located with reference to
the general Negro population of the country.

"I'm awfully proud of you, Donald," she declared,
"and of the success you're making. I feel fully repaid for
all the time and money and love I've lavished upon
you. It hasn't been exactly cheap to support you like a
gentleman, but you're worth every penny of it. I read
your book with joy and delight, read all the reviews
you sent me, and listened to all the compliments which
our friends have paid you and me. I know you must
have smiled sometimes at my old notion that I was
training you to be the Moses of our people, but in view
of what you've already done it doesn't seem at all absurd. You've always been too modest, Donald. You're a
brilliant young man and destined to be a great Negro.
I wouldn't be satisfied for you to be just a great man; I
want the Negro race to have credit for what you do. If
you should desert the race and go off and marry some
white woman, it would break my heart. No doubt you
could do it, especially over in Europe, where there's
not so much race prejudice. I've kept track of you, even
when you didn't know it, and I was rather alarmed
about the nice white girl you were going with during
your second year at Columbia. You're good enough for
any woman on earth, but the race needs you, and I
don't want it to lose you."

Donald laughed. "Never mind, mother," he said,
soothingly, "you needn't worry. I shan't marry for a

long time yet, not till I get started in life. You've been awfully good to me, but I couldn't let you support my wife, and I'll not marry until I have an income. I'm going to write a book and publish it with this dedication: 'To my dear mother, in grateful appreciation of all she has done for me.' I shall probably not make any money on it—such books rarely become best sellers— but it will be, I hope, a credit to the race and give me a leg up."

They lunched at the same restaurant where they had breakfasted, and then went for an automobile ride through Harlem and the Bronx. Mrs. Glover had business with her agency in New York but deferred it until after Donald should have sailed. She wanted to spend as much time with her son as possible.

During the afternoon Donald had got the Browns on the telephone and stated that his mother was in town and would like to call on them. They responded promptly with an invitation to dinner that same evening. Mrs. Glover and Donald went, and talked over with the Browns their early days in Cleveland. Donald was the chief subject of conversation.

"It was a fortunate day for Donald," Senator Brown remarked, "when I referred Mr. Seaton to you. You made Donald a good mother and were fortunate enough to be able to give him the best of educations."

"And he's paying me back with interest," replied Mrs. Glover. "I certainly thank God that he gave me that beautiful baby, who has grown up into this beauti-

ful young man—you needn't blush, Donald, everybody knows how handsome you are—I know what I
am talking about, I have spent many years of my life in
helping to make people beautiful. If Mr. Seaton had
kept him in the first place, or had taken him when he
was growing up, as he wanted to, he might have become a great man, but he wouldn't have been known as
a great Negro, and the race would have got no credit for
him. I brought him up to be a leader of our people and
I shall die happy when I see that day."

Mrs. Glover occupied the bedroom at Donald's
apartment for the night, Donald making shift with the
couch in the sitting room. He had sold or stored what
personal belongings he had not packed to take with
him. The rest of the furniture belonged to the apartment, so that when he left there was nothing to do but
turn the key over to the janitor.

The steamer was to sail at noon. Mrs. Glover accompanied Donald to the pier, where they met Isador Rovelsky and several of Donald's young colored friends
who had come to bid him bon voyage. Mrs. Glover
waved to Donald as the steamer drew away, and was so
preoccupied with him she did not notice several ladies
at the steamer's rail who were waving their handker-
chiefs frantically at her.

CHAPTER XXV

———➤●◄———

I T WAS DONALD'S first ocean voyage, and he had looked forward to it with pleasurable anticipation. The *Campania* was a seven-day boat, and therefore not overcrowded with millionaires, prize fighters, movie actors and *prime donne*. The passengers were mostly Americans, among them many teachers—one of these a friend of Donald's—with a few Europeans, an Egyptian, an Arab and a Turk. There were some minor notabilities, such as judges, small-town mayors and an economical Texas congressman with a large family.

One unpleasant incident threatened to mar the serenity of the passage for Donald. He noticed on the deck, shortly after sailing, a colored woman with a young girl, evidently mother and daughter. They were obviously people of refinement, and Donald observed that the girl wore a University of Chicago pin. He did not speak to them, but meant to do so later.

When the first meal was served, Donald, looking around the dining saloon for the ladies, saw them come and take their places at a table across the room, at which several white passengers were already seated, and to his surprise and delight, recognized in a second young woman who was with them his old friend and companion in crime, Bertha Lawrence. At the same moment, a white woman at the same table, whose dress and bearing suggested a person of importance, accustomed to command, left her seat and went over and spoke to the purser.

Donald's place was not far from that officer's, his hearing was acute, and he heard the lady ask for another seat, giving as her reason that "her grandmother came from Georgia and she would rather eat with a dog than with a nigger." He was sincerely glad that the women he was interested in were beyond hearing, though he suspected they divined what was going on. Colored people, he knew, had an almost clairvoyant consciousness of such things, a sort of sixth sense, sharpened by experience, which was seldom at fault. They might sometimes see offense where none was intended, but they would almost certainly never miss it where it was. To spare their feelings, Donald rose immediately and offered to change seats with the lady. The coolness of her "Thank you" made Donald wonder whether she thought his prompt action a rebuke to her intolerance, or whether she had conceived a low opinion of a man who was willing to eat with colored people.

Donald crossed the saloon and spoke to Miss Lawrence, who introduced the other ladies as her mother

and her sister Rose. They were going to Europe, they
informed him, to meet the head of the family, who had
been promoted from archdeacon to bishop, with a special see which embraced most of the colored Episcopal
churches in the South. He made his headquarters in
Chicago, where he lived with his family when not traveling. He was in Europe, attending an ecumenical conference in Geneva, at the close of which he would join
them at Avignon, in southern France.

The ladies were plainly delighted at the change of
their seat mate from a lady of the "domineering angry-
Saxon race" as Rose later characterized her, to a charming young man of their own breed.

"We saw your mother on the pier," said Mrs. Lawrence, "and waved at her, but she was so wrapped up
in you that she didn't notice us."

The ladies furnished his chief society on the
steamer. The colored women were distinctly cold-
shouldered by the white passengers. One exception
was Donald's former professor at Bethany College and
instructor at Columbia, Dr. Arthur Dean, who accosted
Donald on the deck, introduced him to some of his
friends and asked for an introduction to Donald's
friends. Dr. Dean was on his way to Paris, he explained,
to lecture at the Sorbonne during the summer, in exchange for a French professor's lectures at the Columbia summer school. Thus a voyage which one narrow-
minded person had threatened to spoil for a group of

passengers who had paid for first-class fare and service, was redeemed and rendered pleasant by the courtesy and liberality of one man who practiced what he had preached to his class at Bethany and at Columbia.

On the morning of the second day out Donald was standing at the rail on the lee side of the vessel watching the long line of the steamer's wake as it feathered off behind her, when two women approached him.

"Good morning—Dr. Glover, is it not?" said one of them. Donald glanced around and lifted his cap automatically. The speaker was a tall woman with a fair complexion in which only an expert could have detected any trace of Negro blood, and a thick main of bobbed hair of a shade of red which would hardly have grown naturally on any woman's head. Her companion was a putty-faced, near white, whose rather insignificant features served as a foil for the more exuberant pulchritude of her friend. They both wore white flannel sport dresses cut short enough to display to advantage their really fine limbs, were highly rouged and evidently out for conquest.

"You're Dr. Glover, aren't you?" said the red-headed one. "I've seen your picture in *The Climax* and I've read your poems."

Donald had written no poems, but didn't feel it necessary to say so. He was sure she would not know the difference between a sonnet and a syllogism, so why waste words explaining.

"Well," was his reply, "I'm Donald Glover. I've been a doctor for so short a time that I don't recognize myself by the title, and I suspect am rather young for so solemn a designation."

"I wasn't quite sure about its being you," the lady went on—"your picture made you look so much darker."

The portrait referred to had been drawn by a New York artist who was wonderfully successful with Negro types. Donald had remarked to the artist on the ebony complexion, the tightly curled hair and the Negroid features with which he had been endowed, and the artist had explained that he had been depicting Donald's psychology, that he had reproduced what he saw under the sitter's skin. Donald had smiled and let it go at that. He had been shown as a very fine looking Negro and sufficiently like himself to be recognizable by those who knew him.

The lady continued, "I'm Pearl Gibbs—Mrs. Henry F. Gibbs, of Chicago. You've heard of my husband, of course, the prominent realtor?"

"Oh, yes," lied Donald, politely.

"I saw where you had won a Morganheim fellowship, and I suppose you are going over now to pursue your studies?"

"Something on that order," returned Donald.

"I've noticed you," Mrs. Gibbs went on, "with the Lawrence party. Is the bishop coming over to join them?"

"I believe he is in Europe already," said Donald, "and they will meet him there."

The lady referred to some social item in the *Chicago Crusader* about a recent colored wedding at which she had been a guest and inquired if Donald was acquainted with any of the parties mentioned. He had to confess his ignorance of the people and the event. The conversation was languishing for lack of any contribution on his part, when he saw Mrs. Lawrence and Rose walking toward them on the deck. They were on the point of passing when Mrs. Gibbs stepped forward, and put out her hand. "Oh, Mrs. Lawrence," she said effusively, "I'm so glad to meet you. I saw your name in the passenger list, and was hoping I might run across you. The captain says we may expect a pleasant voyage. I went to California last summer, but decided that I should have to run over to Paris this year and buy some new clothes. Where are you going to meet the bishop?"

"At Avignon, France," replied the elder lady. "He is in Switzerland now, but will meet us at Avignon."

Several other remarks were exchanged, and Donald bowed to Mrs. Gibbs and her companion and accompanied the Lawrence ladies as they moved on. Donald had noticed that Mrs. Lawrence was not especially cordial, and that Rose held herself almost insolently aloof while the other woman was talking.

"How did she get acquainted with you?" Rose asked of Donald, somewhat sharply, when they were out of hearing.

"She came up and spoke to me on the deck," he replied, meekly, sensing her disapproval. She was evidently the conductor of the Lawrence party.

"Umph!" returned Rose. "That's just like her. If there was a good looking man within a mile she'd spot him."

"Who is she?" asked Donald.

"She's the wife of Henry Gibbs, an alderman and ward politician who owns some old shacks in the Black Belt of Chicago, which he rents for evil purposes. They say he runs a policy shop, and a gambling saloon where the sky's the limit. I'm surprised she isn't passing for white, as she often does, but she saw you with us and decided that you were white enough for her to vamp. She's not in our set, and we never speak to her when we can avoid it without being openly rude. Her husband is a very dark man, and she's rarely seen in public with him, her enemies say because she is ashamed of his color, and his friends say because he doesn't care to embarrass her or subject her to unpleasant comment by being seen in his company."

"Who's her friend?" asked Donald.

"She's a Mrs. Nichols. Mrs. Gibbs was so stuck on herself and on you that she probably neglected to introduce her. Her husband is 'one of our most successful bootleggers,' as the colored newspapers do *not* say. She and Mrs. Nichols go away together every summer without their husbands, in search of adventure."

"You seem to know a lot about people you don't associate with," said Donald teasingly.

"I live in the same town and keep my eyes and ears open," she retorted.

"To say nothing of your mouth," said Donald.

"That's unkind," she came back, "when I'm speaking entirely in your interest."

"I beg your pardon," said Donald, contritely. "Of course I'm only fooling."

At this point the breakfast gong rang. Donald and Mrs. Lawrence went into the dining saloon, and Rose ran to get Bertha, who, she said, was dressing.

Donald and his friends were together most of the time during the voyage. Occasionally he managed to be alone with Bertha, and her beauty and charm grew upon him. She spoke to him of his book and of how much she enjoyed it, and he told her of his projected work. She confided to him her present ambition, which was to become a teacher of languages in the Chicago schools. She had received an appointment at the Wendell Phillips High School and was going to Europe to brush up her accent and her French conversation in time to begin teaching that language at the fall term. They practiced speaking French together. In the Chicago high school system the teachers were required to give instruction by the oral method, which demanded a degree of speaking facility.

Mrs. Gibbs hovered in the offing and accosted Donald whenever she caught him alone. On one such occasion, on the fourth day out, he was sitting in his steamer chair on the deck, by himself, with a volume of

Bergson's *Creative Evolution* on his lap, when she came along and lowered herself into the next seat, which happened to be unoccupied. She was carrying a small Kodak in her hand.

"And how do you like the voyage, so far, Dr. Glover?" she inquired.

"Very much indeed," was Donald's reply. "The passage, I'm told, has been unusually smooth."

"I've been taking some snapshots on the boat," she went on. "I got one or two of you when you weren't looking, and I'm sure they come nearer doing you justice than that libel in the *Climax*. At least they don't make your beautiful hair look kinky."

Donald felt annoyed at her having taken the liberty of photographing him without asking his permission, but dissembled his annoyance.

"I suppose I ought to feel complimented," he answered, politely.

"Don't be so sure," she returned, "until you've seen the photographs. I meant to bring them on deck with me, but forgot them. Come on down with me to my stateroom—it is number 108 on the second deck— yours is 115, isn't it? And I'll show them to you."

"Would it be proper for a lady to receive a gentleman in her stateroom?" he inquired, quizzically.

"Why not?" she replied. "We're not living in the Victorian age. Besides, Alice is in the stateroom—we share it, you know—so she'll chaperone us, if a chaperone were needed. I suspect one might be, for I fear you are a *very* dangerous man."

The look she gave him was more than arch, it was inviting. She was a very handsome woman, and he was susceptible to feminine beauty. He would not for the world become involved in an intrigue with her, but he was good-natured and the voyage would soon be over, and he might as well be polite.

"Why, yes," he assented, "I'll go down with you."

They descended to the second deck. She knocked on the door of her stateroom, and there being no answer unlocked it with her key.

"I left Alice here when I went up," she explained, "but it seems she has gone out. But never mind, we don't need her. Sit down, please, on the couch here."

She brought out a box of snapshots.

"I had these developed and printed on the boat," she informed him. "I don't think they are at all bad, do you?"

Donald admitted that they were not, and commented on several of them. She had seated herself beside him on the couch—there were two berths in the room besides—and leaned toward him as she picked up the photographs. Her eyes were avid with desire and she was breathing quickly. Donald was almost expecting her to throw her arms about him when someone knocked at the door.

Mrs. Gibb's handsome features assumed an almost murderous expression.

"Oh damn!" she muttered. "I suppose it's Alice, and I'll have to let her in. She said she was going up on the top deck to watch for whales or porpoises. If I don't open the door she'll unlock it with her own key, and it won't look nice to find us locked up together."

While she hesitated, however, Mrs. Nichols unlocked the door and entered the stateroom.

"Oh," she exclaimed, in mock embarrassment, "excuse me. I didn't know there was anybody here. I wouldn't want to be a spoilsport for anything, I'll go right away."

"Oh, no," said Donald, "don't. I'm the intruder and I'm just leaving. Mrs. Gibbs has been showing me some of her very fine snapshots."

He left her with her friend. As he thought over the incident he wondered if Mrs. Nichols' return had been unpremeditated or whether it was part of a plan to surprise him in a compromising position and thus give Mrs. Gibbs a hold on him.

He had further light on the subject that night. He had eaten dinner at the table with the Lawrences, had walked the deck with Bertha, and sat in the saloon and listened to the orchestra until ten o'clock, when supper was served, and a little later, having bid the ladies good night, went to his stateroom. On his way he had to pass room 108 and saw a light over the transom.

He had undressed, donned his pajamas and lain down on his berth when someone tapped lightly at the door. Thinking it was the steward he called to him to unlock the door and come in. The steward had a pass-key which unlocked all the doors on the corridor.

Instead of the steward coming in the tapping was resumed, in what seemed like a very secretive, almost furtive fashion. He rose and opened the door. Mrs. Gibbs was standing before it, clad in a very attractive negligee and with her red gold hair fluffed out around her head like an aureole.

"Pardon me, Dr. Glover, for disturbing you, but do you happen to have any aspirin or antikamnia? I have a headache, and I don't like to call the doctor for so small a thing."

She was edging nearer the door, which Donald was holding partly open from the inside.

"I'm sorry," he said, sharply and decisively. "I haven't a thing. If you'll call your maid she'll get you something from the apothecary shop or you might try wrapping a wet towel around your head. Good night."

He closed the door and locked it. He was tired of Mrs. Gibbs, and hoped he had made his boredom apparent. He thought he knew women pretty well, but he did not know Mrs. Gibbs. She was aware that she had failed, for no young man would turn from his bedroom door a pretty woman for whom he had any desire whatever. But she had still another arrow in her quiver—or perhaps it would be more modern to say another cartridge in her six-gun. If she couldn't get the man, she would have her revenge on those who kept him away from her.

Next morning after breakfast she watched her chance to catch him alone. He had gone into the bar to get a package of cigarettes, and she waited until he came out and then accosted him.

"Good morning, Dr. Glover, I hope I didn't disturb your virtuous slumber last night. I think you were rather abrupt, not to say rude, in the way you slammed the door in my face, but I bear you no ill will and, indeed wish you well. In proof of it I want to give you some good advice. You seem to spend most of your time on the boat with that Bertha Lawrence. I should think that a young man of your ability and your prospects would be more careful of his company."

"Just what do you mean?" demanded Donald, sharply and frowning portentously.

"Did you know," she continued, "that Bertha Lawrence had been arrested in Athena for disorderly conduct and had served a term in the Athena workhouse?"

Donald lost his philosophic calm; it became as one of the things which were not and had never been. He reverted to the primitive.

"It's a damn lie!" he cried, subduing his voice as much as his anger would permit, lest he be overheard, "a vile and baseless slander. There's not a word of truth in it. Miss Lawrence is a pure and clean-minded woman, and her character is above suspicion."

"Maybe so," returned Mrs. Gibbs, with deceptive calmness, "I only know what I was told by someone who was in Athena at the time. But why are you so positive? Your defense of Miss Lawrence is very gallant and all that, but appearances are sometimes deceptive. What do you *know* about it?"

"I know all about it," returned Donald. "I was with her at the time."

"Oh, I see," said Mrs. Gibbs with an evil smile. "That accounts for it! So there *was* some truth in it."

Donald explained with great vigor of speech and at sufficient length to cover all the details, the incident at Athena. But he was conscious, as he did so, of the weak points in his defense. The arrest, the incarceration, the charge, and his own conviction and punishment he could not deny, and to talk about them was no slander. Miss Lawrence, he could honestly insist, was entirely without fault and the victim of circumstances.

"Well," concluded Mrs. Gibbs, as she turned to meet Mrs. Nichols, who was coming along the deck toward them, "I got it from Link Dixon, who was in Athena at the time. Your story sounds plausible and I'll take your word for it—and everybody knows that Link is a liar. He didn't say who the man was, so I had no idea it was you. But Bertha Lawrence is a snob anyway, and a lot of people in Chicago don't like her, so it's not surprising they are willing to believe the story. However innocent she may be, I'm sure she'll never be able to live it down."

Mrs. Gibbs felt quite cheerful as she moved away with her satellite. The Lawrence women had high-hatted her, and Donald had repelled her advances and shown no reaction whatever to her personal charms, which few men on whom she had tried them had been able to resist.

Donald's first impulse had been to tell the Lawrences what Mrs. Gibbs had said, but on second thought he decided not to do so. It would only wound Bertha, and could accomplish no good purpose. Of course the story, if repeated and believed—and such things are easy to believe and hard to forget—might seriously interfere with her chances of marriage. She had grown very dear to him during the voyage, though he had not meant to marry until he should have become settled in life or at least well-launched upon a career. But he could get an option on Bertha's hand, at least, until that time, which need not be long deferred, and she might wish to pursue her own career, for a time at least.

In accordance with this idea he set siege to her in real earnest. He walked with her, danced with her, sat apart with her, and told her what a wonderful girl she was, and the more he was with her the more he loved her. On one occasion when he was alone, her sister Rose joined him on the deck.

"See here, Donald," she said, "you must be feeding Bertha an awful lot of applesauce. She moons around like a woman in a dream and is so sickeningly filial and sisterly that mother and I hardly know her. And I notice that you know longer speak to that Gibbs woman, while Mrs. Nichols glares at you like a basilisk—whatever that is. Have they been talking to you about us?"

"Has Bertha ever told you," asked Donald in a moment of expansion, which he was before long to regret exceedingly, "about our Athena experience?"

"Yes, indeed. I learned it seven years ago. Does that woman know about it?"

"Yes, one of our fellow pupils at Athena circulated a lying version of it, and Mrs. Gibbs says that the story is all over Chicago."

"That woman is a snake," declared Rose. "I should like to stamp on her. Just what did she say?"

"I'll tell you, Rose," he replied, "if you'll promise not to tell Bertha."

"Of course I won't," she declared.

But of course she did, as soon as she saw Bertha, who burst into tears and would not be comforted. And when Donald told her the next day that he loved her, and asked her to marry him later on, she replied: "I do love you, Donald, and should love to marry you, but I can't do it now, for several reasons. In the first place, you're not ready to marry, and may change your mind before you are. In the second place, although you may love me, I fear you want to marry me to protect my good name, for I know that a garbled version of our Athena episode is in circulation, and I wouldn't let you marry me for any such reason. I want to be married for love and not from pity. Another thing, I fear I couldn't be sure of you, Donald. You're too good looking, and too white. When, or if, you tire of me there'll be too many women anxious to take my place. And if I should marry you and learned to love you any more than I do, it would kill me to have you leave me."

"Such a thing is unthinkable," protested Donald vigorously. "I love you too much."

"But it has happened," returned Bertha. "You must give me time to think about it."

CHAPTER XXVI

⟩⟩⟩⟩⟨⟨⟨⟨

THEY LANDED at Liverpool next day, and Donald took the boat train to London. He kept with the Lawrences until they reached Paddington Station, where a friend staying in Bloomsbury was to meet them and put them up for a few days. They were to spend a couple of weeks traveling in Holland, Belgium and northern France, and then settle down for a month or so at Avignon, in the Provençal. Donald got several addresses and promised to keep in touch with them.

Bertha and he were the last to leave the train.

"When you've made up your mind, Bertha, let me know, by letter, by wire or by wireless, and I'll come running. *Au revoir*, dearest."

"*Au revoir*, Donald, I'll write."

Donald took her in his arms, drew her close to him and kissed her fervently, regardless of the guard at the door, who, casehardened against anything short of murder, was equally indifferent.

He took a cab to a hotel, and spent several days visiting points of interest. So wide had been his reading, so many were his intellectual interests, that he soon perceived that it would take months to "do" London thoroughly and weeks to even skim its surface. Every foot of its soil was replete with literary and historical associations, and the cursory view that he was able to take in these few days merely whetted his appetite for more. So he decided that he would get at his business and get in touch with Mr. Bascomb before he settled down to the projected book which was to justify his fellowship.

Mr. Bascomb had a London address, at the office of the West African importing firm of which he was chairman of the board. He also had an address in Kent, not far from London. Donald called him by telephone at his office. Mr. Bascomb had been advised, by letter from Dr. Jefferson, of Donald's impending visit. He was going to be engaged in a director's meeting during the morning, but asked Donald to drive with him to the country, starting about the middle of the afternoon. His car would call for Donald at his hotel, the Metropole, on Northumberland Avenue, off Trafalgar Square, at four o'clock, and they would arrive at home in time for dinner. He had notified Lady Merrivale, who would be expecting them.

After a pleasant drive in a big black Daimler driven by a chauffeur in livery, through the city, then through a rather drab and uninteresting suburb, then through a beautiful countryside, they reached The Beeches. The estate belonged to Lady Merrivale, with whom her brother, who was unmarried, made his home. He had chambers and a manservant in London, but spent most of his time at The Beeches.

The house was a fine old Elizabethan manor, built of red brick, the end walls overgrown with ivy. Although small compared with the seats of the great noblemen, it was of marked distinction, and was mentioned in *The Stately Homes of England* as a beautiful example of the architecture of its period. As they entered the hall, Lady Merrivale came out of the drawing room and gave both hands to Donald in cordial greeting.

A manservant carried the guest's bags upstairs to a spacious second-story room, with a southern exposure, which looked out through leaded windows over the gardens and beyond them a small park, to a beautiful though rather flat countryside beyond. That part of Essex was not a hilly nor hardly even a rolling country. The interior of the house had been modernized, without spoiling its original beauty, by the installation of bathrooms and electric lights.

"I'm to valet you while you're here," announced the deferential footman, a tall side-whiskered man in plum-colored livery. "Would you like a bawth, sir, before you dress for dinner?"

"Thank you," replied Donald. "I think I should."

"I'll draw it for you, sir. You may call me Simms, if you like, sir. Do you prefer it 'ot or cold, sir?"

"Medium, Simms."

"Thank you, sir. While you're taking your bawth, sir, I'll unpack your bag and lay out your dinner clothes."

When Donald had finished his bath and donned the handsome dressing gown which hung on a hook in the perfectly appointed bathroom, he found that Simms had unpacked his traveling bag and made ready his dinner jacket and shoes and a pleated white shirt, and had laid out his comb and brush and shaving materials on the old mahogany dresser.

"Can I hassist you further, sir?" asked Simms.

"No, thank you," returned Donald. "I can make out by myself now."

"Thank you, sir," said Simms, as he backed out of the room. "If you need anything more, please ring."

Donald had never been helped to dress by any one but his mother, but he found the atmosphere of luxury and deference, which, he soon learned, permeated the whole household, a very pleasant thing. He had never before worn evening clothes except when he was going out to a formal dinner or to some evening function. When he had completed his toilet and had found his way downstairs without the assistance of the solicitous Simms, Lady Merrivale, whom he found in the library, looked up at the tall, handsome, athletic youth who confronted her, and realized that she had never seen a handsomer young man. Donald looked his best in a dress coat or a dinner jacket, as many men do not. He reminded Lady Merrivale somewhat of the Italian gentleman Count Angelo Milfiore, who had proposed to her the year before, but whom she had sent away because she suspected he cared more for her money than for herself.

"We dine at seven," she said. "If you like, while you're waiting, I'll show you the gardens."

She led the way through a French window to an open terrace at the side of the house, and down several brick steps into a wonderful rose garden, and thence to another adjoining it, which was filled with wisteria and other blooms. While they were looking at the flowers, a slightly bowed gray-haired Scotchman came up and tipped his cap.

"This is my gardener, Sandy McAllister," said Lady Merrivale. "Do you think we'll have time, Sandy, to show my friend Mr. Glover the greenhouses before dinner?"

"I think so, mah leddy," was the answer. "There'll be enough time for 'im to gi'e 'em a wee glance, and if he's here another day, we can go into details."

The gardener led the way into one of the spacious greenhouses. There were tables and stands and decorative plants in pots, with many orchids and other exotic flowers.

"And this is our century plant, sir," said McAllister, indicating a large pot on a pedestal. "It's due to bloom varry soon now. I've been tellin' mah leddy that she ought to marry again, so that I might pluck it to adorn her weddin' breakfast."

"Oh, Sandy," returned Lady Merrivale, "you embarrass me. I'm an old woman."

"You're younger than many o' these flappers about, and he'll be a lucky mon that gets you," he declared, with the freedom of an old retainer.

Dinner was served as Donald had never seen a dinner served before. The clear soup was a dream. The sole was delicious. The roast pheasant had been cooked to a turn. Coming from a "dry" country, the fine, smooth, old sherry tasted to him like nectar. When they had finished the dessert, Lady Merrivale had coffee served on the terrace, after which Mr. Bascomb offered Donald a cigar, which, he explained, was made in Jamaica from a specially imported Cuban leaf, and Lady Merrivale joined them with a cigarette in a long jade holder. Donald had eaten well-served meals in some of the great hotels in New York, but this was his first introduction to the prandial luxury of a wealthy household. It was one of the things he had read about but had hardly expected ever to share.

"I suppose we ought to go over Jefferson's plans," said Mr. Bascomb, "but you'll be with us several days at least, and we'll defer it until tomorrow. Meanwhile, the house is yours and everything in it."

"Perhaps Mr. Glover'll sing for us," Lady Merrivale added. "The victrola and the radio have almost ruined amateur chamber music, but I can strum an accompaniment, and the real human voice is better than its best reproduction."

"Yes," interjected her brother, "though Caruso dead still sings, he doesn't throw out his chest in such sheer delight as he did on the stage. I suspect one element of his success was his keen enjoyment of his own performance. But that is true, I imagine, of any artist."

They adjourned to the music room, and Lady Merrivale played the accompaniments on a magnificent Steinway grand, while Donald sang "O Sole Mio" and the torreador song from *Carmen*. The excellent food, the good wine, the fine cigars, and the presence of a beautiful and gracious woman, brought out all that was best in him, and he could hardly have sung better had he been trained for the concert stage. It was an immediate exemplification of Mr. Bascomb's theory. Then Lady Merrivale, still at the piano, sang "O Promise Me," Mr. Bascomb in a very good bass, "Rocked in the Cradle of the Deep," and Donald wound up with "Deep River," as harmonized by Harry Burleigh.

They breakfasted next morning at eight o'clock, since Mr. Bascomb had planned to be at his office by ten.

"I'll see you tonight, Glover," he said as his car drove up to the door. "We want you to stay with us a while. Tell me where to find your trunk and I'll have it brought out. And I'll take care of your hotel bill to date."

"I checked out yesterday," returned Donald, "and left my trunk in the luggage room."

"Very well, I'll send for it. I want to go over the school plans with you soon, but I shall be too busy with other matters for several days. In the meantime Lady Merrivale will look after you—won't you, Blanche?"

"I sure will," returned Lady Blanche, who had picked up a few characteristic American expressions during her visit to the United States.

She was as good as her word. There were several cars in the garage, among them a little maroon-colored two-seater Citroen in which she took Donald for a long drive that same morning in the beautiful English lanes of the neighborhood. They visited the old parish church, where Lady Merrivale showed him the tombs of her father and mother and grandparents. They drove by the ruined castle which had been the ancient seat of the earls of Essex. As they were passing a certain lodge gate, a young lady, coming out on foot, waved her parasol at Lady Merrivale.

"Cheerio, Blanche, how do you carry yourself?"

"I'm all right, Bella. How's your mother?"

"She's well. Don't forget the garden party tomorrow evening."

She smiled at Donald. "Who's your boyfriend?" she asked.

"Oh, pardon me, both of you. This is Donald Glover, a doctor of philosophy, an author and a very serious person, and this is my friend Bella Dexter—the Honorable Isabelle Dexter, to be precise. Her father, Lord Dexter, is a justice of peace and master of the fox hounds."

"Mr. Glover has an English name, but he looks like a continental," suggested the Honorable Bella.

"He's an American, born and bred."

Donald was on the point of explaining that he was an American Negro, but caught himself in time. Since these good people were treating him as an equal, there was no point in suggesting anything that might imply any difference between them. If Lady Merrivale cared to tell her friends what he was, well and good, he would be glad to have her do so; but he was her guest and at her disposition.

They stopped for lunch at a wayside inn, The Boar and Spear, as proclaimed by a swinging sign on an old projecting bracket of wrought iron, for which many a collector would have paid his weight in silver, where they cut roast beef from the joint and split a bottle of stout. Lady Blanche had a wholesome English appetite, and Donald was a good trencherman. In the afternoon she drove him through several small towns and villages, to the seacoast. Before they reached home, she was calling him "Donald," and Donald had dropped the "Merrivale" and was addressing her as "Lady Blanche." They arrived at The Beeches at about seven. Donald bathed and dressed for dinner, under the supervision of the efficient Simms.

"I 'opes you 'ad a pleasant day, sir," said the valet, during his deft ministrations.

"A delightful day, Simms. Lady Blanche is a splendid driver and a wonderful hostess."

"You never said a truer word, sir. She's the best there is. She grieved over her late 'usband, Captain Sir Henry, until she went to America last winter, but she's been very cheerful since she came back. It's fine for her to 'ave young comp'ny in the 'ouse. I hope you stays a long time, sir."

The next day was Saturday and in the afternoon Lady Blanche drove him over to the garden party. There were a number of young ladies and others not so young, the vicar, his curate and several young and middle-aged men of leisure. The weather was fair and warm, and the party was held on the lawn. There were seats and tables for bridge or other games, and a red and white striped marquée from which refreshments were served.

As Lady Blanche and Donald were making their way across the lawn toward their hostess, a beautiful blue-eyed, corn-haired blonde ran up to the Honorable Isabel.

"Bella," she demanded, "where did Blanche dig up the Greek god? Take off his clothes and he could pass for the Apollo Belvedere. Introduce me quick, before somebody else kidnaps him."

Donald was presented to several of the ladies and gentlemen. The blond young woman, Miss Clara Decies, engaged him in conversation, but neither she nor any other could get him far or keep him away long from Lady Blanche. Nor was Donald, aside from his acquaintance with Amelia Parker and his brief affair with Mitzi, accustomed to social intimacy with white women, and the unfamiliarity of the surroundings enhanced his natural shyness. He was introduced to the vicar, who asked him how he liked England. One of the young men, with a military title and one arm—he had left the other at Saloniki—inquired if the United States was going to demand its whole quivering pound of England's flesh according to the terms of the war debt settlement, and compared America, none too politely to Shylock. Donald agreed with him entirely and said as much.

"Well, Donald, how did you like it?" asked Lady Blanche as they drove away.

"It was the ideal garden party that Trollope wrote about and Marcus Stone painted. It might have furnished the setting for *Barchester Towers*."

"It was a bit tame compared with things as they were before the war, before most of the men were killed off and the rest ruined," she returned.

Donald wondered what could have been better. He had read, in the society columns of the American newspapers, of more lavish and ostentatious entertainment at Newport and on Long Island, but could not imagine anything more genuinely hospitable and friendly.

He met Mr. Bascomb at dinner, and they talked about the happenings in the world. The Locarno Conference was in session and the Balkan states were very restive. The British government still refused to reestablish diplomatic relations with Soviet Russia, but winked at trade which brought profit to British merchants and manufacturers.

After another excellent dinner and a glass of sherry, they had more music and Donald retired to his room, at the end of a perfect day. He did not like to think that he would have to leave this beautiful place, but his practical mind suggested that he enjoy it while he might, for the stern battle of life was confronting him and could be not long deferred. However, a short vacation would leave him all the better fitted for strenuous work on the new book to which he meant to devote his stay in Europe—a further elaboration of his system of philosophy with a special application to present-day problems and the future of the American Negro.

He had discussed with his friend Dr. Lebrun, before he left New York, the plan of this new book, and Dr. Lebrun had tried to persuade him to broaden its scope to include all the dark races of the world. But Donald was quite sure that his mother, to whom the book was to be in part payment of his debt to her, was not so internationally minded as Dr. Lebrun, but that she was interested in Africa merely as the mother country of her race, and that the welfare of one Negro in the United States meant more to her than that of a hundred Bantus or Croos or Kaffirs in Africa, not to mention Japanese or Chinese or East Indians.[1] He had talked over the book with Dr. Dean during their voyage over and found that the professor's opinion coincided with his own. There might come a time when the interests of all the darker races would be one, waiting on the millennial epoch when the interests of all races would be one, but for the time being the only common interest of the dark races lay in resisting the encroachments of the white race, for which Donald feared that philosophy would not be a very effective weapon, and the time had not yet come and he hoped would never arrive, when the question of equality or supremacy between the white and colored races of the world would be decided by war—a war in which the cumulative insults and hatreds of centuries would make the German *Schrechlichkeit* of the World War seem like the ferocious blood lust of a sparring match with soft gloves in a YMCA gymnasium.

On Sunday, the day after the garden party, Mr. Bascomb showed Donald his library. Lady Blanche had kept him so busy that he had had time to give the bookshelves little more than a casual glance. The house was built with a wide hall, from which a broad stairway of carved mahogany ran up to a corresponding hall on the second floor, on which the library was situated. It was on the sunny side of the house, with wide windows and no trees near enough to cut off the light, nor any dark shades or heavy curtains. It was evidently intended not only for the storage of books, but for free and unhampered use. The glass cases opened easily, and the books were so arranged as to be convenient of access.

There was one shelf of incunabula, several of the

books, a Gutenberg among them, dating back to the middle of the fifteenth century, the very dawn of printing from moveable types. There was a first folio Shakespeare and a fine collection of the older English poets and dramatists. The library was rich in serious books, especially works on philosophy and scientific subjects. Donald, with a feeling of youthful elation, discovered among them his own *Essay on the Imagination*, which at Mr. Bascomb's suggestion, he inscribed with his name and an appropriate sentiment. Travel, poetry, the drama and modern fiction were well-represented. Many of the books, besides the incunabula, were rare and curious, and there were numerous examples of fine binding by the French and English masters of the art.

"And these," explained Mr. Bascomb when they reached a certain section of the shelves, "are my books on Africa."

There were many of them—the travels of Livingstone, Stanley, Speke, Sir Harry Johnston and others, the standard histories of ancient Egypt, government colonial reports, and among the later additions a copy of René Maran's *Batouala*.[2] There were several American books on the Negro, including one by Dr. Jefferson and another by Dr. Lebrun.

Donald admired the collection and said so, displaying a knowledge of books and bookmaking remarkable, Mr. Bascomb thought, in so young a man. Isador Rovelsky's father was an ardent collector, and Donald had visited his library several times with Isador. Senator Brown's library, with which he was familiar, had contained a number of rare examples, especially along the line of these books on Africa.

"This would be a wonderful place to write on the Negro," observed Donald. "One would only rarely have to refer to the great national collections."

"Of course," said Mr. Bascomb, "the British Museum and the Biliothèque Nationale have more books, but I imagine my library includes the important ones.

"You are entirely at liberty to use it," he added, "as long as you like or whenever you like. I never went in for writin' but I enjoy readin' a good book and try to keep my library up to date. Part of the books are mine and part are my sister's, but I never married, and we have lived together, even during her husband's life, ever since she was born, and the books have never been separated."

"These books on Africa," said Donald, "remind me of my shamefully neglected mission. Lady Blanche and you have given me so good a time that I'd almost forgotten the project for the West African school."

"Ah, yes, and I've neglected it as well," returned Mr. Bascomb. "But it has waited ten years and it won't hurt it to wait another week. I'll bring the papers out from the office and go over them with you next Sunday morning."

But when next Sunday morning came and Donald was all primed and ready to shoot, Mr. Bascomb seemed to have forgotten the papers. Lady Blanche decided to go to church, and, of course, Donald must go with her. The service was conducted at St. Christopher's, the parish church, by the Reverend Benedict Taliaferro, whom Donald had met at the Decies's garden party. The regular Episcopal service was intoned—the church was rather high. The music was good but nothing out of the ordinary. The sermon, though perhaps instructive, was neither inspiring nor illuminating. There was nothing by way of exposition or argument to make Donald revise any of the opinions on religion he had expressed, by inference at least, in his *Essay on the Imagination.*

Then after luncheon, callers came in and several hours passed in conversation, after which Lady Blanche took Donald for a drive in the runabout, while Mr. Bascomb finished the London Sunday papers and skimmed a new book. Then dinner, a walk around the grounds, music and to bed.

Next day, which was Monday, Lady Blanche drove Donald to Kew Gardens. It was after lilac time, but the roses were in bloom, and they walked hand in hand through the garden like any 'Arry and 'Arriet, defied the criticism of Mrs. Grundy, quoted Alfred Noyes and enjoyed themselves immensely.

And not until Donald went the next day but one to Mr. Bascomb's office and retrieved Dr. Jefferson's documents, did they find their way to The Beeches. The following Sunday morning, at Donald's request, Mr.

Bascomb and he set to work. He had helped Dr. Jefferson prepare the plans and had the whole subject at his tongue's end. Mr. Bascomb suggested some changes by way of adaptation to special native needs, but approved the plan as a whole and said he would write to Dr. Jefferson and arrange to have him send men to Africa to install it. Lady Blanche was present during the latter part of the discussion and made several pertinent suggestions.

"How would you like, Glover, to go down yourself and help launch the enterprise?" Mr. Bascomb asked.

"Would his health be at all endangered?" asked Lady Blanche, with a touch of anxiety.

"I don't think so," returned her brother. "I've been down there more than once, and our administrators live there all the time, with an occasional visit home. Glover is dark and claims some tropical blood, which should help him to endure the climate for a while. And it would give him a new slant on the race question. He would see the Negro on his native soil, and find out what progress he is making under our comparatively just and liberal policy in that part of the dominion."

Donald said he would think the proposition over, and write to Dr. Jefferson about Mr. Bascomb's decision. He made his report, but said nothing about the offer to send him to Africa. Indeed, after the luxury of his visit to The Beeches, he doubted whether the hardships of a sojourn of any length in tropical Africa would appeal to him, though he would like at some other time to visit the country and study conditions there long enough to write about them intelligently.

One evening in the latter part of the following week, Mr. Bascomb and Donald were sitting on the terrace alone after dinner. Lady Blanche had excused herself and driven off to a neighbor's on some peculiarly feminine errand where no masculine distractions were desired.

"Glover," said his host, "you've been with us nearly a month. I hope you've found it pleasant."

"Beyond expression," returned Donald. "It has been a delightful experience."

"And I've enjoyed every minute we have been together," added Mr. Bascomb. "You know more than most older men of my acquaintance, in fact far more, so far as books go, than I myself, and yet you are so modest about it. You have none of that cocksureness which characterizes our younger intellectuals, besides whose feeble lucubrations your clarity of thought and felicity of expression shine resplendent."

Donald's dark cheek flushed with real embarrassment. "You overwhelm me, sir," he replied. "I hoped you had been pleased with me but had not expected any such—panegyric—is that the word?"

"Not at all—a mere cold, calm, simple statement of fact. As to Blanche, your visit has made a new woman of her; indeed, she has grown young again. I don't what are your views about marriage—are you engaged by any chance?"

"No," said Donald truthfully, because Bertha Lawrence had given him no definite answer nor had he heard from her but once since they had parted, though he had addressed several letters to her.

"Very good. That clarifies the situation. I don't know how you feel about my sister. She's a lovable woman."

"She's the finest lady I've ever met or ever hope to meet," declared Donald.

"I think," continued the lady's brother, "that she's in love with you. I'm quite sure that, if you should ask her to marry you, she wouldn't say no."

Donald was overwhelmed with astonishment. He had never dreamed of such a thing. That the lady was kind had been obvious. That she might be in love with him was possible. But ladies had loved before and had not married where they loved. That a woman of Lady Merrivale's position should seriously consider marriage with a man so much her junior and of obscure and socially ignoble origin would never have occurred to him. Her reference to her colored blood he had looked upon as more or less of a pleasantry. It had meant nothing in her life. Whereas, in his own case, it had made him a social pariah in his own country and had so narrowed his outlook on life that only by extraordinary ability or exceptional opportunities could he overcome his handicap.

Mr. Bascomb, perceiving his embarrassment, tried to help him out.

"You have, I know," he said, "as you have told me,

plans for the uplift of your race, as you call it. I haven't said anything to our friends about your blood, because it isn't important and we care nothing about it, at least in your case, but there's no use challenging dormant prejudice by advertising it. You wouldn't need to cease working for your people. You could stay here and write your books and develop your philosophy, and should you want variety you could serve as a sort of general advisor for your wife on her West Indian property, or even live there for part of the time, and you can help me in the same way with my African interests. Should you tire of the role of reformer, I can make an opening for you in business, or you can lead the life of a country gentleman—hunting, fishing, polo, airplaning, yachting or any of the time-killing pursuits the idle rich indulge in. As I say, my sister loves you, and I would like her to be happy."

"I'm frightfully upset, in fact I'm completely bowled over, Mr. Bascomb," said Donald, as soon as he could command his composure. "Of course, Lady Blanche has been kind to me, and I've learned to admire her very much. I am conscious of her great condescension and would do anything I could to make her happy; but to give up all my plans, to deflect the line of my life in an entirely new direction—I should have to think about it. Give me a day or two. It is an alluring prospect, and one not lightly to be dismissed."

CHAPTER XXVII

———⇒➤●⇐———

DONALD SLEPT little that night, and it is not unjust to say that he was strongly tempted. He had never thought very highly of people who sought the easy way, nor yet had he severely criticized them. As a philosopher, he knew that life, to be at all tolerable, was a matter of compromise, and that no one could be sure that one would be always wise, always just, always honest, always loyal.

He had thought himself loyal to his race, but how far did that loyalty go, and was it consistent with the life of a wealthy Englishman? He had believed himself loyal to his mother; indeed, it had been the prime motive in marking out a career for himself. But could he convince her that to seize this golden opportunity would be loyal or wise? He doubted it, but—there was another one of the hurdles which had marked his course through life.

But the most important obstacle was Bertha Lawrence. Were it not for her, assuming he could dispose of the other objections, he could find it easy to love a rich and affectionate wife. True, Lady Blanche was some years older than he, but the compensating advantages were so great that the difference of a few years was negligible. The temptation was great, and, had he not met Bertha on the steamer, might well have proved irresistible. It was a conflict between mind and heart, between intellect and emotion, between self-interest and sentiment. As a practical philosopher, he would be a fool to turn down Lady Blanche's proposal, for such it undoubtedly was, although her brother had been the self-appointed ambassador.

Donald had not quite made up his mind by morning. After breakfast Mr. Bascomb went to London, and Lady Blanche received a telegram from an old friend who was lying ill and wanted to see her for perhaps the last time. She excused herself, and was driven to the nearest railroad station where she would take the train, to be gone until the late afternoon or the next morning. She would wire the hour of her arrival, and Donald could, if he liked, drive to the station in the runabout and meet her.

Donald was not in the mood to read or write, so he walked about the grounds until the next mail delivery, which was at eleven o'clock. There were several letters for him, among them one from his mother, which he opened first and read. In it she asked him not to forget their vision nor permit any distraction to wean him from it. Another letter, postmarked Avignon, France, was addressed in a flowing hand with which he was not familiar, but at the sight of which his heart thrilled. His intuition proved correct; the letter was from Bertha:

Avignon, July 10, 1928

Dear Donald,

We're having a delightful time here. I'll tell you all about it when we meet. I've made up my mind, too, and will tell you what it is, too, when we meet. I miss you, Donald, and would like to see you. Another man is coming from America soon, whom my father wishes me to marry. So hurry, Donald, and get here first.

Bertha.

The simple signature, with no qualifying adjective or adverbs told Donald all he wished to know.

The vision of the gracious English lady faded, and Donald saw before him the slender, clear-eyed girl who had walked down the hill with him at Athena seven years before. He saw her sitting, with apprehension in her eyes, in the sordid police court, amid the ruck of the Athena underworld. He visioned her as the more mature, polished and graceful young woman with whom he had passed those delightful days on the steamer. He recalled the love in her eyes and the tender tones of her voice when she had said she was afraid to marry him, and the fervor with which she had returned his parting kiss when they left the train at Paddington Station.

For the moment, all his practical doubts took flight. No other man should possess her. No cause, no crusade, no mission should interfere with their union.

He seized pen and paper, and, seated at the Sheraton writing desk in the Elizabethan library, where all the surroundings appealed to his love of the beautiful and the aesthetic, he renounced them all and wrote a letter to Mr. Bascomb.

He thanked him for his kindness toward him and for his interest in his future. He could think of nothing he had done to deserve it. It had been dictated by a fine and generous spirit, and he would cherish its memory all his life. The prospect Mr. Bascomb had unfolded to him was alluring; it had been a great temptation which only the realization of prior obligations and loyalties could enable him to resist.

He had received a letter in the morning mail, he continued, calling him immediately to France, and he was leaving The Beeches during the day and would not be there when Mr. Bascomb returned in the evening. He had also written to Lady Blanche. He subscribed his letter, "Respectfully and gratefully yours, Donald Glover."

He was rather glad Lady Blanche was away for the day, for it would have been very awkward to take leave of her. From his own observation, enlightened by Mr. Bascomb's disclosure, he was sure the parting would be painful to her, as it would be embarrassing to him. It would be much better to write her a letter.

The letter proved only less difficult than a personal farewell. And while the regretful Simms was packing his things, he did the best he could with his letter. He did not wish to refer to her brother's proposition, since the lady was supposed to be ignorant of it. To "turn down" a beautiful, lovable and loving woman might seem, in theory, to be easy for a practical philosopher, but for a man of sentiment—and Donald was both, and at this juncture sentiment was to the fore—it was the hardest task he had ever undertaken. This is what he wrote:

Dear Lady Blanche:

A sudden summons in the morning mail is taking me away from The Beeches before your return. I hope you will pardon the abruptness of my departure and believe me when I say that the past two weeks have been the happiest period of my life. The privilege of living in your beautiful home and of enjoying your delightful society will always remain a sweet and pleasant memory. And if I can feel, as I am sure I can, that you wish me well, it will be an inspiration to me for the best and finest things all the rest of my life. With sincere thanks for all your kindness, and the best of wishes for your future happiness, believe me always,

Your devoted friend and beneficiary,
Donald.

He had meant to stop there, but to write his whole name would be less personal, and he added the "Glover."

He enclosed and addressed the two letters and left them lying on the desk while he waited for his trunk and bags to be brought downstairs. And while he

waited he kept on thinking, and as he considered the
situation, sentiment gave place for a moment to the
practical. Suppose Bertha's answer should not be what
he expected? She had not been definite and might well
give him a negative answer. Her father's influence
might outweigh her own inclinations. If these letters
reached their destination he would have definitely severed his relations with these liberal and generous people who were willing to take him into their hearts and
into their life. The more he thought of Lady Blanche
the more he shrank from hurting her. Before the re-
ceipt of Bertha's letter he had not definitely decided
upon his course.

He had thought he could foresee what his mother
would think, but he could not be exactly certain, and
he was not where he could consult her. She might regard a marriage with Lady Blanche as placing him in a
position to be extremely useful to his people. And if he
should properly stress Lady Blanche's West Indian origin it might be easy to convince her that he was not
abandoning the cause of their people but merely approaching it from a different and, though indirect, perhaps more effective angle. They could claim as their
own anything he might accomplish, and wherever he
might spend his days he would always be in spiritual
sympathy with them. It was not inconceivable that by
his writings he might help to promote a more tolerant
attitude in the white world toward dark people. Certainly in the freer atmosphere of Europe he could make

intellectual and social contacts which would widen his views and sharpen his intelligence. For while he had confidence in his powers and in his future, he was essentially modest, and his head had not been turned by the adulation of the critics and plaudits of his friends.

The ocean of philosophy was so broad and so deep that the greatest minds of all the ages had only skimmed its surface and had not begun to plumb its depths. If, as Herbert Spencer put it, the true aim of philosophy is to promote human happiness, if he could outline and inculcate a philosophy of life which would contribute to this end, his own people would profit by it as well as others and, besides, it would be, so to speak, a feather in their cap. This at least was his attitude of mind when he sat down at the desk and took up again the pen he had laid down.

With a prudence which he had inherited, along with his philosophic outlook on life, from some unknown ancestor in the long line from the first man down, not to mention the intelligent anthropoid who first learned to use his thumb and to correlate in his brain cause and effect, he decided not to burn his bridges behind him. So he set match to the other letter, threw it into the empty grate, watched it turn to ashes, and then wrote this short note:

Dear Lady Blanche:

A sudden summons in the morning mail is taking me away from The Beeches before your return, and I may not see you again for some days or weeks. Believe me when I say that the past few weeks in your beautiful home, with the privilege of your delightful society, have been the happiest period of my life. With grateful regards,

Yours, until we meet again,
Donald.

Much of the same reasoning applied to his letter to Mr. Bascomb, so he decided not to leave it, but to see Mr. Bascomb in London before he left the city.

Simms came in to announce that his things were ready, with the dogcart to take him to the station.

"It's too bad you're goin', sir," he said, sorrowfully. "I'd 'oped you might stay a long time. I'm sure mah leddy'll be 'art-broken when she comes and finds you've gone. I 'opes you'll be back soon."

The other house servants had come to the door to see him off. He tipped them liberally and then climbed into the dogcart and was driven along the beautiful Kentish lanes to the station. When he had bought his ticket and taken his seat on the train he experienced a decided feeling of relief, mingled with a certain sense of shame. He was running away, from a gilded prison it is true, but mainly because he did not dare to face his jailers, which was not a brave man's part.

CHAPTER XXVIII

⟹➤●◄⟸

COINCIDENTALLY WITH these happenings in Europe, certain other events vitally bearing upon Donald's past and future, were transpiring in America, which it were well to review at this point.

A few days after Donald had sailed, Dr. Douglas Freeman, former superintendent of the Columbus, Ohio, City Hospital, while attending a meeting of the American Medical Association in New York, read in the *Times* one morning at the breakfast table in his hotel, that Mr. Angus Seaton was in the city, and having looked up the millionaire's New York address, called him on the telephone to arrange for an interview, saying that he had something important to tell him about the boy he had adopted so many years before. Mr. Seaton invited him to dine with him that evening at the Waldorf, at seven o'clock. It chanced to be the day on which Donald was sailing for Europe.

When Dr. Freeman arrived at the hotel, Mr. Seaton had already secured a table in the dining room and left word at the desk for his guest to be shown to it. Dr. Freeman had not, Mr. Seaton thought, changed a great deal, except that his hair, which had merely been shot with gray when Seaton first met him, was now snow white. Mr. Seaton rose, and when they had shaken hands, the two men seated themselves at opposite sides of the small table. They inquired after each other's health, and when they had ordered what they wished and were waiting for the hors d'oeuvres, Dr. Freeman broached, by way of question, the subject of which he wished to speak.

"What ever became of the little boy you adopted from my hospital? I severed my connections with the institution several years ago, and meant to write to you at the time. You may remember reading in the papers about a certain confusion in the hospital records, which led to some very distressing complications. There were several lawsuits to determine the parentage of children who had been born at the hospital. The management, of which I was at the head, was severely criticized, and an investigation was ordered by the governor, as a result of which I left the institution. It developed, in the course of the inquiry, that the secretary who kept the records—Wilson was his name—you may recall him, a tall thin fellow with a face like a rabbit's—had been suffering from a slow and an insidious form of paresis—which was not discovered until a lot of damage had been done. I didn't like the findings of the committee, though they were probably just enough, and resigned my position—I imagine just ahead of the boot. Before leaving the hospital, however, I checked up all the records of births and adoptions and in doing so learned something about the boy which I think you, and he, if he is still living ought to know."

"He is living," replied Mr. Seaton, "and so far as I know, is here in New York."

"Did you bring him up in your own home?"

"No, but I wish I had. After the talk with you in which I learned his parentage, I placed him with a colored family, who adopted him and brought him up. He turned out to be a very bright, indeed, a brilliant boy, and never developed any of the bad traits of his immediate ancestors. Neither did the law of averages in physical heredity work out in his case. When he grew up he showed no signs of African descent. Some years later I offered to take him again and educate him and provide for his future, but he was so attached to the good people who had adopted him that he declined my offer. They have given him a good education. He is a Ph.D. of Columbia University, and has already distinguished himself as a writer and thinker. He has won a Morganheim fellowship, and is going to Europe to study. He means to devote himself to literature or to teaching, or both—it seems difficult to make a living at either alone. I was talking with an old friend about him only the other day."

"He isn't, by any chance, married?"

"No, I believe not. At least I haven't heard of it," replied Seaton.

"I'm glad of that. It might have complicated his life very much, in view of what I have to tell you."

"And what is that, Doctor?" inquired Seaton, somewhat intrigued by this announcement.

"Well," answered Dr. Freeman, "it transpired that Wilson, the secretary, had mixed the hospital records. We had an ideal registration system, but nothing human is foolproof. He put the wrong history card in the child's file. Instead of the parentage shown, the right card, when the records where straightened out, disclosed that the boy was of exceptionally good descent on both sides, judged by the highest standards, both social and intellectual."

"You don't mean it," interjected Seaton.

"Yes. His father was Reverend Sinclair Marvin, who had been a Congregational minister. The history of this old and prolific New England family is quoted by writers on sociology, crime and heredity as conclusive proof of certain theories. It seems that back in colonial times a certain young gentleman of this family, whose grandparents had come over on the *Mayflower*, had a passing amour, while yet unmarried, with a feeble-minded maid at an inn where he put up one night. This meeting proved fertile and the girl bore a child. Careful records were kept and verified, showing that every generation of the descendants of this child produced thieves, prostitutes, murderers, forgers, drug addicts and drunkards. The workhouses, asylums and jails of New England swarmed with them. Female virtue was almost unknown among them, and most of their children were illegitimate.

"Shortly after his affair with the chambermaid," Dr. Freeman went on, "the gentleman, having sown his wild oats but unaware of what the fearful crop would be, married a young lady of his own caste, reared, like himself, within smelling range of the sacred codfish. Among their descendants were a long list of talented people, among them a governor, a famous general in the Revolution, college presidents, ministers, senators, authors—indeed they were found in the very front rank of the intelligence and culture of the nation.

"The boy's father came of this line. He was not one of the most brilliant of them, although a graduate of Harvard and of Andover Theological Seminary. He had filled several charges acceptably, but much reading and thinking had undermined his faith, and his New England conscience would permit him no longer to preach a creed which he did not believe. But he was a lover of humanity, and when he put off his clerical garb, went into social service, and at a settlement in Columbus, where he was working at the time, he met Teresina Milfiore.

"This young lady, last hope of a noble but impoverished Sicilian family, had come to America to sing in Italian opera. She sang first in the chorus, but she had an excellent contralto voice and had been promised a minor role for the next season. Her salary on this lower rung of the musical ladder was not large, and to eke it out she joined a summer opera company which was touring the country. During their week at Columbus, she complained to the director one day of a slight swelling in the throat. The throat of the singer, like the hands of the violinist or the legs of a dancer, is his or her most valuable member, and the director took her to a physician, who examined her throat, diagnosed the ailment as tonsillitis, and sent her to a specialist to have her tonsils removed.

"The specialist botched the job, whether through ignorance or carelessness is not important in view of the result. In removing the offending glands, he injured Teresina's vocal chords, and it soon became apparent that she could never sing again in opera. The company left her at Columbus and went on to the next city. It was the law of the pack and the usual fate of those who fall by the wayside."

"Did she sue the surgeon for malpractice?" asked Seaton.

"No, she had no money to speak of, and the surgeon none to amount to anything, so a judgment for damages would have meant nothing. She had no friends in the city, but when her small savings were exhausted, some good ladies in musical circles to whom her predicament became known, took an interest in her and found her employment as a music teacher. Among other activities she conducted a singing class for small children in the settlement where the ex-preacher Marvin lived. They met, fell in love with each other and were married. Nine months later the husband died of flu. A few weeks afterwards the mother went to City Hospital, where she was delivered of a male child and died in childbirth. No one claimed the child, and it was kept at the hospital until your wife and you came there in search of a baby. The rest you know. Instead of a poor kitchen slut, the child had for its mother a lady of noble birth and lineage, and for father, in lieu of a wastrel mulatto, a man of education and ideals, of a family of thinkers, statesmen and writers."

"His character and intellect are quite consistent with such a heredity," returned Mr. Seaton. "It was a tragic mistake on the part of us all."

"I suppose you'll tell him?"

"I suppose so, but I want first to talk to the man who helped me out once before when I consulted him about the boy. It is a difficult situation, and there are several intricate problems involved which ought to have careful consideration. I'll let you know the outcome."

"I wish you would," returned Dr. Freeman, "for I feel quite guilty in the matter. Of course, it wasn't directly my fault, but the responsibility was mine. I hope I haven't injured him irretrievably."

And Dr. Freeman, having thus relieved his mind and his conscience, now passes out of the story.

CHAPTER XXIX

———⟶●⟵———

NEXT DAY Mr. Seaton called on Senator James L. Brown at the office of the Invincible Life Insurance Company, on lower Fifth Avenue, and repeated the story told him by Dr. Freeman.

"And now," asked Mr. Seaton, "what shall I do about it? I won't promise to adopt your views, but I should like to know what they are. I've a very high regard for your opinion. I think that in justice to Donald he ought to be told of his origin. What do you think about it?"

"You consulted me more than twenty years ago about Donald," replied Senator Brown. "You didn't ask my advice on whether or not you should keep him, but without being asked, I expressed certain opinions with regard to Donald and the race problem which you did not see fit to adopt. My views have not changed at all."

"But the situation as to Donald has changed, Brown," argued Seaton. "I thought then that he was colored. Now I know he is white."

"The boy was as white then as you think he is now," admitted, Brown, "but that's begging the question and doesn't get us anywhere; I didn't know he was white, but had every reason to believe the contrary. I did what I thought was best for Donald."

"You did what a white man thought was best for a Negro, which in most cases is nothing of the kind. For fear of bringing up as a white man a child with no sure sign of Negro blood, you ignored entirely his white blood. The scorn of white people for their own blood, of which they have so low an opinion that thirty-one thirty-seconds of it cannot override one thirty-second of dark blood, is something I could never understand. It seems a crime against their own race."

"I'll not argue with you about that, Brown," returned the millionaire, "but it's the custom of the country, and to live comfortably in a country one must conform to its customs. I never claimed to be any better or wiser than other people."

"Even if the history the paretic secretary in Columbus had scrambled had turned out to be true," Mr. Brown went on, "you might have brought the child up to be a man of whom your race might well, and as it has turned out, justly have been proud. The teachings and influence of the woman to whom you gave him, a woman of character with high ideals and a great heart, together with the environment in which he has been reared, have made of him a Negro, devoted to his people, of whom the race is proud and to whom they look for great things. Race consciousness is a complex thing; it is not entirely a matter of blood. Nature made

Donald white; man has made him, in sympathy, in outlook upon life, a Negro. Why spoil a good Negro by telling him this fairy tale, which, however alluring, may be no more true than the other? There was one slip-up in a perfect system. There may well have been another."

"My dear Brown," returned Mr. Seaton, "your argument is specious, and may be convincing to a colored man or from an impersonal viewpoint. But I'm considering this matter from the standpoint of a certain individual who happens to be white. If it is not a decided advantage to be white, then some five or six hundred million people in the world are fooling themselves badly."

"Of course," returned the lawyer, "it's still a tremendous handicap to be black, but things are looking up a little for the colored people. Their education for the past two generations, limited though it has been, is raising their level of culture. Negro wealth is increasing—we have few if any millionaires, but our combined holdings amount to many millions. The insurance company I represent, which is only one of several, has two hundred thousand dollars of paid up capital, and a million dollars of outstanding policies. Present indications are that the color line is weakening in spots, despite assertions to the contrary, and that all colored people may not always be social pariahs. And men of real parts, like Donald and some of the younger men, may find it in the future no great hardship to be classed with that race. It may even work to their advantage for a considerable time to come. They will have a smaller constituency, more closely welded in interest and sympathy, and may be able to accomplish more than they would as mere scattered and more or less alien units in a white world."

Mr. Seaton shook his head in doubt.

"That may be true," he said. "I hope it is, but I can't imagine a white man deliberately choosing to be a Negro for the sake of any problematical advantage to be gained. Even the colored man who can pass for white and get by without undue emotional stress or strain, gains materially."

"Undoubtedly," said Senator Brown, "and many of them are doing it. And another thing, being white isn't all glory. The page of the white race in history is by no means clean. It is soiled and bloody with a long record of cruelty, of treachery, of greed, of calculated crimes against humanity."

"But with some fine achievements on the other side. The abolition of slavery, for instance, and the enfranchisement of the Negro."

"That I will grant you," admitted Brown, "but the white people had introduced and fostered slavery, and its abolition, at the best, only balanced the account and left no credit surplus. The enfranchisement of the Negro in the South has been only a joke. At this very moment the white race everywhere has its iron heel on the neck of the darker world, and shows no intention of lifting it. I see no ultimate future for the Negro in the Western world except in his gradual absorption by the white race."

"But is that probable?" asked Mr. Seaton.

"It is already far advanced," returned Brown. "There is obviously much white blood among the so-called Negroes, and among the white people much black blood that is not obvious. We'll not live to see the day, but as sure as the sun rises and sets the time will come when the American people will be a homogenous race."

"That may well be," returned Mr. Seaton, "but it is of the future, the distant future, and Donald's case is of the immediate present. I'm arguing it from the white viewpoint."

"And I from the Negro. But there is a third viewpoint, which will be the controlling one, the viewpoint—"

"Of Donald himself," said Mr. Seaton. "I quite appreciate that. I shall hold the matter in suspense until I have checked up Dr. Freeman's story, but the chances are, when I am sure of the facts, that I shall tell Donald. I think he ought to know. After he learns the facts, he may choose his own course. With the best intentions in the world, I made one ghastly mistake about Donald because I didn't know the truth. All through my life I have followed the truth as I saw it. It was this very reason which led me to relinquish the boy in the first place—I didn't want his life to be a lie, even without his knowledge, so I turned him over to what I believed were his own people. The truth demands that he have his chance to correct, if possible, that mistake, and I want the opportunity, personally, to make amends to him for the past by opening up to him the future. As I say, I'll check up on the facts and be absolutely certain before I take any action."

With the promptness and thoroughness which characterizes the modern businessman of ample means, Mr. Seaton set in motion the machinery to obtain the information of which he was in search.

In carrying out his intention as announced to Brown, he wrote to a genealogist at Rome, who, in search of a family tree for Donald, eventually cut his way through the jungles of Italian genealogy and made his report. Mr. Seaton explained that he was not interested in building up or tearing down a family history for social purposes, but wanted merely the facts about the family of one Teresina Milfiore, a young opera singer, who had left Italy in 1901, when she was about twenty-five years old, and had gone to America to sing in grand opera. He also communicated, through a New York office engaged in the same line, with a private inquiry agency in Naples, asking for the same information.

When reports were received from these sources somewhat later, they confirmed substantially the story told by Dr. Freeman. There were some slight discrepancies, but they agreed, in effect, that the Milfiore fam-

ily was one of the oldest of southern Italy and had contributed many distinguished men to the country, running back to the days of Julius Caesar. The older
branch was extinct, but of the cadet branch one member was attached to the papal court, another was a
colonel in the Italian army, and there was a Professor
Milfiore on the faculty of the University of Turin. Teresina Milfiore had been the only daughter of Count
Luigi Milfiore, of Palermo and Taormina, Sicily, at one
time a man of large estates. The Castello Milfiore, the
ruins of which were still extant, had in medieval times
been the seat of the family. Count Luigi had impaired
his fortune by too many visits to Monte Carlo, and in
the effort to recoup it had speculated in African mining
shares, with disastrous results. The remnant of his fortune vanished, and he died of diabetes shortly after his
daughter Teresina had gone to America. Inquiry made
of former members of the company, which had long
since disbanded, revealed that she had left the troupe,
on account of illness, at Columbus, Ohio,[1] where she
had died of childbirth at City Hospital. Whether she
had left a child or not, of if she did, what became of it,
the investigators were unable to ascertain.

CHAPTER XXX

————⟫◉⟪————

MR. SEATON had retired from active business and was devoting much of his means and leisure to good works. He was not at all an easy mark for professional uplifters, but a genuinely good cause could always command his support. Of course, no one man is rich enough to finance every philanthropy, but Seaton's range of sympathies was broad, and his name could be found in the list of contributors to many colleges and schools, including several Negro institutions. He had built and presented to the congregation the imposing John Knox Presbyterian Church in Cleveland, and his benefactions to hospitals and foreign missions were numerous.

Just at the juncture when Donald's affairs were brought to his attention by Dr. Freeman, his time was hanging rather heavy on his hands, and he welcomed a new interest. He determined that as a matter of conscience he must do what he could to right the wrong which Donald had suffered. He spent many hours considering how this could best be accomplished. There would be no trouble on the personal side. The young man was white, of a very fine mixed type. He could find him a place in a bank or a corporation office if he cared to go into business. He could get him a professorship in a college if he cared to teach. He could help him to assume his true position in his mother's country, if he had any such inclinations.

He could procure his reception into the best American society. If Donald wished to devote himself to philosophy, he could finance him in a career which was not likely to be financially profitable. Most philosophers had been poor men—Will Durant had not yet written his *Story of Philosophy*. The mind had small chance in competition with the pocketbook.

If he could be of service to Donald in some direct and positive way, it would compensate in some measure for the mental sufferings Mr. Seaton assumed that the young man must have undergone through the deprivation of his rightful social heritage.

He imagined Donald's delight when he should learn who and what he was, and his gratitude to his benefactor for the information and for his patronage. Donald would be the Horace to his Mecenas, the Goethe to his Frederick, the Aristotle to his Alexander. What glory his protege might achieve would be reflected upon his happy patron.

He inquired of Mr. Brown about Donald's whereabouts and learned that he was in London, and could be reached there in care of Mr. John Culver Bascomb, at 10 Fenchurch Street, E.C. He engaged passage on the *Ruritania* and set sail for England about three weeks after Donald's arrival in London.

⟩⟩⟩⟨⟨⟨

CHAPTER XXXI

ALIGHTING FROM the train at the London station, Donald took a taxi to Mr. Bascomb's office, where he was informed by the managing clerk, Mr. Peters, that Mr. Bascomb was attending a meeting of the West African Importing Company, Ltd., of which he was president, and would be engaged for an hour or more.

"By the way, Mr. Glover," said the clerk, "there's a letter here for you. Mr. Bascomb meant to take it out this afternoon, but you may as well have it now."

Donald thanked him and opened the letter. It was from Mr. Seaton. He was in London, he said, on business, and was stopping at the Savoy Hotel. Would Donald call on him immediately on a very important matter? He would remain in all day, so as to be sure not to miss him.

Donald, leaving word that he would see Mr. Bascomb later in the day, went out on the street and hailed a passing taxicab, which soon deposited him at the entrance of the Savoy. Inquiry at the clerk's desk revealed

that Mr. Seaton was in his room, to which a page conducted Donald. It was a comfortable suite, composed
of a bedroom, sitting room and bath. Mr. Seaton was a
man of simple tastes, and despite his wealth, not given
to extravagant luxury. From his viewpoint there were
so many useful ways to spend money that it was hardly
less than a crime to waste it, and useless expenditure
would be no less than waste.

He welcomed Donald warmly, more warmly, Donald
thought, than their previous acquaintance could account for. Although he knew of Mr. Seaton's connection with his past, they had not met since he had declined, ten years before, Seaton's offer to educate him.

"Well, Donald," he said, "I'm delighted to see you. It
was my principal reason for coming to England. I had
some other affairs to attend to but they could have
waited. But I felt that the matter on which I wished to
see you should not be permitted to wait longer. It is
something you ought to have known many years ago.
You're not married yet, I hope?"

"No," replied the young man, "not yet."

"I'm glad to know it. Your marriage might have
made things difficult."

Donald wondered why Mr. Seaton should be interested in his marriage, but he was not left long in ignorance. He had never known any more of his origin than
his mother had told him, and that had simply been
what she knew, that he was an adopted child. He had
cared no more about it than his mother had. He knew

by the simplest principles of heredity that he must have good blood, and he had accepted the fact as a human inheritance, with no curiosity as to its particular source. His mother had trained him to be proud of his race, and proud of their progress against obstacles he well might be. One might be proud, or at least glad, to be a man, but to arrogate to one's self special privileges because of belonging to a certain type of humanity, was unphilosophical and anti-social.

Nevertheless, the history of his origin which Mr. Seaton proceeded to unroll was profoundly interesting. He told the story in detail, and told it dramatically, beginning with his visit to the hospital, including the first hospital record and the true history as reported recently by Dr. Freeman and verified later by himself. For a while Donald could find nothing to say, while Mr. Seaton went on talking.

"On your father's side," said he, "you belong to one of the best American families, and on the other side to a noble Italian house. Of course, so many people of good descent have gone wrong, so many good families have run out, that the mere fact, standing by itself, doesn't count for much. But the record of your father's family may easily account for your own intellectual brilliancy. For I have read your two books, and allowing for some few signs of immaturity which time will correct, they stamp your mind as that of a sound philosopher. It might have been that of a Scotchman, of the race which produced Hume and Carlyle."

"You overwhelm me, sir," demurred Donald.

"I mean every word of it," averred Mr. Seaton. "On your mother's side you are by birth Count Milfiore of Palermo and Taormina. Since the World War the world is cluttered up with ruined counts and dukes and grand dukes and princes, so that the title, should you use it, would of itself be of no value, except perhaps as a social asset."

It was like a fairy tale, a romance of a bygone type, though Donald's case proved it still a possibility and in this instance a fact.

"I thought you ought to know this, Donald—I always think of you by the name I gave you, and by which I called you when as an infant you sat on my knee. Your position is potentially far better than it has heretofore been. Instead of being colored, with all the disadvantages which that status entails in our country, you are white, with a family history which, with your talents and your education, would normally open every door to you. Of course, you will make a career for yourself, perhaps along the lines you have started on, but your field will be the world, instead of one group of one type of humanity. You're a brilliant young man, Donald, and I shall count it a privilege to see that in future you have every opportunity you would have had if I had reared you as my son, as I intended when I adopted you."

One of Donald's finest intellectual attributes was the faculty of prompt decision. In the case of Lady Blanche he had hesitated, it is true, conscious all the time, however, that it was a mere emotional hesitation. But in practical matters he could follow an argument to its logical conclusion in his own mind, in a very brief space of time. To be an Italian count, or any other kind of Italian made no appeal to his imagination. The race had a glorious record in ancient time, and during the Renaissance, but in the United States it was chiefly mentioned in the newspapers in connection with blackmail and bootlegging and their attendant homicides. To come of a fine New England family would have been gratifying, no doubt, had the fact been known and recognized from his childhood. Any intellectual inheritance from such a family, however, was his by virtue of his birth, so he had lost nothing there. Even the presumption of illegitimacy, very natural and almost inevitable in the case of an adopted child of unknown origin, had never disturbed him. Some very great men in history had been illegitimate, and among his own people, except for the past generation or two, such a birth had involved no social odium. Since he had never known of his supposed early history as disclosed to Mr. Seaton after his adoption of the boy while an infant, Donald had never even heard that he was illegitimate. He had rather assumed it, believing that, had his mother known otherwise, she would have told him. He had so many privileges—a sound mind in a sound body, a good home, loving parents, a fine education, that to worry about so immaterial a matter would have been foolish.

He had never suffered from any sense of inferiority because of his assumed mixed blood. He shared this distinction with many millions of people. Indeed, all the great races historically were mixed races, and all through history the white race had industriously and joyously mingled its blood with that of every darker race with which it came in contact. He had always resented the assumption by white people that they had a monopoly of courage and honor, as well as most of the Christian virtues, and their common and almost universal use of the word "yellow" as a synonym for weakness, cowardice and baseness. He had known black and brown and yellow men to perform acts of bravery and daring and to suffer with a fortitude which disproved any such assumption—the records of our national wars and the history of their race were full of examples—and the persistence of the epithet in spite of these facts he regarded as an insult springing solely from racial conceit and arrogance. The Negro, like the Jew and the Indian and the Chinaman, had been the victim of a crass and cruel generalization.

He was, first of all, a man. Circumstances had made him one of a certain group. He had been reared as one of them. He had been taught to see things as they saw them, he had shared their joys, their griefs, their hopes and their fears—in fact he had become psychologically and spiritually one of them. He could no more see them with the eyes of the white man of the street than he could make himself over. While recognizing the weaknesses they shared with all mankind, he could never despise them or slight them, or hear them reviled or derided without a disclaimer. He would carry to the grave a scar on his right shoulder from the knife of a drunken marine from a United States battleship, who was attempting with others of his crew to eject some Negro passengers from a Broadway subway car, to whose assistance he had come. He could only desert this group at the sacrifice of love and loyalty and the whole setup of his life. There might be a potential gain in being white, but the game was not worth the candle, the god was not worthy the sacrifice. Manhood and self-respect were more important than race.

These arguments had rushed through his mind in less time than it has taken to record them. But the decision he reached thus logically was in accordance with his feelings and his principles.

"I thank you very much, Mr. Seaton," he said at length, "for your interest in me and your efforts in my behalf. But on thinking the matter over I have decided to let things stand as they are. I hold nothing against you for the mistake you made. It was a perfectly natural thing to do, and no one could justly blame you for it, so do not disturb yourself on that score. I have been very happy, and all that I am or hope to be I owe to the good people who brought me up as their child, and I should feel that I was doing an unworthy thing should I abandon them and their people. Of course, it is easy for one to overestimate his powers or his value to others—it is quite possible that I would be no loss to them—but whatever good thing I may do, however unimportant it may be, I feel that they should have the credit for it. And between you and me, sir, I am sure I shall be happier and more comfortable. The roots have struck too deep to be easily eradicated."

"Perhaps you are right," returned Mr. Seaton regretfully. "Time alone will tell. I had hoped that I might help to right the wrong I unwittingly did you in your infancy. My friend Lord Rothmere has offered to lend me his yacht, and I was looking forward to taking you on a cruise to Italy, where you might study at first hand the scene on which your mother's people played their mighty part in history. I had thought that we might visit Sicily together and look over the former home of your ancestors, and if you should have felt the call of the blood, I was willing to buy the Castello Milfiore and make you a present of it. Undoubtedly you will make own your career in the world of intellect, but, if you like the place, it might be interesting to possess it.

"But perhaps it serves me right," he sighed, "that I shall not be permitted to atone for my early mistake. Of course, if you continue to be known as a colored man, you won't want me to make public the story of your origin?"

"No," returned Donald. "It would make a sensational item for the newspapers, but to publish it would probably break my mother's heart and impair any usefulness I might have to my people. So I shall merely thank you and ask you to keep it secret."

"I have told it to but one man, Senator Brown, whom you know and with whom I talked over the matter before coming to you. His opinion is the same as your own, and he need never know that I have told you. Dr. Freeman does not know your present name and to make your story known would be of no credit to him, so I think the secret is reasonably safe. I wish you all success and happiness. You are going to do what I imagine few men would be capable of, and should you change your mind or should your courage fail, I still stand ready to do all that I intended."

"Thank you, sir," Donald replied. "You are more than generous. Will you be long in London?"

"No," said Mr. Seaton, "I have already attended to my principal business, which was to see you, and after a few weeks with friends in Scotland, I shall sail for New York. Keep in touch with me when you come home. I shall watch your career with a lively interest. It will be perhaps the most unique case of the kind on record."

"It will not be on record, dear Mr. Seaton, if we keep silent about it."

CHAPTER XXXII

———»◄•►◄———

UPON LEAVING the Savoy, Donald returned to 10 Fenchurch Street, where he saw Mr. Bascomb, thanked him for his kindness and explained the reason for his absence. He hoped it would not be protracted and said that he would see Mr. Bascomb on his return.

He crossed the channel late that afternoon, stayed at a hotel in Paris overnight, took the Mediterranean express the following morning, and the afternoon found him in Avignon, the old pontifical seat of the French popes, in the Provençal, not far from the city of the immortal Tartarin. He had telegraphed Bertha the hour of his arrival, and she was at the *gare* with Rose to meet him. Mrs. Lawrence was waiting outside in an automobile.

Bertha flew to Donald's arms with the light of love in her eyes.

"Oh, my dear, my dear, but I'm glad you've come," she exclaimed. "Rose thought I ought to write you, but I said no, if you wanted me badly enough you'd come without a letter."

It was only quick thinking, prompted by a violent and repeated contraction of the left eyelid which Rose made over her sister's shoulder, that saved Donald from the *faux pas* of asking the obvious question. When Bertha had disentangled herself, he gave Rose a brotherly kiss, and they went out to Mrs. Lawrence in the car. She gave him a motherly kiss—all in all it was quite a family party, and the amiable Gauls within sight or hearing smiled appreciatively—it was quite in keeping with their attitude toward life.

They drove to the *pension*, where a room had been secured for Donald. Bishop Lawrence had not yet reached Avignon but was expected daily.

"And now," demanded Donald, as soon as he found himself alone with Rose, "explain this mystery. Is Bertha suffering from loss of memory, and if not, who wrote me that letter?"

"I plead guilty," returned the lively soubrette. "When I saw her pining away for you—it really affected her appetite, Donald, which is a sure sign that something is wrong with Bertha—but too proud to write, I decided that you were altogether too handsome to be left running around London by yourself, and something would have to be done. My handwriting is exactly like Bertha's, so I wrote you a letter and signed her name to it. But keep your mouth shut and be nice to me and I'll not give you away."

"I like your nerve," said Donald. "Was the letter entirely a work of fiction," he asked, "or was there some truth in it? Who, for instance, is the other fellow, if there is one?"

"Oh, he's Phil Reed, Dad's pet young rector, the bright hope of the church. He's coming from Rome with Dad in a few days, but I want him for myself, if I can't have you. So hurry up and fix things with Bertha or you'll find yourself up against a hard proposition, in the shape of little Rose."

"*Dieu me garde!*" said Donald. "I should never be able to defend myself."

"Oh, go along," retorted the girl, "you're talking through your hat."

A colloquialism now seldom employed, and which the uninformed might easily suppose to be of American origin, but it is found in Molière, and much farther back, in one of the Greek dramatists.

CHAPTER XXXIII

———⫸●⫷———

U PON HIS RETURN to America, Mr. Seaton called once more upon Senator Brown and informed him of Donald's decision.

"It is what I hoped for," returned the lawyer, "though it may not prove easy to carry through. While he is young and full of hope it will be comparatively simple. He has the opportunity to become the intellectual leader of our people, which may win him fame and honor. Because of his complexion and talents he will get many things even as a Negro that few of us can expect. But as the years go on there may come times when he will wish he had chosen differently—one can never tell.

"By the way," he continued, "I wonder if you know something I discovered the other day?"

"That depends upon what it is. Enlighten me."

"I was in Cleveland, looking up the title of a piece of real estate, and in so doing had occasion to examine the county records of legal adoptions. I ran across the one in which you adopted Donald, but I could find none for the second adoption. Are you sure it was ever legally made?"

"By George!" exclaimed Mr. Seaton. "I don't believe it was! I didn't attend to it, and I probably just assumed that the Glovers would."

"If that is so," said Senator Brown, "he is still legally your son, and entitled to a son's rights."

"He's welcome to them," replied Mr. Seaton. "If I should die intestate it would be another way for me to make amends. But I have already made provision for him in my will, which I shall revise and give him a larger portion—or perhaps a personal trust would be better. Had I known this ten years ago when I wanted him back, I might have demanded as a right what I asked as a favor—not that I should have, but I could have. Years ago I was willing to assume a father's duties toward him. Had I done so I might have claimed a father's rights and won a son's love. But God, or Fate, or whatever the destiny that shapes our ends, saw fit to deprive me of that pleasure. So runs the world."

Several years later, after Donald's third book had been published, Mr. Seaton accepted an invitation to dine at Donald's home in New York and for the first time met his wife. He had married Bertha shortly after their return from Europe. Doctor and Mrs. Glover, who had moved to New York, were present.

When the visitor left, Donald went down in the elevator with him to the door.

"Well, Donald," he said in parting, "I'm glad I came.

Your wife is a beautiful and charming woman and the boy is the image of you at his age. I'm not at all sure that you didn't make the wise choice."

NOTES TO
THE QUARRY

CHESNUTT was inconsistent in handling certain details of punctuation and spelling. Sometimes in a given text he would conform to the practices of an earlier era, and sometimes in the same text he would follow modern practice. To give two examples: Chesnutt frequently separates contracted words—"does n't," "would n't"—and he sometimes follows a dash with other punctuation; however, he follows neither of these practices in all cases. In the interest of consistency, I have chosen, in these instances, to follow contemporary practice; thus contracted words are not separated, and there is no punctuation after dashes in the manuscript I have prepared.

CHAPTER V

1. Davis, the barber with close ties to white political and social leaders, resembles Chesnutt's friend George H. Myers, proprietor of the Cleveland Hollenden Hotel barbershop. Frances Richardson Keller writes that Myers served for years as "a one-man clearinghouse for racial affairs and as a liaison center between the black population of Cleveland and the Republican Party" (*An American Crusade*, 240). Chesnutt also portrayed an

influential Negro barber in his story "The Doll" (1912), which is included in Render's edition of Chesnutt's short fiction.

2. Elbert Hubbard (1856–1915), an American author influenced by William Morris, founded an artist's colony and a publishing house in East Aurora, N.Y. His most famous literary work, "A Message to Garcia," was based on an incident in the Spanish-American War. Chesnutt mentions in a letter dated October 31, 1903, that Hubbard had appeared in the Temple Course of Lectures in Cleveland, a series in which Chesnutt also participated (*"To Be an Author,"* 195).

Chapter VI

1. Senator Brown's career resembles that of Chesnutt's cousin John Patterson Green, a black North Carolinian who moved to Cleveland, where he practiced law and served in the Ohio General Assembly. Chesnutt wrote an introduction to William Rogers's biography of Green.

2. The possibility of Robert Browning's Negro ancestry, as well as that of Elizabeth Barrett, was a matter of speculation in Browning circles during the poet's lifetime and after. See Julia Markus, *Dared and Done,* 110–13.

Chapter IX

1. Mrs. Glover's reaction to this publication echoes Chesnutt's attack on William Hannibal Thomas's *The American Negro*. The book, written by a Negro, went further in abusing the race than did many Southern whites. Chesnutt suspected a fraud and led a campaign against the book, causing Macmillan to withdraw it from circulation. See Keller, *American Crusade,* 210–11. For Chesnutt's correspondence documenting Thomas's unsavory career to the publisher, see *"To Be an Author,"* 198–209).

2. Donald's experience with Professor Neuman recalls Chesnutt's own experiences as a young man. His journal (July 25, 1880) records that he studied German and French in Fayetteville with Professor Neufeld, and that Professor Neufeld kept him as a student even when white students objected. Richard Brodhead, in his edition of the *Journals*, identifies Neufeld more specifically as Emil Neufeld (141, n.71).

3. Donald's education recalls the program of disciplined study which Chesnutt undertook and which he records in his journal from the late 1870s and early 1880s. Both young men, for instance, devoted hours to patiently translating the *Aeneid*. However, Donald's readings are more philosophical than the literary readings—Dickens, Dumas, Goethe—discussed in the journals. Chesnutt has also brought Donald's readings into the more recent period. Royce and Drummond's publications, for example, had not yet appeared during the period Chesnutt records in his journal.

Chapter X

1. Ernest Hogan (1860–1909), the minstrel entertainer and songwriter, was, during the first decade of this century, one of the most popular African American entertainers. Many of his compositions belong to the "coon songs" genre.

2. The Fisk manuscript has "desired."

Chapter XII

1. Mrs. Glover's career in the cosmetic business resembles that of two black women entrepreneurs, Annie Turbo Malone (1869–1957) and Mrs. C. J. Walker (1867–1919), both of whom successfully marketed beauty products for black women.

Chapter XIII

1. The Ohio University manuscript identifies "Bethany College" as Berea College in Kentucky. Helen Chesnutt reports her father's disappointment at the United States Supreme Court decision in the Berea College case. "Berea College had been doing a noble work among the mountaineers of Kentucky and Tennessee. It had received its charter in 1865 and had admitted both white and colored students until 1904, when, by an act of the Kentucky State legislature, education of Negroes and whites at the same institution was prohibited. This act was fought through the courts up to the United States Supreme Court which in 1908 upheld the act" (*Charles Waddell Chesnutt,* 206–207). Chesnutt refers to "the destruction of Berea College" in a March 5, 1904, letter to Booker T. Washington, *"To Be an Author,"* 197). Chesnutt could also draw on the history of Maryville College in Tennessee. Frances Richardson Keller reports that Samuel W. Boardman, Maryville President Emeritus, told Chesnutt that "his college refused Negro students in 1904 though it had been endowed on the condition 'over and over pledged, in the strongest possible language by Synod, Directors and Faculty, that all citizens should have equal rights.' Boardman deplored these conditions when all this had not a feather's weight with the Gov. & Legislature of Tenn." (*An American Crusade*, 209).

Chapter XIV

1. The Ohio University manuscript identifies Athena University as Atlanta University, a historically black educational institution chartered in 1867.

2. Dr. Lebrun (Dr. C. B. Lebrun in the Ohio University manuscript) is based on W.E.B. Du Bois, who taught economics and history at Atlanta University from 1897 to 1910. For a discus-

sion of Chesnutt's relationship with Du Bois, see Keller, *An American Crusade*, 249–56.

3. The Ohio University manuscript has "the propagandists of race purity—Lathrop Stoddard, Madison Grant and other pseudo-scientists of their school—" Stoddard was the author of *The Rising Tide of Color Against White World-Supremacy* (1920) and *The Revolt Against Civilization: The Menace of the Under Man* (1922). Grant wrote *The Passing of the Great Race, or the Racial Basis of European History* (1922).

4. The Atlanta riot of September 22, 1906, resulted in the death of twenty-five black men, and one hundred and fifty serious injuries. It climaxed a campaign of unsubstantiated rumors of sexual assault by black males against white women.

5. In 1913 Leo M. Frank, a Jewish superintendent of an Atlanta pencil factory, was convicted on flimsy evidence of the rape and murder of Mary Phagan, a white girl. He was sentenced to death, but his sentence was commuted to life in prison by the governor of Georgia. Frank was assaulted in the state prison at Milledgeville by another prisoner, and while recovering, was taken from the prison by a mob and lynched on August 17, 1915.

Chapter XV

1. Chesnutt based Boaz on Franz Boas (1858–1942), a founder of modern anthropology, who taught at Columbia University from 1896 to 1936. Boas sought to put thinking about race on a more scientific basis. Among the ideas he attacked were the assumptions that intelligence is racially determined and that race mixing leads to degeneracy. For a discussion of Boas's importance for the Harlem Renaissance, see Hutchinson, *The Harlem Renaissance in Black and White*, 62–77.

2. Theodore Parker (1810–60), Massachusetts theologian and reformer, was an antislavery activist.

Chapter XVI

1. Samuel Coleridge-Taylor (1875–1912), a British composer, was the son of an African Negro father and an English mother. His *Symphonic Variations on an African Air* (1906) developed an African motif within a traditional European musical setting. Chesnutt heard him conduct a performance in Washington, D.C., in 1904; see *"To Be an Author,"* 220.

2. John Rosamond Johnson (1873–1954) and his brother, James Weldon Johnson (1871–1938), edited several collections of American Negro songs and spirituals in 1926 and 1927. Chesnutt may also have in mind Hall Johnson (1873–1970), who formed the Hall Johnson Choir in 1925 to perform Negro musical material.

3. Henry Thacker Burleigh (1866–1939) arranged Negro spirituals, such as "Deep River," using the chromatic harmonies in the style of art songs.

4. Roland Hayes (1887–1976) was the first African American to establish an international reputation as a singer of classical art songs. He was also influential in bringing the African American spiritual to integrated concert audiences.

5. Charles S. Gilpin (1872–1930) created the title role in Eugene O'Neill's *The Emperor Jones* in 1920.

6. The Ohio University manuscript has "Negro American." Chesnutt reversed this in the Fisk manuscript, making "Negro" the noun and "American" the modifying adjective.

7. Paul Robeson (1898–1976) appeared in *The Emperor Jones* on stage in 1925 and on film in 1933.

Chapter XVII

1. The publications listed here are probably based on *The Crisis*, the NAACP magazine, edited from 1910 to 1932 by

W.E.B. Du Bois, and *Opportunity*, the National Urban League publication, edited from 1923 to 1926 by Charles S. Johnson.

2. The Universal Negro Improvement Association (UNIA) was founded by Marcus Garvey in 1911.

3. Marcus Garvey (1887–1940) urged world-wide black unity and the creation of an autonomous black state in Africa. He entered jail after a mail fraud conviction in 1925 and was deported to Jamaica in 1927.

CHAPTER XIX

1. Most of the names listed are well known or are identified in the passage. Two names which may require further identification are Blanche K. Bruce (1841–98), United States Senator from Mississippi from 1875 to 1881, and John Mercer Langston (1829–97), Ohio's first black lawyer, the first president of Virginia State College, and Virginia's first black congressman.

CHAPTER XX

1. Mamie Wilson's career as a black woman entertainer-entrepreneur echoes that of Ida Cox (1896–1967). Born Ida Prather in Cedartown, Georgia, Cox sang in a local church choir before running away in her teens to join a minstrel group. She toured widely, establishing herself on the Harlem and Chicago stages as a leading blues and jazz singer. Cox was an astute business woman, managing her own road shows.

CHAPTER XXI

1. In these references to national organizations for black women, Chesnutt had as possible models the National Association of Colored Women, a philanthropic and service organiza-

tion formed in 1896, and Alpha Kappa Alpha, the first black Greek-letter organization for women, founded in 1908.

2. The name of Donald's club recalls *The New Negro*, the anthology edited by Alain Locke in 1925. Locke, in his title essay, asserted that fifty years of freedom and the recent northern migration had brought a new confidence and maturity to Negro artists and intellectuals. His volume gave proof of this new spirit with work by sociologists, historians, and musicologists, as well as by poets, fiction writers, and visual artists.

CHAPTER XXIII

1. Booker T. Washington (1856–1915) founded Tuskegee Institute at Tuskegee, Alabama, in 1881. Chesnutt was on good terms with Washington, and they corresponded frequently. This correspondence is included in *"To Be an Author."* Frances Richardson Keller has summarized some of the key differences that emerge in this exchange: "Chesnutt believed in integration at all levels. Washington accepted a postponement of rights and privileges until the Negro should be prepared to exercise them, but Chesnutt insisted that all rights and privileges should be accorded 'now.' Washington would entrust the management of Negro destinies to benevolent white people, but Chesnutt would trust only black people to control their affairs. Washington thought the vote was relatively unimportant; Chesnutt thought it was crucially important" (226).

CHAPTER XXIII

1. *The Chicago Crusader* is based on *The Chicago Defender*. *The Defender*, founded by Robert Abbot in 1905, was an important voice for African Americans in the 1920s. It generally supported an integrationist approach to the racial question.

Chapter XXVI

1. Donald and his mother's position on Africa is much closer to that of Booker T. Washington, who placed primary focus on the condition of American blacks, than to the position of the more internationally minded W.E.B. Du Bois. However, Washington's influence in Africa was considerable, and he and his graduates offered assistance and advice to the German colony of Togo and to the Republic of Liberia.

2. Réné Maran (1887–1960) was born in Martinique and educated in France. His novel, *Batouala*, won the Prix Goncourt in 1921. Chesnutt read it in French and praised it in a letter to Benjamin Brawley: "While he [Maran] is not a United States Negro, I think his triumph is one of which all those who share the blood of his race—for from his portrait he seems to be of the full blood—may well be proud."

Chapter XXIX

1. The Fisk and Ohio manuscripts both have "Cincinnati, Indiana." But several times earlier in the novel Chesnutt placed the hospital of Donald's birth in Columbus, Ohio.

WORKS CITED

Chesnutt, Charles W. *The Colonel's Dream*. Upper Saddle River, NJ: Gregg Press, 1968.

———. *The Conjure Woman*. Ann Arbor: University of Michigan Press, 1969.

———. *The House Behind the Cedars*. New York: Penguin, 1993.

———. "Introduction." William Rogers. *Senator John P. Green and Sketches of Prominent Men of Ohio*. Washington, DC, and Cleveland, OH: Arena Publishing Co., 1893.

———. *The Journals of Charles W. Chesnutt*. Ed. Richard Brodhead. Durham, NC: Duke University Press, 1993.

———. Letter to Benjamin G. Brawley. 24 March 1922. Chesnutt Collection. Western Reserve Historical Society, Cleveland, OH.

———. *Mandy Oxendine*. Ed. Charles Hackenberry. Urbana: University of Illinois Press, 1997.

———. *The Marrow of Tradition*. New York: Penguin, 1993.

———. *Paul Marchand, F.M.C.* Ed. Dean McWilliams. Princeton: Princeton University Press, 1999.

———. *Paul Marchand, F.M.C.* Ed. Matthew Wilson. Jackson: University Press of Mississippi, 1998.

———. "Post-Bellum—Pre-Harlem." In *Breaking into Print*. Ed. Elmer Adler. New York: Simon, 1937. 47–56.

———. *The Short Fiction of Charles W. Chesnutt*. Ed. Sylvia Lyons Render. Washington, DC: Howard University Press, 1981.

———. *The Wife of His Youth and Other Stories*. Ann Arbor: University of Michigan Press, 1968.

Chesnutt, Charles W. *"To Be an Author": Letters of Charles W. Chesnutt*. Ed. Joseph R. McElrath, Jr., and Robert C. Leitz, III. Princeton: Princeton University Press, 1997.

Chesnutt, Helen. *Charles Waddell Chesnutt: Pioneer of the Color Line*. Chapel Hill: University of North Carolina Press, 1952.

Greenslet, Ferris. Letter to Charles W. Chesnutt. 31 January 1931. Chesnutt Collection. Western Reserve Historical Society, Cleveland, OH.

Hutchinson, George. *The Harlem Renaissance in Black and White*. Cambridge, MA: Harvard University Press, 1995.

Keller, Frances Richardson. *An American Crusade: The Life of Charles Waddell Chesnutt*. Provo, UT: Brigham Young University Press, 1978.

Locke, Alain, ed. *The New Negro: Voice of the Harlem Renaissance*. New York: Atheneum, 1992.

Markus, Julia. *Dared and Done: The Marriage of Elizabeth Barrett and Robert Browning*. New York: Knopf, 1995.

Rogers, William. *Senator John P. Green and Sketches of Prominent Men of Ohio*. Washington, DC, and Cleveland, OH: Arena Publishing Co., 1893.

Thomas, William Hannibal. *The American Negro*. New York: Macmillan, 1901.

DATE DUE

			Printed in USA

HIGHSMITH #45230